RED CANVAS

A LISE NORWOOD MYSTERY

ANDREW NANCE

Red Canvas
Red Adept Publishing, LLC
104 Bugenfield Court
Garner, NC 27529
http://RedAdeptPublishing.com/

Copyright © 2020 by Andrew Nance. All rights reserved.

Cover Art by Streetlight Graphics

No part of this book may be reproduced, scanned, or distributed in any printed or electronic form without permission. Please do not participate in or encourage piracy of copyrighted materials in violation of the author's rights. Thank you for respecting the hard work of this author.

This is a work of fiction. Names, characters, places, and incidents either are the product of the author's imagination or are used fictitiously, and any resemblance to locales, events, business establishments, or actual persons—living or dead—is entirely coincidental.

Prologue

T*he Artist*
A delicious dizziness struck the moment he found himself in the presence of true art. An inability to breathe lessened until he could take shallow breaths. With oxygen came the rush, tingles along his flesh and tremors in his limbs. Soon the tears arrived—joyful, rapturous tears. Such a magnificent sculpture in so mundane a dwelling. A polished gem displayed within a dreary heap. The woman, carved from marble, absorbed light from the surrounding candles and reflected it back with an angelic glow.

The sculptor captured a split second of time when the woman was in the process of falling to her knees. Her right elbow pointed skyward, her left at the ground, as both hands tried to grasp the arrow shot into her back. The arrow was not part of the sculpture, but he knew it was there; that was why her body arched so. In scrabbling for the shaft, her robe had slipped from her shoulders, displaying her breasts, one full thigh, and a hint of mons pubis. The sculpture stirred him sexually, and it was then that he realized his own nakedness. His memory often failed when his passion burned at a blue-heat intensity, so he couldn't remember if he'd had a recent orgasm. Inhaling deeply, he smiled at the heady aroma of sweat mixed with sex.

What is her name? Is this her apartment? He wondered if they'd made love in front of the sculpture, which brought new tears at the glorious possibility. He walked around the masterpiece, kicking away torn and discarded clothing in his path, her garments. He deemed the sculpture perfect, no matter from what angle it was viewed.

He looked toward the apartment window. Dawn was close. *Time to go*. He took his eyes from the sculpture long enough to locate his clothes. He put them on, went to the door, and paused for one last look. The smooth marble seemed luminous. The impending death of the carved woman made it that much more beautiful, as did the splendor of blood that trailed down the statue to pool on the floor.

Chapter 1

Every eye in the room focused on me. This was oddly similar to every student's nightmare of standing before a class to give a report only to realize they're naked. In this case, it was the subject matter that was nude, not me.

"Our next example is from the seventeenth-century Baroque style. *Drunken Hercules* by Peter Paul Rubens is another fine example of the male nude." I used the cursor to rapidly circle Hercules's crotch, looking at the two men seated at the side of the dais, making sure they were paying attention. They appeared stoic and intrigued, but I knew better. On the inside, they were giggling like elementary school boys waiting for the teacher to sit on a whoopee cushion. "Note that though his flaccid penis is somewhat covered by the woman's translucent robe, it is still visible." After a couple more circuits with the cursor, to emphasize the penis, I added, "See what I mean?"

The class watched me, most with confused expressions. What they saw was an attractive, fit, thirtysomething dishwater blonde spouting off about limp dicks and doing it with a straight face. What they didn't know was that I was one floppy comment away from all-consuming laughter. Normally, I chose to wear casual clothes when working as a private investigator, but I felt a dark skirt, white button-down shirt, and red-framed reading glasses added to my gravitas as guest speaker.

"You've been a great class," I told them. "I hope Professors Weldon and Turner will have me back."

The men on the dais stood and applauded.

Nick, the younger of the two professors, said, "Okay, class, let's thank our guest lecturer and former San Marco University art major, Analise Norwood, for her presentation on classic male nudes."

A few in the class joined in with tepid clapping, while the others rapidly packed their books and supplies, eager to leave the classroom in case the insanity they'd witnessed turned out to be contagious.

The men on the dais strolled over, and Gabriel Turner said, "Lise, once an overachiever, always an overachiever. You used the term *flaccid penis* four times in your presentation."

"I couldn't remember whether I'd used it two times or three," I said, shutting down my laptop. "So I added another to be sure I settled the bet."

"And not just anyone's floppy member, but Hercules's floppy member. You settled the bet and then some," Nick said. "I hope you've learned your lesson."

"I know, Nick. Never bet on the Jaguars when they're playing your team."

Gabe wagged his finger at me. "Don't bet on the Jaguars when they're playing *any* team."

"Hey, those are the old Jags you're talking about," I argued. "They're getting better now, right? Kinda sorta?"

Nick shrugged. "Fine with me if that's what you think. When you lose your next bet, you'll teach another class on nudes, utilizing the term *perky breasts*."

Not as bad as flaccid penis, *but then again...* "Maybe I will give up game-day bets."

Gabe put a hand on my shoulder and said, "That was the most entertaining thing since Abbott and Costello argued about who's on first." We all had a fondness for the old black-and-white Hollywood movies, especially the comedy teams. Gabe was Nick's mentor and had once taught a couple of my classes when I'd been a student at San Marco University. Head of the art history department, he resembled one of those timeless actors who seemed to never age. He had to be approaching sixty, if he hadn't already crossed that line, but in the right light, he could be mistaken for a man in his forties. Being in the Sunshine State, his wardrobe was Florida formal: dark jeans, a white T-shirt, boat shoes without socks, and a navy sport coat. Fit and healthy, he had a head full of brown hair, which he swore did not come out of a bottle. He was as handsome as all get-out.

I pointed at a stain on his T-shirt. "We've talked about this, Gabe. Anytime you wear white, you're going to end up with a red wine stain, ketchup stain, or, as in this case, a coffee stain."

Gabe gazed down at his chest. "Damn it."

Nick and I laughed. Gabe wasn't exactly Pigpen from the "Peanuts" comics, but he did have more stained clothing than any adult I knew.

"Ah, screw it." Gabe brushed at the now-dry blotch of coffee then looked at his watch. "Gotta go. I'm late for a department head meeting that's guaranteed to be a real snoozefest. Take care."

After Gabe left, I made sure all the students were gone, stepped up to Nick, and pulled him down for a kiss. At five-eight, I didn't have to pull him far. I held him close while gazing in his blue-gray eyes that sometimes seemed intense and at other times washed out. In tan slacks with black sneakers and a Frank Zappa T-shirt, he wasn't the stereotypical university professor. He was good-looking, not out-and-out hot, but darn close. I loved his tousled brunet hair, which always appeared uncombed, so I slid my fingers in his longish locks and ruffled his hair, adding to what he claimed was windswept and what I called unkempt.

I kissed his lips, moved to his cheek then his ear, and whispered, "I brought you something."

"And I am loving it." He moved his hands down to my posterior, and I pushed him away.

"Slow down, cowboy. Not that, and not now. Let's go to your office."

"Now you're talking."

"Not that. Not now," I repeated with a laugh. "I really do have something you'll want to see."

"Hmmm." He scratched his chin. "Still sounds dirty to me."

We linked arms and made the short walk to his office, a ten-by-twelve mess of paper, books, and cheap furniture. I took a manila folder from my bag and smiled at Nick. I couldn't wait to see his reaction. "Ready for something you've never seen before?"

"What've you got?"

"This." I opened the folder, displaying an eight-by-ten photo of a sketch.

"And here I was hoping for a suggestive selfie." Nick's attention turned to the picture. His concentration took over, and his body tensed as he became more focused. Levity gone from his expression, he fell into his chair. "This is something special."

"Yes."

"It's a ballerina."

I looked over his shoulder at it.

"She's in a unique pose, something I've never seen. A hint of cubism, certainly surrealism."

"Very good. Give yourself an A."

"It's from a master." He slapped his desk and glanced up at me, his eyes shining. "I'd bet on it."

"Sorry, I just paid off one bet." Grinning, I asked, "Which master?"

Nick rolled back to take advantage of sunlight shining through the window. "It's ink on what? Doesn't look like paper."

"Linen."

"Linen?" He stared at it longer.

"A napkin. Which master sketched it?"

When Nick came across something in art he couldn't understand, he got frustrated. When that happened, he massaged his left temple, which he was doing now. "A napkin? Why a—"

"Which master?" I raised my voice, excited by his excitement.

"If I had to guess, I'd say Picasso, maybe? I mean, so many elements of his style are present, but there are elements that aren't." He brought the photo closer so that it almost touched his nose, then he held it out at arm's length.

"Congratulations," I said. "You're half right."

He spun his chair to face me. "Half?"

"The original is signed. I cropped it out to see if you could guess."

"But it is a Picasso?"

My voice reverent, I said, "Picasso *and* Dali."

He hardly took his eyes from the photo as I sat on the edge of his desk and told him the story. "It's tied to a case I'm working." I wasn't sure whether to start my story from when I was hired or when I realized how important the sketch was. I decided to begin with the history. "Picasso and Dali were friends, right?"

"Yes."

"In 1931, they met for lunch at a café in Barcelona. Their young waiter was star-struck at serving the two masters. He lingered near their table when not actually bringing food, so he could eavesdrop. Picasso said he was thinking of creating a painting of a ballerina unaffected by gravity, but he was having trouble with how to convey her dance as if she floated. Dali was intrigued, and they took turns sketching out ideas on his linen napkin. When they had a figure they were happy with, they took Picasso's napkin and drew that sketch, working at the same time. Dali worked on the ballerina's left side and Picasso on the right."

I knelt by him so I could watch his expression as I told him more. "The two artists were simply having fun while kicking around ideas, and they left the napkin behind when they finished their meal.

The waiter chased them down, begging that they sign the sketch. He framed it and passed it down to his son, who passed it to his daughter, who is my client."

Nick's gaze finally left the photo as he looked to me. "You're sure it's real?"

"No," I admitted. "If I could get my hands on it, I'd get it authenticated."

"She hasn't?"

"No. She said she knows it's real because of how it's been handed down within the family."

"What's the case?" Nick asked.

"Could be burglary, certainly a theft, and probably divorce."

"Throw in a murder, and you'd have a great noir film."

I got up and went around his desk to sit in a chair. "My client is a woman named Shari Stephens. She's probably late thirties. Blond. Attractive in a PTA-mom sort of way. Her house had been broken into. Several valuable items were taken, including the sketch. That's how she found me. She saw my resume included a degree in art history. She figured that would give me an advantage over other private investigators."

"Bet your jaw dropped when she told you about the sketch," Nick said.

"It did. And then she showed me a photo, and my jaw damn near landed in my lap. She thought I might have a line on black market art dealers and fences and such. Told her I didn't, but she hired me anyway."

"How's the divorce tie in?"

"Hey, there's a thing called *confidentiality* involved here."

"Oh."

"Lucky for you, I told her I'd probably have to discuss the case with colleagues, and she said that'd be fine. And since you're a colleague—"

Nick grinned. "And lover and friend—"

"I can spill the beans. Several weeks ago, her husband, Ricky Stephens, left his laptop in the kitchen, and she used it to look up a recipe. She stumbled onto what she first took to be pornography but was actually several websites for people who want to meet up for random sex. He had a collection of dirty photos his internet sweethearts had sent him."

"Not a great hobby for a married man."

I nodded. "It gets worse. Around this time, she'd had a low-grade fever, along with discomfort, tenderness, and swelling in that most private of places."

"Oh boy."

"Yep, chlamydia, the gift that keeps on giving until antibiotics get involved."

"Poor lady," Nick said, leaning back.

I leaned forward. "Not poor. She comes from a fairly wealthy family, and he comes from a poor one. He makes good money now—he's the sales manager at a car dealership, Jack Todd Ford—but he also enjoys the fruits of being married to a well-to-do woman. She told him about discovering his philandering and was having her lawyer draw up divorce papers. A couple of days later, their house was burglarized. The thief took the sketch, her jewelry, and a rare coin collection that belonged to her father."

Nick's eyes widened. "Wait a minute. Are you saying her husband faked a burglary to get her valuables before the divorce happens?"

"I'm saying it's a good possibility. She's not so sure. They have three kids, and she can't see him stealing what would basically be their inheritance."

Nick thought a moment. "Maybe he doesn't see it that way."

"Either the house was hit by real burglars, or Ricky staged it. If he did, he did a good job."

"Have you spoken with him yet?" Nick asked.

I shook my head. "Not going to. Right now, I'm following him, and my anonymity is key. Anyway, what I learned from Shari and from the police report is that a window set in the back door was broken from the outside. The house was trashed like someone rushed through searching for valuables. She put up a ten-thousand-dollar reward, and I've contacted galleries and pawn shops around San Marco. I decided to be vague and only tell them I was looking for a valuable sketch."

"Good idea," Nick said. "A heretofore unknown sketch by both Picasso and Dali somewhere on the black market would make news, and that probably wouldn't help you find it."

"Imagine how many people would be clamoring to see it, if not own it. So along those lines, don't tell anybody about it or show anyone that." I pointed to the photo. "If Ricky is responsible, Shari made a mistake by giving him a heads-up about the divorce. So I advised her to tell him that she wants to work at reconciliation. That way, if he did take it, he might not be as eager to get rid of it if the divorce is on hold." I moved behind Nick's chair and peered over his shoulder at the picture. "What would you guess *The Floating Ballerina* is worth if it's real?"

"*Floating Ballerina*?"

"That's what her family calls it."

"You say it's signed?"

"Yeah, here." I brought up a photo of the sketch on my phone and zoomed in on the bottom right of the linen napkin. The top signature was Picasso's, in his recognizable fashion of separate letters except for the *C*, *A*, and first *S* being joined. Below that and to the left was Dali's, and he'd continued with the big loop at the top of the D, turning it into a crown over his name.

Nick laughed in amazement. "Those appear authentic. That'll send its value through the roof."

"You're the expert, what do you think it's worth?"

Nick blew out a breath of air. "That's hard to say. I mean, sketches by either artist could bring in anywhere from tens of thousands to hundreds of thousands. But this—there has never been a record of them working together like this. I wouldn't be surprised, as they've both signed it, if some collectors would pay seven figures to own it, maybe even eight."

"My client doesn't have a clue."

Nick sat back and crossed his legs. "How are you going to find out if her husband is responsible?"

"Right now, I'm following him around. If he took it, maybe I'll learn where he's hidden it, or at the least, make sure he doesn't sell it."

"Sounds time intensive."

"Three days in and counting. But I have help. I wait outside his house in the morning, so I can follow him to work. I have an associate who watches his workplace while he's there."

I could tell Nick was trying to remember his name but failed. "That homeless guy?"

"Yeah, Elliot the Slim. And then I get there about the time Ricky leaves and follow him home. His wife gives me a heads-up if he leaves the house and stalls him if I need time to get there, but they're only a couple of miles from my house."

"Hmm." Nick pursed his lips then asked, "Seen anything out of the ordinary yet?"

"Nope."

"What if he didn't take it? Or if he did and hangs on to it for months? Or years?"

I shrugged and sat back. "That'd suck, but I'll keep following him as long as I get paid."

There was a knock at the open door, and we looked up to see two men in suits, holding out badges.

Chapter 2

Upon seeing the two cops at the door, I pointed at Nick. "He did it."

The men entered without smiles, making the office claustrophobic. One in his late forties asked, "Nicholas Weldon?"

"Guilty," Nick said then quickly added, "Guilty of being Nicholas Weldon, not of committing a crime or anything."

"I'm Detective Baker, and this is Detective Ortega."

They had little in common. Both wore dark suits, though Ortega's was wrinkle free, and as he approached, I saw that the creases on his pants looked dangerously sharp. His bright-orange tie with little blue gators on it indicated he was a University of Florida graduate or maybe just a fan of their sports teams.

Beneath his wrinkled jacket and slacks, Baker was a solid man. He was either too busy or too lazy to take care of his shoes as neither had seen polish for months or more. The same could have been said of his brown hair, which was long overdue for a trip to the barbershop. I didn't take him for lazy, so I assumed he was a busy man. His face brought to mind adjectives that all began with S: stone-faced, serious, and scary.

Nick, still grasping the photo of the ballerina, put it on his desk and stood. "What can I do for you?"

Baker turned to me. "We'd like to speak to Professor Weldon alone, please."

"I can take a hint," I said, gathering my belongings.

"Nonsense," Nick said. "Lise is a colleague. What can we do for you?"

Baker chewed on that for a minute. Ortega scratched his military-style buzz cut as he watched him.

When Baker shrugged, Ortega blinked his brown puppy-dog eyes and said, "Okay. But what we tell you has to do with an ongoing investigation and needs to stay confidential."

"No problem with me," I said. "Nick's the blabbermouth."

Nick shook his head. "No, I'm not. We'll keep what you say between us."

As he and Baker approached the desk, Ortega explained, "A couple of years ago, you helped a colleague, Detective Ramirez, with a cache of stolen artwork. She recommended you."

"You helped cops on a case?" I asked, mildly annoyed that he'd never said anything about it. "You never told me."

"We weren't an item then. And it really wasn't much work. She had me ID recovered paintings after the bad guys were caught. Most were contemporary pieces in the middling range, though there was one Cézanne still life."

"Stolen art?" I asked.

Baker glared at me like I'd just insulted him. "We're with homicide."

Nick and I exchanged a look of surprise.

Ortega said, "A murder took place a couple of weeks ago, a particularly ugly one. The victim was in her twenties; she was raped, tortured, and murdered in her apartment."

A terrible thing that someone so young died so horribly. "That's awful."

"You have no idea," Baker said.

Ortega glanced down at Nick's desk, and his eyes caught the photo of *The Floating Ballerina*. Ortega's scrutiny inspired Baker to look at it.

I picked it up and replaced it in the folder. "Don't be nosy."

"We're cops. Nosy is our job," Baker said.

"And you're here because..." Nick widened his eyes.

"Because we hope you can help us with something," Baker said. "The killer posed the body in a particular fashion utilizing wire and rope. Initially, we thought that he was trying to communicate something with that display."

"This morning, he gets an idea"—Ortega nodded at Baker—"that maybe the killer isn't trying to communicate, but considers his victims his works of art."

"I'd like to show you a picture of the victim at the scene," Baker said, "to see if you think I'm heading in the right direction."

Nick sat, picked up a pencil, and ran his thumbnail up and down its length. "How bad is it?"

"Bad," Ortega admitted.

"Well, I suppose I can take a look, if it will help." Nick didn't sound eager.

How odd, I thought, as Baker removed a glossy photo and handed it to Nick. For the second time today, Nick was looking at an unexpected photo.

"Ah shit," Nick muttered. A moment later, his tone changed to one of interest. "Lise, check this out."

Baker started to protest, but I went and leaned over Nick's shoulder. I tried—and failed—to keep a neutral expression as I took in the photo. The girl had been reduced to a beaten corpse. Naked but for a sheet draped over her right thigh, she was held in place by ropes and wires that angled in from walls and the ceiling, tied around arms, elbows, legs, and torso. She was reaching to her back with both hands. Gruesome torment on her face, she was caught in the middle of a giant spiderweb spun in a small living room. Once I got past the horror, something else came through.

"Is it?" I asked.

Nick looked up at me for a brief second, then his eyes returned to the photo. "You recognize it, don't you?"

"Is it *The Dying Niobid*?"

"I think so," Nick said.

Ortega pulled a notepad from his jacket pocket and held a pen at the ready. "The dying what?"

"I don't know if the killer is trying to send a message or not, but I'd bet dollars to donuts that he copied a famous Greek statue," Nick said.

"The artist is unknown," I said, "and the sculpture dates back several hundred years B.C."

"Four hundred to four hundred and fifty B.C.," Nick added. "It's based on Greek mythology. Queen Niobe had seven sons and seven daughters, and—"

"She's supposed to be this queen?" Baker said.

"No." I explained, "Queen Niobe bragged that she was more fruitful when it came to having babies than the goddess Leto. That pissed off Leto's children, Apollo and Artemis."

"As punishment, they killed all of the queen's children. This poor girl depicts a daughter who was shot in the back with an arrow." He held up the photo toward Baker and tapped on it. "That's why she's reaching like that and is in the process of falling to her knees."

"We didn't find any arrow," Ortega said.

"It wasn't part of the sculpture, either," Nick said. "Only implied."

Baker stared at Nick, as if waiting for more, and finally muttered, "Fuck me. I'm more confused than ever." He took a stick of gum out of a jacket pocket and gazed vacantly as he unwrapped it then popped it into his mouth. "Say, Professor, would you mind acting as a consultant for the PD, should the need arise?"

Something strange took place. Nick opened his mouth to reply, then he shut it. His gaze shifted from the policemen to me, and he bit his lip. Finally, he settled on Baker. "Normally, I'd be happy to help, but I'm leaving for Vienna in four days."

With those words, Nick delivered an invisible sucker punch to my gut.

Leaving for Vienna? That was news to me.

"I've accepted a fellowship to study in Vienna and teach a semester at the Academy of Fine Arts." He stared at me as he said that. His expression was blank, but I knew he was watching for my reaction.

Despite the anger churning in my gut, I didn't give him one.

"Got a colleague you could recommend?" Baker asked.

"I supposed you could ask the head of—" Nick was going to suggest Gabe, but he stopped, looked at me, and smiled. "The head of her own investigative firm. I highly recommend Analise Norwood. Lise knows her art and art history, and she's a private investigator. Right, Lise?"

Okay, score one for Nick for mentioning me. However, he was still down a couple of touchdowns, a few three-pointers, and a whole lot of runs for this Vienna thing. I didn't respond.

"Yeah, well, the last thing I need is a private detective dogging the case," Baker said.

"What's your art background?" Ortega asked.

Giving Nick a shot of angry eyes, I answered, "I attended San Marco University, majored in art history. I met Mr. Vienna here when he was a grad student and taught one of my classes. Got my degree and worked at a few galleries and a couple of museums, which had been the plan all along, except I wanted those to be in New York or Chicago. Instead, I ended up working in Tampa, Jacksonville, and Savannah. I found the work unsatisfying."

"And blah, blah, blah, you became a PI," Baker said, feigning boredom.

"No, Detective. Through a business acquaintance, I got a job at an insurance firm based out of Atlanta that insured high-priced art. They used me on an investigation into an art theft, decided I was good at it, and moved me into investigations. I got homesick and took a job at Monroe Kettleman Private Investigations in Jacksonville."

Ortega raised his eyebrows. "Big firm."

"Yep. I worked for them until my accumulated experience qualified me for my private investigator's license, and last year, I returned to San Marco as my own boss."

Baker sniffed and said to Ortega, "Guess she'll have to do."

Have to do? I felt like I was stuck in a room full of guys trying to see who could piss me off the most. "I can help you out in the role of a *professional* consultant. In other words, it'll cost you."

"What?" Baker said. "What makes you think we'd pay you?"

Ortega was more diplomatic. "We'll have to see how things shake out, Ms. Norwood. For now, can we exchange phone numbers? We'd like both of yours," he said, indicating Nick and me.

He gave us his and Baker's numbers, and both Nick and I programmed them into our phones. "In case you think of anything else. Thank you for your time. We'll see ourselves out."

"Yeah, shake yourselves outta here," I muttered as they went through the door. After a couple of breaths, I added, "God, that makes me mad."

"Yeah, Baker was a tool," Nick said.

I aimed my index finger right at his nose. "I'm talking about you!" My eyes narrowed as his widened.

Nick sank into his chair and put his hands on his desk. "I'm sorry, Lise. I was planning to tell you tonight over dinner. Speaking of which, how about dinner tonight?"

I grabbed my bag and laptop then snatched the photo of *The Floating Ballerina* out of the folder. I held it up to him. "See this? I made you a copy of this photo because I knew you would appreciate it, which is proof that at least one of us values the feelings of the other."

"Lise, really. I was going to tell you tonight."

"Fellowships don't fall out of the sky. Why didn't you discuss it with me?"

"I really didn't have any choice." He gazed down, collecting his thoughts, then looked up. "Gabe surprised me with it. The Academy of Fine Arts initially asked him, but he couldn't leave, so he arranged for me to go in his place. In his mind, it would be this big wonderful surprise, and he hadn't factored our relationship into the mix."

"But you waited to tell me until four days before you leave?" I meant to flip the photo onto his desk but put a little too much oomph to the effort, and the photo spun like a Frisbee, hitting him between the eyes.

"Lise, don't be like that," he said, rubbing at the point of impact.

"Okay. I'll be like this." I turned and walked out.

Chapter 3

I drove out of the university parking lot in my cream-and-black MINI Cooper, ignoring the rent-a-cop signaling me to slow down. It was early September, classes had just started, and students wandered around haphazardly as they looked for buildings and classes. Turning right onto Columbus, I drove past the western part of San Marco University, a mishmash of new buildings built to look old and large old homes dating back to the late 1800s and early 1900s. Those had been refurbished for scholastic use. It was a beautiful campus with maintained lawns and lots of shade from massive oaks and towering palms, but I wasn't in the mood for it.

"Shit," I blurted, hitting my steering wheel.

I was mad at my boyfriend and perturbed at Gabe. I felt like the two of them were keeping secrets from me. But it really wasn't Gabe's responsibility to keep me apprised of my boyfriend's career. So that let Gabe off the hook. That brought my raging mind back to Nick. Okay, so maybe we weren't exactly a dedicated couple. We'd been down this road before. When I was a student, I'd requested a private study session with him in a feeble attempt to get close to him. He'd said he would happily help, in a feeble attempt to get in my pants. We were both wildly successful at what we wanted.

Three months later, our relationship shifted into an on-again, off-again drama highlighted with angry arguments about nothing. Well, not nothing. A difference of opinion about what to watch on television, what to have for dinner, or where to go for the weekend could devolve into pitched battles. And though the subjects of the arguments were trivial, the subtext wasn't. I suspected we were really fighting over fidelity, levels of commitment, and the possibility of a future together—things neither of us had the courage to bring up at that point in our relationship. And since the arguments that inevitably ended in tearful apologies were something neither of us wanted, we'd mutually broken it off. As Nick had put it, we were both mature enough to recognize that we were too immature for a relationship.

I turned onto the beach road, and though the ocean wasn't visible on this stretch of the A1A, I could hear the pounding of the waves through my open windows. I breathed in that organic smell of the ocean—salt mixed with life and decay, a cleansing tonic borne on the air—but it didn't help this go-around.

Nick and I had remained friends over the years. After I graduated, we'd floated in and out of each other's lives from time to time. Upon my return to San Marco to open my own business, he was the first person I called. He was single. I was single. So we spent time together.

Three months ago, after an evening of pizza, wine, and The Marx Brothers in *Duck Soup*, something fell from my mouth almost of its own volition: "I think we're both mature enough to recognize that we are now mature enough to have a relationship."

The rest of the night, we'd spent engaged in the horizontal tango. It had been passionate and feverish, and it'd felt right. But then, Vienna popped up. *Four days? Shit!*

I wasn't upset that he was going. That he hadn't said a thing to me, hadn't allowed me time to prepare for his departure, was infuriating.

I pulled into the parking lot at San Marco Eldercare too fast and nearly nicked a car backing out of a space. I needed to calm down, especially if I was going to visit Mom. I parked, got out, then had to wait for the car I'd nearly hit to drive past. The old man driving gave me a dirty look. I figured he'd been visiting his wife and didn't need aggravation from me, so I raised my hand in a signaled apology. He gave me the peace sign. I needed that.

I entered the building and passed the main desk with a nod at Greta, who welcomed visitors each weekday. I took the elevator up to my mother's floor. Mom had been wheeled into one of the communal rooms in front of a giant TV on which Gene Kelly, Donald O'Connor, and Debbie Reynolds were dancing. I pulled a chair beside her and sat, taking her hand. She looked at me curiously, not knowing who I was, but smiling just the same. She always loved company.

I pulled out a brush and started on her hair. She closed her eyes and made a sound of appreciation. In better days, Mom had liked to see her stylist once a week and always fussed over her hair. Pops had first started brushing her hair on visits. I'd continued the tradition after his death. As I brushed, I told her about my day and teaching the class, though mainly, I talked about Nick and Vienna, asking if she had any advice. She mumbled now and then. Maybe in her mind we were having a mother-daughter conversation, though for that to happen, she would have to recognize me. And while I couldn't understand what she was muttering, I imagined her speaking in her voice from years ago, cogent and rational.

"First," Mom from days gone by said, "ask yourself if you love him and want to be with him. I assume the answer is yes, or you wouldn't bring it up. While it was inconsiderate of him to spring it on you at the last minute, I can understand that he'd worry how you'd take it. You do have your father's temper, you know. That's why he put off sharing the news."

I thought about what I imagined she'd said. I patted her hand, though her attention seemed glued to a romantic Gene-and-Debbie scene. "How would you handle it if it were you and Pops?"

Mom leaned forward and swung her head to me, surprise on her face. She lay back and closed her eyes, instantly asleep. But in my mind, Mom said, "I'd support him in his venture and let him know I was proud of him. But you should also let him know that finding out the way you did hurt you. Tell him you will always be open and honest with him, and that you'd appreciate it if he did likewise."

"Good advice, as always." I stood, and she mumbled something in her sleep when I kissed her cheek. I left as the *Singin' in the Rain* credits began to roll and ran into Arlene Fruman in the lobby as she was on her way to visit my mother. Mom had a lot of friends, many who visited her regularly. I just wished Pops was still alive so he could visit her, as well as give me some fatherly wisdom concerning Nick.

I turned west out of the parking lot, heading past a new, fairly upscale neighborhood called Leaning Oaks. Ten minutes later, I was tempted to stop at Merrill's Fish Camp for a cold one, but I drove on by, giving my horn a quick blast to say hi to all the retirees who either fished or just sat at Merrill's bar. Finally, I pulled into the little strip mall a quarter of a mile from the San Marco Municipal Airport. Sandwiched between the Kwik Stop at one end and my little office at the other were a tattoo shop, a sewing shop, a pizza place, and a yoga-slash-Pilates studio.

After using my key to open the dead bolt on the door, I stepped in. My office wasn't much, and I could have probably worked as well from home, but an investigator I'd worked with in Jacksonville had said an office would make me more credible in the eyes of clients. Set up as a storefront, it had a glass front wall and door, which I'd covered with beige drapes. Clients and potential clients stepped off the sidewalk and right into my office, where an abstract Jaison Cianelli giclée was mounted on the wall across from my scarred desk bought from a secondhand store—and an expensive chair, because I treasured my comfort. The other walls held framed black-and-white beach shots that a photographer friend took. Someone had given me a green filing cabinet, and even though all my files were computerized, it added credibility. The cabinet held mostly office supplies, along with snacks, a bottle of Bulleit rye, gym clothes, and other assorted knickknacks. A pastel-blue love seat sat in a cluster with a couple of chairs. As a nod to my profession, and more art than functional, there was a coatrack in the corner holding a raincoat and fedora.

I sat and opened *The Floating Ballerina* file on my computer. I hadn't had the *honor* of meeting Shari Stephens's husband. One of the first things I'd learned about working a divorce case was not to believe everything when it came to one spouse, even my client, detailing the shortcomings of the other. Divorces involved a lot of emotions, biases, and skewed viewpoints. On the other hand, some cases were simply a matter of a woman being married to a douchebag. Shari Stephens was one of those women. She'd accepted her husband's general doucheyness and resolved to stay married because, in her mind, that was what people should do. Then he'd given her chlamydia.

She'd provided me with copies of what she'd found while poking around his computer. He was a member of not one, but three sites devoted to random sex with strangers. His username was StudlyHungwell69.

Before I could get sufficiently grossed out reviewing the online antics of Mr. StudlyHungwell69, my cell phone played Barry White's "Can't Get Enough of Your Love, Babe." I'd picked it as Nick's ringtone specifically because of the cheese factor.

I held my sigh until I answered so I could share it with him. "Hello, Nick."

"Still mad?"

I thought carefully about how to answer, because though I still felt a fire burning, it was dwindling. "Look, I'll get over it, but yeah, I'm still ticked off. Not telling me, well, you hurt my feelings."

"I know, and I'm sorry. At least let me explain."

"Go ahead."

"Gabe didn't ask me. He *told* me I was going. I suppose I could have backed out of it, but it is a huge honor. I figured we're doing so good right now that we'd easily survive a few months at a distance, and then we can return to our illicit affair."

"It's not illicit."

"I know, but it sounds cool."

I laughed a little. "It does, doesn't it?"

"I started to tell you a few times and then chickened out and then tried working up the nerve, and then we'd get back into illiciting."

"Neck deep in illiciting."

He laughed, sensing my thaw. "To be honest, Lise, I did plan to tell you tonight over dinner."

"Okay, I believe you. It just sucks that you're leaving when we're getting along so well."

After a moment of silence, he said, "So how about it? Dinner tonight?"

I felt it in the lower left quadrant of my gut, a little kernel of anger sizzling away. "Not tonight."

I could hear his disappointment. "Tomorrow night then?"

"We'll see."

"Aw, Lise, c'mon. I'm leaving in four days."

"Call me tomorrow."

"All right. And, Lise..."

"Yeah?"

"I'm sorry."

After ending the call, I held my phone for a good five minutes, staring at nothing and thinking about my life, future, and a life and future with Nick.

Is that something I want? I thought I did. I was pretty sure, anyway. It was funny—I could be decisive when it came to most things, but with relationships, not so much. It boiled down to my personal freedom. Anything that threatened that, real or imagined, scared me. But Nick wasn't a threat to my independence, and he certainly wouldn't want me to change. In fact, we supported each other's careers and independence. My anger had dwindled to a crumb of irritation, and a bit of guilt had been tossed in. Nick was sweet and smart, and he treated me well.

As a child, Nick had spent years under the care of his aunt. She was quick to anger and meted out harsh punishment, and I wondered if his reluctance to tell me could be attributed to that. Nick's mother and father had married young and bought a small farm west of Saint Augustine. When Nick was five, they were killed in an accident on the way to a farmers market with a load of spuds. He went to live with his father's older sister, Penny. Aunt Pen, as Nick called her, lived on welfare, started to drink early in the day, often left Nick on his own, and saw no problem in bringing her temporary boyfriends to her mobile home late at night for a rollicking good time while Nick attempted to sleep in the next room.

I was tempted to call Nick back and agree to dinner, had it not been for one obstacle—my pride. Still, I would get over it. I had to. With him leaving for Vienna, we only had hours to spend together.

Getting back to Shari Stephens and *The Floating Ballerina* case, I reread some of the printouts of her husband's online conversations with other women but then decided I didn't want to delve into that muck right then. I was too curious about those two detectives who'd stopped by Nick's office. *What would it be like to work a murder case like that?*

My conversation with Baker and Ortega was probably as close as I would ever come to an actual murder case. For me, the work was cheating spouses, dirt digging, and process-servicing. All that was a job, which I felt suited to and was content with. But to work serious crimes, like murder, seemed like more of a calling. I wondered about that poor girl. The suffering she'd undergone, and the terror, must have been gruesome. The way the killer had left her body, considering the work he'd put into posing it, was equally horrific and remarkable. The killer was evil, and to be responsible for putting away just one evil person would be life-affirming. I could make a difference.

Baker and Ortega hadn't told us much about the case, and I wondered if there was more to be learned. I clicked on the website for the local newspaper, the San Marco Ledger. Since I had the general time frame, and San Marco didn't have many murders, I quickly found the first news item. It didn't give details other than that she had been found murdered in her apartment. The other three articles offered little, except her identity—Kristin Harmon, a twenty-three-year-old student and waitress. That last article included a head-and-shoulders photograph. Her head was turned slightly, and she was smiling. Her blond shoulder-length hair caught my attention. It was wavy, like my cousin Gracie's hair. Though the face didn't match up exactly, the way she held her head and the sincerity of her smile added to the likeness. The next thing I knew I was getting teary-eyed. Through watery eyes, the photo could very well have been Gracie.

"Ah shit." I sniffed back snot and refused to get all emotional. It was hard because they also shared something besides a passing resemblance—they had both been murdered.

Something occurred to me, something about family. I made a call.

"Baker," a voice answered.

"Hi, Detective. It's Lise Norwood. We met at the university earlier."

"Yeah?" His tone added an unspoken, *So what?*

"I was just thinking."

"Were you now?"

He wasn't making this easy. "In the myth of the Dying Niobid, all of the Queen's children are killed."

"So you told us."

"Well, on the chance that part of the myth is important to the killer, maybe you should see if the victim has any brothers and sisters. Maybe warn them to be extra careful."

Baker took a breath, and I was expecting another smartass comment. Instead, he said, "Good point. We'll handle it." And he hung up.

Chapter 4

The Artist

A burnt smell, smoky, a hint of scorched rubber. Lying on top of her, moving, shifting, it was too dark to see her. He tried to learn more about her by scent and by touch. She remained a mystery. He caressed her naked body as she moved against him rhythmically, leaves and dirt their bed.

His fingers dug into her flesh and anchored the struggling woman in place.

A twig poked his knee each time he pushed against her. With a gasp, her mouth traveled over his skin, gently kissing down his arm.

Pain flared as she put her duct-taped mouth against his forearm and managed to bite through the tape. He made a fist with his free hand and hammered her head twice, stunning her.

He nuzzled along her collarbone and up the side of her neck. Her breathing became a pant, and his followed. He pushed himself up into leaves and limbs. His face broke a web, and a spider skittered over his ear and onto his shoulder. An insight: dark hair, almost black. With his hands he felt her body, trim and soft, full in the right places. The tip of his tongue traced behind her ear. Her panting changed to moans, so he stayed at her ear, licking and nibbling.

She screamed through the torn duct tape, loudly enough that had anybody been nearby, they would have heard. Nobody was, so he ground his teeth harder.

Hips moved, her legs spread, and he slid into wet heat. The odor of burned rubber intensified. Her long groan turned into rapid gags like she was choking. He exploded in an orgasm so intense that it was painful, and he bit her shoulder throughout his release. Her skin tasted of salt and copper. Rolling off, he collapsed deeper in the brush and waited for his heartbeat to settle. She crawled from him, exiting their nest.

Her wrists, bound by wire behind her back, prevented her from moving quickly. She crawled like an inchworm, her cheek in the dirt. Her panicked breathing grew louder now that she'd chewed through the tape.

A light source reached through the foliage, casting shadows of branches and leaves across her body. Out of the growth, she stood. Her dark hair fell midway down her back, between wide shoulders. Her narrow waist and Frazetta ass, wide and full, swayed as she walked away.

Struggling to her feet, she screamed for help through the tattered tape then ran without looking back.

She strolled to the right and headed down a hill, disappearing into night. Arms extended, he pushed from the undergrowth and felt cool air on his skin. He scrambled back, patting at the ground. He grabbed his clothes and reemerged from the brush. A distant glow, the moon stood sentinel as he hurried after her. When he came to a small lake, he paused to slip his legs into damp trousers and buttoned his shirt. Dancing on one foot then another, he slid on his shoes.

Footprints in the muddy shore led him to a tree line, and she moved behind a pine. He entered the trees and emerged under the moon in a grassy field that gently ascended a hill. Between him and the moon was the silhouette of a form surrounded by a low circular wall. He recognized her as she sat on a large rock within the wall, gazing into the distance. The water surrounding her reflected the moon. She sat atop a still fountain.

"Hi," he said.

She sat stoically, facing away from him.

"Where... How did we..." He moved around to face her, and when the moonlight was behind him, he saw her hair was now a dark copper color, as was the rest of her body. He stepped over the wall and into ankle-deep water, creating hushed splashes. He wanted to laugh, or maybe he did, when he saw that she was made of bronze and anchored to the rock she sat upon. His hands went up and touched solid thighs that he'd caressed earlier. She stared out, unaware.

Chapter 5

After an English muffin and two cups of coffee, I was out of the house early. I followed my client's husband to the car dealership where he worked then met Elliot the Slim, who would watch the place throughout the workday. Before getting to the office, I stopped at the gym. I tried to work out seven days a week, which really meant three to five times a week, unless it was only once or twice a week. In reality, the gym was a sporadic thing for me. I would work with weights and machines for thirty minutes then spend another thirty on one of the cardio machines. I hated cardio, which was probably why my workouts were so sporadic and definitely why I wasn't a jogger. I could, however, tolerate a stair-climbing machine, rowing machine, or stationary bike. As I was trying to decide which of those torture devices to mount, my cell phone trilled with an old-fashioned ring. *A pity...* I had hoped to hear the dulcet tones of Barry White.

By the time I got the phone from my pocket, it had already rung four times, so I answered without checking the caller ID. "Analise Norwood Investigations."

A gruff man said, "All right, we'll take you on as consultant."

After a moment of confusion, I managed to respond, "Who's this?"

"It's Baker, San Marco Homicide. We'll pay your consultation fee. We'd like to hire you."

Surprise, surprise. "How much do you usually pay? Is it a flat fee, or an hourly consultation? It's more if I have to go to—"

"I don't care what you charge," he said. "You're hired, and we need you at De Leon Park right now. Do you know where it is?"

"Yeah, I know where it is. Why there?"

"We have another one. Get here now." He hung up.

I ran out of the gym in my workout clothes, black tights with gray swirly designs, an old gray tank top only months from becoming a rag, and a pair of old ankle-high Keds sneakers. Once in the car, I headed east, struggling to keep my speed low enough that I wouldn't get ticketed. De Leon Park was a couple of blocks from the ocean. It was surrounded by nice neighborhoods, including the Dunes, an upscale gated community. Most of the beachfront homes there were neo-Florida cracker style: wood frame with metal roofs, oversized windows, and surrounded by wide verandas. They were beautiful homes, but considering the price tag, they better be.

When I took the turn to reach the front entrance of De Leon Park, I was treated to a display of flashing lights atop all manner of law enforcement and emergency vehicles. I felt like I was in a TV cop show as I took in the yellow crime scene tape holding a dozen or so gawkers at bay. A young uniformed officer stopped me at the entrance, and I started to explain why I was there, but at the mention of my name, he instructed me to drive in and leave my car in the main lot. Remembering the photo that Baker showed Nick and me, I parked and sat in my car, preparing myself for whatever I was about to witness. There was a tap on my window. It was Ortega.

I got out. "Detective."

"Ms. Norwood. Thanks for coming."

"Call me Lise. Sorry about the..." I used my hands to indicate my gym clothes. "Baker said to come right now."

Without responding, Ortega took my arm and guided me through a small contingent of uniforms to the head of a trail blocked off with more crime scene tape. He held it up, and I ducked under. He followed.

"We'll get you files for both murders," he told me. "At least what we can share."

That sounded like they wanted me for more than a onetime crime scene interpretation. "Baker said there was another one."

Ortega muttered, "Another sadistic slaughter. Another pose we need you to identify. This way." He pointed down the trail and started walking at a brisk pace.

I caught up and asked, "Wires and ropes?"

"Yes."

"Another young woman?"

"Yes, but a different type. The first one, the Dying whatchamacallit—"

"Dying Niobid," I said.

"Right. Twenty-three-year-old Kristin Harmon. By the way, thanks for calling Baker with your idea to warn any of Ms. Harmon's siblings."

"You're welcome."

"A good notion, but she was an only child. She was going to cosmetology school and paying for it working as a waitress at Capello's Ristorante."

Capello's, fine Italian cuisine, always busy. She probably made good tips.

"She lived in the North," Ortega added. The North was officially San Marco North, an old neighborhood that was mostly affordable housing and rentals. "In a duplex with a longtime friend. Kristin was blond."

"And this one?" I asked, as we continued down the trail.

"Our new vic is Hispanic. The ID we found with her jogging outfit says Angela Lopez. She was eight years older than our other vic. Kristin's neighborhood is pretty much blue-collar. Angela lived a couple of blocks that way." He pointed south of the park, where a number of upscale condominiums were located. "I don't think our killer has a specific type, other than female and attractive."

"Kristin was found in her apartment, right?"

"Uh-huh. Her roommate spent the night with her boyfriend and came home the next morning to find Kristin murdered."

I thought about what it would be like to make that discovery then about how my cousin Gracie's body had been found by an eleven-year-old boy whose mother had taken him to the park. That boy, who would be in his twenties now, probably still saw Gracie in his dreams.

"You okay, Lise?" Ortega asked, interrupting my morbid reflection.

"So the killer doesn't have a particular type, and he's not picky about where to do it."

"Apparently indoors or outdoors are both fine with him. C'mon, she's over there." The trail ended at a small meadow, and Ortega pointed to a fountain in the middle.

I'd harbored hopes of appearing cool and calm when I got to the crime scene; instead my Catholic upbringing took control. "Mary, Mother of God."

"Yeah," Ortega said. "I know what you mean."

A couple of uniforms and a suit were huddled nearby, talking. The suit called out to Ortega.

"You can get closer," Ortega said before he left me. "Just stay out of the way."

I inhaled, exhaled, and started across the grass. The fountain was twenty feet across and ringed with a low coquina wall. A massive coquina stone rose about five feet from the center of the fountain, upon which Angela Lopez was affixed. She'd been perched naked on the stone, knees bent, her legs together and to the left. Her left arm was draped casually across her lap, and her right hand rested on the stone beside her as if she were leaning on it. I moved south of the fountain to where I could best see her, and my first real thought was how beautiful she was. Then I noticed both the insects and techs buzzing around the corpse, some seeking nourishment, some seeking clues. I had no doubt about what statue the crime scene copied, but the famous bronze wasn't beaten and bloody like this poor woman, who was wired in place. Stepping closer, I noticed specific wounds, one on her shoulder and another on her thigh—bite marks caused by enough force to create deep wounds. Blood matted her hair to the right side of her head and had splashed down her neck and shoulder. Her nose had bled, as well, covering shredded duct tape over her mouth and her chin.

"Did he recreate another famous piece of art?" someone behind me asked.

I turned to find Detective Baker. He looked exhausted.

"Yes," I said. "He copied *The Little Mermaid*, a bronze sculpture by Edvard Erikson, a Danish-Icelandic sculptor."

"*The Little Mermaid*? Okay. Yeah. Even I know that one."

"Based on the Hans Christian Andersen story. If I remember correctly, it was commissioned in 1909 and put in a park in Copenhagen a couple of years later."

"I don't suppose there's any connection between the two statues?" Baker asked.

"Well, they're both female nudes, but that's about it. They were sculpted a couple of thousand years apart. *The Dying Niobid* is marble, and *The Little Mermaid* is bronze."

Baker grunted, shut his eyes, and massaged his temples.

"Find anything helpful?" I asked.

"Michelangelo left plenty of DNA. At both scenes."

"Michelangelo?" I asked.

"He's earned a nickname. Hopefully, it stays in the department."

"Hopefully."

"He didn't kill her here. We haven't located that spot yet."

"So he killed her and then moved her here and created that?" I nodded toward the fountain.

"Yeah, killing elsewhere and moving the body is different than the first."

I pointed to the corpse. "He's a biter."

Baker took out a pair of sunglasses and placed them on his face. Though he covered the dark circles under his eyes, he still looked like he'd been awake for the past few days. "Yeah. There's a couple more, on the underside of Angela's other thigh, as well as on her right buttock. Also chewed on her right ear, worried at it like a dog with a rawhide bone. Some of the ear is missing. Bit Kristin too, the first victim."

"Twenty-three, waitress at Capello's."

"Which pisses me off even more. My wife and I love that restaurant. Anyway, we've got DNA. We've got bite patterns. What we don't have is a match to anything on record."

"Anything else?"

"Medium-length brown hairs at both scenes. The tech geeks feel sure the ones recovered here will be a match to the ones at Kristin's apartment."

"You call victims by their first names?"

He gazed at me. "It helps me to remember that they're people, feeds my drive to solve the crimes."

Hmm, maybe I found a reason to like Baker after all.

"Here's something interesting. Even though Michelangelo sprayed semen around Kristin's apartment like a garden hose, left saliva, hair, and bite patterns, he hasn't left any prints at either scene."

"Luck? Gloves? Cleans up?"

"Techs say that he probably wipes everything when he's done. Both of these cases confuse the hell out of me. On the one hand, the rape, torture, and murder seem spontaneous, fueled by passion. But the careful placement of the bodies indicates a cool calculation that's further backed up by wiping the scene." Baker took off his sunglasses and used his tie to wipe the lenses. "I think Michelangelo has his prints on file."

"Criminal background?"

"Maybe, but people get printed these days for all sorts of reasons. He could volunteer with children or help with a church youth group. Maybe he's in education or security."

"Or he's a private investigator."

"Got someone in mind?"

"No. Just know I had to get fingerprinted for my PI license."

"Want to get closer?"

"Not really," I said but halved the distance to the fountain anyway.

We walked around the back of Angela. A few lengths of wire and rope had been run into the fountain and tied off at a couple of drains. The rest ran from her body to what appeared to be tree limbs hammered into the ground like tent stakes. Baker said, "Same baling wire as the last crime. You could pick it up in any hardware store. Same with the rope. He used some wood with Angela."

Michelangelo had made a rudimentary base out of tree limbs wired to the boulder with another sturdy branch acting as a support that ran up Angela's back and to her head. Her head was tied loosely enough to list toward her shoulder, matching the statue.

"He's strong," I said.

"To do that? Yeah."

"He's a serial killer, isn't he?"

"Officially? Not until he's killed three people. But if I was a betting man, which I am, I'd bet that he's killed before, but the connection with those other murders hasn't been made yet. So yeah, I think he's a serial nutjob."

Tired of taking in Angela's degradation, I stared across the meadow. "Even if Kristin and Angela are his first two, there'll be a third, won't there? Another to make it official?"

"Probably. And then I lose the case to the FBI. They'll probably take over for a serial killer."

My attention was caught by a man in his early thirties, in a suit, running out of the trail. A uniformed officer ran right behind him, yelling at him to stop. The man stumbled when he saw the dead woman on the rock, and he fell to his knees. His face contorted in grief and horror.

Baker muttered, "Ah, shit."

Chapter 6

The man's lips moved, but no words escaped his mouth. He tried again and shouted, "Angela? Oh God, no. Angela!"

He rushed toward the fountain. Baker ran toward the man, intercepting him before he got close. The man struggled, trying to free himself.

Baker got in his face and shouted, "There's nothing you can do for her!"

The man stopped struggling, stopped all movement. Panting like a dog, he stared past Baker.

Baker called to another uniform, "Take him back up the trail. I'll be up to talk to him in a few minutes. You," Baker called to the cop who'd chased the man. "What the hell?"

"Sorry, Detective." The uniform nodded at Angela's body. "He's her boyfriend. I knew you'd want to talk to him, so I led him halfway down the trail, told him to wait, and the next thing I know, he's flying past me."

Baker shook his head. "Thanks for the help. Come on."

When we got to the path, I stopped for one final look at Angela. "That's the last image he's going to have of her."

"Yeah, that sucks," Baker said.

As we worked our way up the trail, I remembered the last image I'd had of Gracie. Thankfully, it wasn't of her dead, but it wasn't nice, either. We'd argued. She'd been arrested on a possession charge, not the first time, and I had driven to Panama City to bail her out of jail.

Out on the sidewalk in the hot Florida sun, not twenty paces from the door to the county lockup, I'd told her, "You have to make a choice, right now. You can either have me in your life, or you can have drugs in your life, not both."

Gracie had kept her gaze down and shuffled her feet. "Aw, come on, Lise. Don't be like that."

"Make a choice. Now." After a full minute of silence, I'd held up a hand in a dismissive gesture. "Fine. I give up." Before I walked away, I'd seen her face reflect both shame and raw anger.

Before Baker and I got to the trailhead, we came across the man sitting on a bench, huddled over and crying. A couple of self-conscious uniforms had placed themselves between the man and the crime scene.

Baker approached the man. "And you are?"

He was one of a kind. I started to head up the trail but changed my mind. I went and sat beside the man. "I'm sorry for your loss."

"What are you doing, Norwood?" Baker asked.

The shock and confusion Angela's boyfriend felt was evident. "Loss?"

Baker gave me a hard stare then turned his attention to the man, repeating, "And you are?"

The man took him in with that same numb expression. Finally, he said, "Me? I'm Jon Murphy."

Baker made a note in a small notebook. "How do you know Angela Lopez?"

Murphy looked down the path, a pained expression in place, as if he could still see her. "She—Angela is my—was my girlfriend."

I opened my mouth, but Baker held out a hand to hush me.

After a long stretch of silence, Murphy said, "I work in IT at the district attorney's office. Angela is a legal assistant there."

"Crap," Baker said. He saw my quizzical expression and explained, "The DA's going to want to jump into things now."

Murphy went on to say, "That's where we met. We've been going out for almost a year."

"How'd you know to come here?" Baker asked.

"Her boss called me, wanted to know if I knew where she was. She didn't show up for work, which isn't like her. I went to her condo." He breathed deeply, released it with a sigh, and gazed out blankly.

After several seconds, Baker said, "Keep going."

Murphy blinked several times. "Huh? Oh. She wasn't there, at the condo. I have a key and let myself in. I noticed her jogging shoes were gone, which is odd because she always runs in the evening after work. Then I thought that maybe she was still mad, you know, because of the fight, and went running this morning to blow off steam and lost track of time. That's why I came to the park—to look for her. But I never in a million years expected..."

"When's the last time you saw her?" I asked.

"Not for a couple of days. We had a fight and haven't spoken since."

"A fight, huh?" Baker made a big show of writing that down. "So what did the two of you fight about?"

Murphy shook his head. "Same things a lot of couples fight about."

"Be specific," Baker said. "Was she mad because you leave the toilet seat up? Are you sick of having to watch chick flicks all the time? Which argument?"

"Am I a suspect?"

Baker acted amused. "At this point? Yeah, you're a suspect. So it's best that you tell us everything you can. Including why you and Angela fought."

"Angela was taking evening classes. She wants to be lawyer—wanted to be. I thought she took too many classes this semester. All her free time went to studying."

"Aren't you supposed to support your loved ones in their educational pursuits?" Baker asked.

I couldn't keep quiet and told Baker, "Don't be such a dick."

He glared at me, anger and surprise both evident. "Why are you still here?"

Murphy didn't register our little clash. "I know, I should have supported her more. But she was growing distant. I was scared I was losing her, so we had that stupid argument." He focused on the ground between his feet and gave a laugh that was empty of humor. "I wanted more of her, and she wanted more freedom."

"Franklin," Baker called to one of the uniforms. "Take Mr. Murphy back up the trail." First, Baker took down Murphy's contact information and passed him a card. "Call me if you think of anything important."

While we watched the officer lead Murphy away, Baker asked, "You called me a dick?"

"Yeah, well—"

"You do realize how often it's the significant other who's responsible for a murder?"

"A stand-alone murder," I said. "Not something like this."

"You don't know. But believe me, we'll find out if there's any connection between Murphy and Kristin Harmon."

"Hey." Ortega hurried up the path, a little out of breath. "We found where he killed her."

"Can I see?" I asked.

Baker and Ortega looked at one another, trying to gauge each other's reactions.

"Might find something that needs my expertise," I said.

Baker nodded and grunted, which I took as consent, and I followed them back down the trail. Ortega led us past the fountain. We passed a couple of men discussing how best to bring her body down, then we cut upward at an angle to the edge of the field and stopped before a tall, overgrown bush with red berries. A tech with paper covers over his shoes was on his hands and knees, his head stuck inside the bush.

"Whatcha got, Busby?" Baker called.

The tech backed out and stood, brushing his gloved hands a few times on his gray slacks. I'd seen his type before in 1940s movies—skinny and short, with slicked-back hair and thick glasses. I'll be damned if he wasn't sporting a pencil-thin moustache. He wore a button-down white shirt, its sleeves rolled up his forearms, and a red bowtie.

"Baker, Ortega," he said then looked at me, waiting for an introduction.

I held out a hand. "Lise Norwood."

He took my hand and smiled at me.

Ortega added, "She's our art consultant."

"Ah," Busby said. I couldn't tell if it was in approval or not, but he still hadn't released my hand.

"Reuben Busby is the best crime scene tech in the state," Ortega added.

"And a helluva dance partner," he said.

It took a moment to realize that he was flirting with me... at a murder scene. It was so surreal that I had no idea how to respond.

"Can we concentrate on the case, Romeo?" Baker said.

Busby dropped my hand. "Sure."

"Michelangelo killed her by the bush?" Baker asked.

"Looks like a bush, and no, not there," Busby said. "That is actually a Brazilian pepper tree, an invasive species. You know we found her clothes scattered from there to there." He pointed to a grassy stretch to the right of the pepper tree. "He forced her from the jogging path, ripping off her clothes as they went, and shoved her into the foliage. Judging from the condition of the tree, she put up a good fight. He bound her arms behind her back with wire, which tore up her wrists as she struggled, and slapped a piece of duct tape over her mouth, which she eventually chewed through. Showed chutzpah. He raped her in there." He indicated the direction of the fountain.

"This is speculation, but I'm guessing she got free, ran a little that way, before he caught and then killed her over there." He pointed to where a tech was putting up tape around a grassy section. "I'd say strangulation, like the last vic. He's strong; strong enough to get her from the path, into the pepper tree foliage, bind her, rape her, chase her, kill her over there, and then carry her body to the fountain. Strong enough to deal with her dead weight while he applied wires, ropes, and wood to hold her in place."

"Anything else?" Baker asked.

"Probably. Just haven't found it yet." Busby started for the pepper tree, stopped, and smiled at me. "And if you ever need a skilled dance partner..."

"You're the first I'll call," I said.

Busby knelt and crawled into the growth.

Baker surveyed the scene. "See anything artsy?"

I took in the Brazilian pepper tree, where she'd died. Then I slowly spun around, scanning the area. "Nothing. Other than Angela's body mimicking *The Little Mermaid*."

"If we don't find him, he'll do it again," Ortega said.

Baker grunted. "Uh-huh, and then we'll be up to our elbows in feds."

Personally, I couldn't see a downside to that. "And that'll be because there's another woman who died horribly. Don't forget about *her* when you're whining about the FBI."

"I don't whine," Baker said. "And why are you still here?" He paused to scrutinize me. "Nice look."

"I was at the gym."

"Bill us," Baker said. "Ortega will walk you back to your car."

"I can find my way."

Still, Ortega escorted me. "It's a crime scene."

We walked in silence, but about halfway up the trail, the images of Angela and Kristin in the photo angered me. "I wish there was something more that I could do."

Ortega nodded. "I understand. But you've already helped us quite a bit. We'd still be stumbling around in the dark if you hadn't told us about *The Dying Niobid* and *The Little Mermaid*."

That made me feel better, but only by a little.

Chapter 7

I went home to change into business attire then drove to my office. After visiting the crime scene, I found myself oddly wired and paced back and forth in front of my desk. It had been a disturbing yet affirming morning. I would never cleanse the image of Angela Lopez from my mind. As bad as the photo of Kristin had been, seeing the aftermath of a murder in person made the brutality infinitely worse. But being involved, even in such a nebulous fashion, by offering my assistance in the pursuit of a killer, confirmed that I had made good choices with my life and the career I was following. I hoped that I could continue as a consultant on the case. I wondered if I could do more to make myself the go-to PI for work with the San Marco PD. Then I realized a police department needed a PI about as much as I needed a second head. The fact that they'd used me was a one-in-a-million chance—and only because of my art knowledge and because Nick was leaving town.

Oh shit. At the thought of Nick, my brain shifted gears to lovelorn. I shook my head and sat at my desk to write up a bill to submit to Baker. The guy was a piece of work, though Ortega was decent enough. I came up with a figure that was reasonable and added an un-notated asshole surcharge for having to deal with Baker. As the invoice was printing, Gracie came to mind, and I started remembering things. I wished they were good memories, like at a family feast or ripping into presents under a Christmas tree, but the remembrances were of my mother calling to tell me Gracie had been murdered. I'd been in my dorm room at school. It was midmorning, and there was a lot of noise from out in the hall. Students were headed to class and coming and going from the showers and bathroom. Doors were open, and music added to the mix. I'd just finished studying for an exam coming up later in the week and was preparing to leave for Professor Turner's class. That was before we'd become friends, and I'd started calling him Gabe.

The printer finished, and I held up the invoice. They hadn't specified an amount, and they *had* told me to charge whatever I normally did. With the un-notated asshole surcharge, it was a little high. And while it felt good tacking it onto the bill, maybe I shouldn't have boosted the cost just because the client was a pain. The surcharge totaled what a client normally paid for two hours of work. I decided to redo the math and print up a new invoice.

Or... I smiled. I could just send the invoice for that amount, which would justify my owing them a little more work on the case—two hours' worth—whether they wanted it or not. And if I did learn something important to the case, maybe the San Marco PD would keep me in mind on the rare occasion they needed a consultant.

Another reason was driving me to poke my nose where it didn't belong: in honor of Gracie and her unsolved murder. With that rationale in place, I called Jon Murphy's phone number, which I'd memorized when he gave it to Baker. While waiting for him to answer, I ignored the little voice in my head telling me how much trouble I could get into if Baker and Ortega found out about this.

Murphy answered with a still-in-shock tone.

"Mr. Murphy, my name is Lise Norwood. I was with Detective Baker at the park this morning. I was hoping I could stop by for a few follow-up questions."

To my surprise, Jon Murphy asked to meet me at Angela's condo. I locked the office and drove off in the direction of the San Marco Beach and Tennis Club, located a couple of blocks from De Leon Park. I bypassed Gordo's, a food truck permanently parked in the

Dicky's Surf Shop parking lot. It took a good deal of self-control, because Gordo's could throw together the best Tex-Mex-style burrito this side of Austin. I promised myself a Gordo's Grande after I talked to Murphy.

San Marco Beach and Tennis Club was a gated condominium, but the security guy let me in when I showed him my PI license. San Marco had taken a page from Saint Augustine and Saint Augustine Beach and put a three-story limit on all construction, especially condos. Nothing could spoil the beauty of a beach more than some ugly-ass twelve-story complex rising like a giant tombstone over the Atlantic.

I quickly found Angela's building, which was closest to A1A and farthest from the beach. Still, she had to make a pretty good salary to afford either ownership or rental at the Beach and Tennis Club. I parked by half a dozen clay tennis courts. The condo buildings borrowed from the Caribbean palette, and Angela's was sunset pink. I thought about how much trouble I would be in with Detectives Baker and Ortega if they knew I was about to interview a possible suspect. The rational side of my brain told me not to do it, to let the police handle it and hope they would seek my services. However, the irrational side kept telling me to work on the case in honor of Gracie. I took the stairs to the third floor and found the unit. The door swung open as soon as I knocked, and I saw Jon Murphy sitting on a sofa, staring at the floor, oblivious to my arrival.

"Knock, knock," I said.

He looked up and motioned me in.

I bypassed the kitchen and dining area on the left and guest bedroom on the right. Besides the sea-blue sofa that Murphy sat on, the living room held a matching loveseat, a white lounger, a coffee table, and end tables. Sliding glass doors opened onto a view farther into the condominium complex. If I stood on tiptoe, I might have been able to see the ocean. If the condo sold, it would be listed as "ocean view," and tens of thousands would get tacked onto the asking price.

Murphy had returned to his staring contest with the tile, and I sat in the loveseat. "Have the police been by yet?"

"Yes. A policeman. He went through the place, said some more would be showing up and not to take anything out." He spoke in a monotone.

I figured it'd be best if I was gone by then. "Did they mention when they'd return?"

"No."

Okay, make this quick, just to be safe. I decided to open with a softball question, something to get Murphy to start talking. "Did Angela play tennis?"

"Huh?"

"She lived at the Beach and Tennis Club. I was wondering if she played tennis?"

"She played some. Angela liked sports and played them all. Her main passions, though, were running and surfing."

I noticed the two surfboards out on the porch, a shortboard and a longboard. "I know you haven't had time to come to grips with this, but is there anything new that's come to mind as to who might have done this, or why?"

Murphy groaned like an old man as he stood and walked to the sliding glass door. "Not a clue. Everyone liked her, and I'm not just saying that. Everyone at work, the places we hung out, our friends. Everyone loved Angela."

"Did that make you jealous?"

Murphy looked at me like that was the silliest question I could possibly ask.

I shrugged. "At the park, you told Detective Baker that Angela was spending more time with classwork, and you felt you were losing her. Makes sense that other people who felt some affection for her could inspire a little jealousy."

"No," Murphy said. "I wasn't jealous of anyone. I mean, I get your point and all, but Angela was focused on school and her job. She barely had time for me, much less someone new."

I stood and went to stand by him, gazing out of the glass door at the condo complex, and waited for him to continue.

After a few more seconds of silence, he said, "I wasn't jealous of the time she was devoting to her studies, I was just scared I was losing her. Have you ever loved someone who, it seemed all of a sudden, lost interest in you?"

Frankly, no, though I hadn't had a lot of boyfriends to compare against. On the other hand, I wanted to be sympathetic. "Who hasn't?"

"Then you know that helpless feeling. If you don't do something, they'll drift that much further, but if you try to do something, it makes you seem desperate and clingy. Then that makes it even worse."

"A lose-lose situation."

"Yeah."

When taking the previous murder into account, I didn't think that Murphy had anything to do with Angela's, unless there was some unknown connection between him and the first victim. That was an avenue I would leave to Baker and Ortega, though I did ask, "Do you know someone named Kristin Harmon?"

"No. The other policeman asked me that. What does she have to do with all this?"

"A possible lead. Has Angela mentioned any strangers following her? Watching her? That kind of thing?"

"No. Nothing like that."

"Where was she taking classes?"

"San Marco University."

They had a decent law program for such a small school. Kristin Harmon was taking classes, as well, but in cosmetology, so she was probably enrolled at SMTI, San Marco Technical Institute.

"Mind if I look around?"

He looked out the glass door. "Help yourself."

The condo was small, but plenty big for one person. The beachy fashion continued over to the dining room, which was the space between the sofas and kitchen counter. There were framed photos of varied beach scenes, including a sunrise and a close-up of a starfish.

"Was Angela into photography?" I asked.

Without turning to me, he said, "As much as anything else. She had a Canon camera and would take it out now and again. She took those on the walls."

I stopped before one that featured an attractive dark-haired surfer in a bikini, on a board, riding a decent-sized wave. *Decent for Florida, at least.* "Who took this photo of Angela surfing?"

"I did."

I couldn't see his face, but from the sound of his response, I suspected he was crying.

I went into the kitchen. The countertops were clean, and the drainer in the sink held a small plate and coffee cup. The refrigerator had a good deal of food for one person, but I noticed that most of it leaned toward healthy and included lots of fruits and veggies. It did include a chilling bottle of Chardonnay and a half-empty bottle of zero-calorie margarita mix. I meandered into the guest bedroom, which Angela had turned into an office space. The bookcase was crammed with textbooks and notebooks. Her laptop perched on a desk pushed up against a windowless wall, a rolling desk chair next to it. There was one framed bit of art in there, and it got my heart racing. The painting was of a famous sculpture, one even more famous than *The Dying Niobid* and *The Little Mermaid*.

The painting was done in realism bordering on pseudo-realism. The subject was the Venus de Milo, one of the world's most famous sculptures. The artist was talented, creating a striking likeness while displaying a sense of humor. The Venus de Milo's arms had broken off at some point in history, though exactly when was a mystery, but whoever had painted the picture had supplied a pair of arms. Oddly enough, they were Popeye's ballooning forearms, complete with an anchor tattoo on each. A whimsical dichotomy to be sure, but on the heels of a killer recreating great art in a bloodier fashion, it stood out. I peered carefully through the framed glass. It was an original on canvas.

"Jon," I called. "Where did Angela get this painting?"

I heard his footsteps approach. He stuck his head in the door. "Oh, that. She said it was funny and bought it, though it was kind of pricey."

"Where'd she get it?"

"First Friday Art Walk, about three or four months ago," Murphy answered.

"In Old City?"

"Yeah."

On the first Friday of each month, all the art galleries in Old City had what boiled down to a street party. Galleries stayed open until at least ten o'clock and served wine and hors d'oeuvres. Nick and I usually went; it was a good time. Old City was part of the historic district of San Marco. Certainly not as old as Saint Augustine just north of us, San Marco was founded by the Spanish in the early eighteenth century. Only a few homes from that era still existed, but there were plenty of nineteenth-century and early twentieth-century homes, restaurants, and shops that made Old City both charming and notable.

There was a title for the piece in the bottom right-hand corner, *Venus de Popeye*, and under that, it was signed *A. Hurst*. "Were you with her when she bought it?"

"Yeah."

"Do you remember where?"

"One of the galleries there. One on Cadiz Street."

There were over half a dozen small galleries on Cadiz. "Can you narrow it down?"

"One of the galleries north of that cigar and jazz club." That whittled the number down to three or four.

I handed him my card. "If you think of anything and would rather talk to me than the police, call me."

He looked at me with confusion. "I thought you were the police."

"I'm a consultant. I'm helping with Angela's case and another one." I considered asking him to not tell anyone I'd been there but couldn't figure out a way to justify it. Instead, I attempted a different tactic. "There's going to be a lot of different law enforcement people asking you questions, many of them the same ones you've already answered. Don't get frustrated with the process. Just answer as best you can and accept the fact that someone else will probably ask the same thing." Hopefully, he wouldn't say something like "I already told that Norwood woman about that" to any real cops.

He walked me to the door, looking at my PI card. "If the police are consulting you, you must be good at what you do."

"I like to think so," I said, while thinking, *I hope I am*.

Exiting the condo, I saw Baker and Ortega heading for the stairs nearest Angela's condo. *Hey, I'm wearing my big-girl panties*. I descended a couple of steps on the way to meet them. But then imagining an angry Baker reminded me of the benefits of avoiding conflict, and I went back up and headed toward another set of stairs. There were ten yards between the concrete staircases, and I got to the other one as Baker and Ortega were almost to the third floor. I held my phone up to ear and let my hair fall across my face so they wouldn't easily recognize me. I made it to the parking lot just as they were entering Angela's condo.

I sent Murphy a mental message: *Don't tell them I was here, Jon.*

Pulling out of the parking lot and heading toward Old Town, I thought about Gordo's, but Murphy's grief had ruined my appetite.

Chapter 8

I cruised up Cadiz, passing restaurants and shops, historic homes and galleries, and found a parking space right in front of Cheroots, the cigar and jazz club Murphy had used as a landmark to locate the gallery where Angela purchased *Venus de Popeye*. I was familiar with the first gallery I went into, a converted gas station from the '40s and '50s called Cadiz Street Station. It was a co-op that exhibited paintings, sculpture, photographs, and jewelry. A friend from college, Nadine Welch, was one of the founding artists, and I'd attended more than one First Friday celebration there. It was her framed photos that graced my office walls.

I wandered through, quickly seeing that Hurst was not a featured artist. The artists manning the main desk said no one named Hurst had displayed work there as far as she knew. Next, I slipped into the Alley, a narrow gallery that required First Friday attendees to go down and back in single file, and there was barely enough space for that. Luckily, no one other than the proprietor was there, so I didn't have to worry about claustrophobic pangs. The Alley was exhibiting pieces from university students, and though there was a promising artist or two, none were up to the quality of *Venus de Popeye*.

Next to the Alley was a gallery I'd never been in. It had been an antique store before, the kind that had a lot of junk to sort through before finding anything of value. I liked those stores; they were kind of like a one-stop collection of yard sales. The junk was gone, though, and a coat of whitewash covered the once-red bricks, and two six-foot-tall kinetic sculptures were spinning and clanking in the wind out front. I stepped into the street so I could read the sign on the front of the building. In cube letters, it read Delve, which sent my pretentious meter all the way up to pompous. I opened a wood-and-glass door and was greeted by a blast of arctic air from a hard-running air conditioner.

The first room was large, each wall painted a dark color: one blue, another purple, one mauve, and the fourth taupe. The colors worked well, helping to delineate the art that hung on the walls. This room held oils, watercolors, and computer graphics. Two open doorways led to more rooms in the back, and I heard voices coming from the one to my left. I moved closer and peeked in at a young couple being shown about the room by a rotund man, who said he would be with me momentarily. I told him to take his time, while thinking how much he resembled the great 1940s British movie star Sidney Greenstreet. He had a similar flabby face and was mostly bald up top, with light-brown hair on the sides. Unlike Sidney Greenstreet, he didn't wear a white linen suit, but a brilliantly colored tropical short-sleeve shirt, white slacks, and on his feet, electric-blue Crocs.

I meandered into the other room and found what I was searching for on the wall directly across from the entry. The first painting was a rendition of the bust of Nefertiti, but instead of the Egyptian headdress, it had Marge Simpson's bright-blue hairdo. I could tell at a glance that it was the same artist who'd painted *Venus de Popeye*. I looked at the others, including one titled *Goophinx*, depicting the Sphinx with Goofy's face. Hurst had painted Rodin's *The Thinker* sitting on a cartoon toilet, and *The Discus Thrower* by Myron set to throw a worn red Frisbee. In the background, a dog poised to chase the Frisbee. As with *Venus de Popeye*, the artwork was signed A. Hurst, and the price tags ranged in the low- to mid-hundreds.

I went back to the main room and heard the proprietor still working with the young couple, so I moved to the counter and took a business card from a pile next to the cash register. "Delve Gallery" was inscribed in the center in the same blocky font as the letters on the sign. The address, website, and phone number were printed in the bottom left corner. In the right bottom corner was the owner's name, Adolph Hurst. So the owner was also the creator of *Venus de Popeye*. I wondered what kind of parents would name their kid Adolph.

I stood by the door to eavesdrop on the proprietor and his customers. They were talking about cost and investment potential of certain pieces.

"What do you think the appreciation in value would be in twenty years, Mr. Hurst?" the young man asked, so I knew the Sidney Greenstreet look-alike was the artist and owner.

I considered waiting to question Hurst, but I didn't know much about him. We were chasing a killer who mimicked famous sculptures, and Hurst was an artist who also mimicked well-known artwork. I decided to first prepare myself and do a little research and find out what I could about Hurst before proceeding further.

Driving back to my office, I realized that if Baker and Ortega hadn't noticed the painting and its subject matter in Angela Lopez's home office, I might be the only one who knew about what could be a valuable clue in solving a double murder. Excited, I ran to my desk and fired up my laptop. Using Google, I found out that Adolph Hurst was from Miami. A number of online news articles highlighted Hurst's extensive knowledge of art. A few hinted at Hurst's carnal craving for women. Others led to detailed articles almost tabloid in nature.

As a young man, Hurst was an artist who never got past the up-and-coming stage. He moved into the business side and spent over twenty years as a big-shot art dealer. Hurst worked with the biggest auction houses and moved pieces that sold into the hundreds of thousands and even millions of dollars. A few years prior, one of his employees, Belinda Vasquez, died at a weekend party at Hurst's home. The young woman had passed out, vomited, and choked to death. Police had found abundant amounts of cocaine and arrested him.

Though the case was aggressively prosecuted, police could never prove the cocaine belonged to him. He'd already spent a fortune on the criminal charges then faced a civil suit from the young woman's family. After a long, public case, Hurst had finally made an out-of-court settlement. The publicity and financial hit had been damaging enough to force him to close his business. There was no further mention of him until a blurb in the San Marco Ledger announced his gallery opening in Old Town.

I sat back. An artist himself, Hurst was knowledgeable about art. His paintings displayed an affinity for classic sculpture. Even with the humor thrown in, they were flawless renderings of the pieces they portrayed. The same could have been said about the murder victims. News accounts weren't shy about highlighting Hurst's sexual proclivities. Maybe his voracious sexual appetite, fed by the stress of his ruin, had turned violent—to actual rape and murder.

My fantasies shifted into high gear as I imagined myself conducting further inquiries, picking up one piece of crucial evidence after another and presenting an airtight case to the police—to Baker himself. It would infuriate him if I were the one to solve the Michelangelo case. As sweet as that sounded, if I pursued that, hiding clues from the police until I had definite proof, I would be partially responsible if Michelangelo killed someone else.

So I picked up the phone and called Baker.

He answered with, "What—"

"Hi," I interrupted.

"—the hell do you think you're doing going over and talking to Jon Murphy? At the victim's own condo!"

Pretending not to hear, I said cheerily, "It's Lise Norwood."

"Yeah, I know. Phones have this thing known as caller ID. Answer my question."

"About that, yeah, well, I went back over my invoice and saw that I overcharged you. So I decided I'd work it off with a little more consultation."

"Three things, Norwood. No, no, and no."

"But—"

"*But* is not *no*. It's no, no, and no. As a consultant, you come when we call, provide your services, and leave. You do not investigate or speak to witnesses or impede my damn investigation. I've already called the Department of Agriculture and Consumer Services, and you know what I learned?"

All at once, it felt like the temperature dropped a hundred degrees. My throat constricted, but I managed, "What?"

"I learned your license is up for renewal in a year and a half. How do you think that'll go if the San Marco PD files an official complaint?"

"Not good."

"Best case scenario is a hearing where you can plead your case. Worst case is they go ahead and suspend your license immediately."

I sat in shock, listening to Baker breathing heavily on the phone. Finally, I asked, "Are you going to file a complaint?"

"First things first, you're fired. To find out if we're filing a complaint, you'll have to wait and see if you get a letter from the state."

Again, we sat in silence. The trepidation I felt slowly changed from fear to insult and, finally, to anger. I spoke softly, because the only other option was to lose control, shout, and scream. "Guess that leaves you in control. That's something you like, isn't it? Being in control, having all the power?" I paused for a breath and heard him start to respond, but I cut him off. "You know it strikes me as somewhat inept that you aren't the least interested in what I might have learned that inspired me to call you."

But for Baker's deep breathing, silence reigned again. In a resigned tone, Baker asked, "Why did you call, Norwood?"

I heard him just fine, but my anger made me petty. "What's that, Baker? Did you say something?"

He spoke through what sounded like gritted teeth. "What do you want?"

"To hand you a lead on a silver platter. Unless you saw the painting in Angela Lopez's condo and made the connection." There was a stretch of uneasy quiet, which I topped with, "Well? Did you? You know, make a connection?"

There was a heavy sigh from Baker's end, and I envisioned him with a hand over his face. "What connection, Norwood?"

I told him about *Venus de Popeye* and Adolph Hurst's interesting and sordid history.

Baker grunted something that could have been a thank you, goodbye, or "kiss my ass." Before I could ask him to repeat it, he hung up. As I stared at my phone, the door to my office opened.

"There's my favorite private eye, right after Spade and Marlowe." Gabriel Turner stood there with a brash grin that would melt most women. Instead, his radiant smile wilted when he saw how upset I was. "Lise? What's wrong?"

"I just got fired." I held up a trembling hand. "I'm so mad, I'm shaking."

"What happened?"

I went to him so we could exchange cheek kisses. "Take off your coat. Can I get you some coffee?"

"No thanks, Lise. I was passing by and wanted to stop in and—well—who fired you?" I started to tell him about the case, but he interrupted. "Nick told me about you consulting with the police. Shocking, isn't it? A murder victim posed like *The Dying Niobid*."

I explained what I'd done, how that had led to my firing, and how Baker was holding an official complaint to the state over my head like the sword of Damocles.

"A complaint would be bad, huh?"

I didn't want to think about it anymore, so I simply shrugged and returned to my seat. I gestured to the chair on the other side of the desk. "So what's up?"

He was decidedly uncomfortable as he sat, as timid as a boy on a first date. It was so adorable, I decided not to tell him he had a quarter-sized stain on the lapel of his jacket. It looked like dried and crusty mustard.

"Come on, Gabe. I can tell something's up."

"Well, I kind of feel responsible for you being mad at Nick."

The anger Baker had stoked was still close to the surface. I didn't want to unleash it on a friend, but I wanted him to know the truth. "When I found out about the fellowship, I wasn't only mad at Nick. I also thought you deserved some of the blame."

"Come on, Lise—"

"But I realized that Nick waiting so long to tell me was what really pissed me off, so I guess that lets you off the hook."

"I'm glad."

"Wait a minute. Nick's talked to you about it?"

"Of course. I'm his mentor and his friend."

"And you're a wonderful mentor," I said.

"Thanks. I'm here as an intermediary. Nick feels terrible about the whole thing. I set it up for him, so I should talk to you." He cleared his throat. "Nick says you were quite angry."

"To be honest, Gabe, I have this fantasy where I'm storming out of his office, but as I reach the door, he calls my name. I stop and turn, and he's right there. He takes my hand and drops to one knee."

Gabe's eyes went wide. "To propose?"

"To beg for forgiveness."

Gabe started to smile but stopped at my stern expression. "Lise, I didn't even consider you when I arranged for Nick to go in my place. It's not that I don't consider your relationship important. It's just that I travel a lot; you know that. I don't think being far away is a big deal.

But then I don't have what you and Nick do. I'm a confirmed bachelor, and so that's how I think. But you know what?"

"What?"

"Even if he'd told you about it that first day you two became a couple, he'd still be going."

"I know. I wouldn't want him to miss the opportunity, but…" I shrugged.

"And when those policemen asked for a recommendation, Nick chose you, didn't he?"

I held up my hand, my thumb and index finger almost touching. "He came this close to giving them your name instead of mine."

"That may be true, but he still gave your name."

"Only because Nick was hoping it'd be a get-out-of-jail-free card." I sighed. "So Nick knows you're here?"

"I told him I'd be happy to talk to you, and he thought it was a good idea."

"Isn't that adolescent, Gabe?" I said it with more anger than I wanted. "Shouldn't Nick be handling this?"

Surprisingly, Gabe laughed. "Come on, Lise. Nick and I are members of academia. We pretend to be adults, but you know very well that we're, to put it in your words, adolescents."

His laughter defused my anger, and I laughed myself.

"What I'm mad at is Nick not telling me until the visit from the cops made him spill his beans." Gabe started to answer, and I silenced him with a raised hand. "You can tell Nick I'm not mad anymore."

"Good."

"Just sad he's going," I admitted. The murders, my cousin's resemblance to the first victim, my getting fired, and Nick's imminent departure all mixed together, putting me in a melancholy mood. "Have I ever told you about my cousin Gracie?"

Gabe took a moment before answering, "I don't think so."

I gazed blankly above Gabe's head. "Her mother and mine were sisters. They were close, so we spent holidays and a lot of summers together. She was three years younger than me and was like my little sister. Her last couple of years in high school, she got in with a pretty bad crowd and ended up addicted to opiates."

"That's tough."

"Anyway, she managed to graduate high school and moved out of the house." Even years later, it was still hard to put into words. "One summer night in a park in Panama City, when she was nineteen, someone stabbed her nine times and left her to die. She managed to walk—or stumble or crawl—a hundred feet toward the road. She didn't make it. Some poor kid found her body the next morning. That was my senior year at the university." I was struck by a realization. "I got the call right before your honors class on Renaissance and baroque art. That's the only class of yours I ever missed."

"Ah, Lise, I'm so sorry."

"I was so angry and heartbroken. But the thing I felt most was helplessness. As much as I wanted her back or to have the killer caught, there was nothing I could do to accomplish either."

"Why didn't you tell me back then?"

"I didn't tell anyone, Gabe. There was just no way I could put it into words. Not for a while. I finally told Nick. He helped me get through it."

Gabe got to his feet and walked around my desk. I stood, and we hugged.

"Why are you telling me about this now?" he asked.

I broke the hug and sat on the corner of my desk. "Something came up in that thing I just got fired from. A victim reminded me a lot of Gracie, and that made it all resurface. As if my stewpot of emotions isn't bubbling enough with Nick leaving."

"If there's anything I can do for you, Lise…"

"I know. And talking to you about it makes me feel better. C'mon, I'll walk you out."

We linked arms, and Gabe said, "I'm glad there is no irreparable damage between you and Nick. You're perfect for each other."

"Perfect?"

"Okay, maybe I shouldn't go that far. You and I, now that would be a perfect pairing, but since Nick already has dibs on you—"

"You dirty old man." I laughed as I hugged him.

I sat back down after he left. I knew he'd been joking about us being the perfect pair. Gabe wore his bachelorhood like a badge of honor. In all the years I'd known him, he'd never been seriously involved with anyone. Gabe did date, with truly beautiful women, but nothing ever lasted more than a few months. And he never seemed heartbroken when a romance ended. I always figured he simply loved his freedom and was truly happy being on his own. He worked when he had to work, and when school was out for holidays or summer, he hit the road and traveled to far-flung places off the beaten path.

Nick's ringtone started up, and I rolled my eyes. Judging by the timing, Gabe had called Nick as soon as he left, and now Nick was calling me.

I answered with "You big sissy. Sending Gabe to see if I was still mad."

"Hell yeah. You're scary when you're mad." He paused, then, sounding guarded, he asked, "So Gabe's right, isn't he? You're not pissed anymore?"

"I'm pissed at circumstance, but not at you. Not anymore."

"In that case, I'm leaving in two days."

I grinned and leaned back, putting my feet on my desk. "Then you better plan on spending the night at my place."

"I'll be there with bells on."

"Bells on and nothing else."

"Yes, ma'am. Me and my bells are going to ring your chimes."

And he and his bells did.

Chapter 9

I climbed over Nick to get dressed. I followed Ricky Stephens to work then waited across the street in the parking lot of a strip mall to be relieved by Elliot the Slim. In my mind, I relived the passionate night before and chuckled, remembering how after making love, I'd become tangled in the sheets and fallen out of bed.

I'd said, "That's another fine mess you've gotten me into," in reference to our love of old black-and-white comedy.

"That's not how the quote goes," Nick said.

"Is too."

"Nope. That's a common misconception."

"You're wrong."

And like the football bet I'd paid off by teaching a class about flaccid penises in classic art, we made a bet as to the accuracy of the quote. We looked for Laurel and Hardy movies online and selected *Another Fine Mess*.

"See?" I said. "It's even in the title."

But Nick gave me a smug grin.

Sure enough, when the line came up, it was "Well, here's another *nice* mess you've gotten me into." *Nice* instead of *fine*. I'd had another bet to pay off, and I had, with lustful passion.

Grinning at the memory, I was startled when Elliot the Slim said, "S'up, Lise?"

I hadn't seen him walk up and kneel by my open window. "Hello, Elliot. How's it going?"

"Kinda pissed," he said and walked from the car to his observation post under trees in an empty lot next to the parking lot.

I got out and followed him to where he was unfolding a blanket onto a flat piece of cardboard.

"You're not mad at me, are you?" I asked.

He sat on the blanket, with a look of surprise. "What? You? Nah, Lise. You're righteous."

"Thanks, Elliot. That means a lot."

Tall and skinny, Elliot the Slim had long dark hair, which hadn't been washed in weeks. His long beard gave him a Viking look, but his clothes and bundled belongings definitely said *Destitute*. His age was a mystery. He was either young and aged dramatically by circumstance and hard living, or he was late middle-aged and held on to a youthful aura.

He handed me a small flyer with a photo of a building on it. "No, I'm mad 'cause this bitch comes up to me outta nowhere and gives me this." His volume grew at the indignation of having to relate what had happened. "How insulting."

Printed on the flyer was: "Homeless? If you need a bed, a shower, a meal, and someone to talk to, stop by Saint Benedict House."

"Well, don't be too mad. She was just trying to be charitable. I've heard good things about Saint Benedict House."

"But, Lise, I ain't homeless," he said.

"No?"

"How can I be homeless when San Marco is my home?"

I smiled at him. "Good point. I guess sometimes people think someone's homeless if they don't have a roof over their head."

"That's just ludicrous."

Elliot the Slim could be found most days within a six-block radius between the university and the historic district; students, faculty, and tourists were good to hit up for a buck here and there. I'd used him on a stakeout before, and he'd turned out to be a great asset. He had infinite patience, which was important for a stakeout. I had met him almost a year ago while trying to serve a summons on an insurance CEO. As the businessman was leaving his office building for lunch, I'd called his name and held out the envelope with the summons inside. He'd started for it, realized what it was, and snatched his hand back. He harrumphed, smiled arrogantly, and walked on without taking it.

Elliot had been sitting on the sidewalk and witnessed my failed attempt. "You want him to take that?"

"Yeah, I do."

"Here, give it to me."

I wondered about how smart it was to let a disheveled homeless man take legal papers then shrugged and passed it to him. He folded it in half, then I crossed the street and sat at an open-air coffee shop to watch. Forty-five minutes later, the CEO returned. He passed Elliot and started into the building. Elliot stood and surreptitiously dropped the envelope on the sidewalk.

"Hey, man, you dropped something," Elliot called and picked up the envelope.

The CEO stopped, walked back to Elliot, and took it. When the man saw what it was, he yelled at Elliot to move away from his building. The CEO checked left and right before finally seeing me as I stood from my table. Cup of coffee in hand, I attempted to mimic his smug smile as I waved. Afterward, I gave Elliot a twenty. Since then, he had delivered four more summonses for me.

I looked at Elliot. "I know what you mean about San Marco being your home, but if you ever want to get a place, you know, an apartment or something, I'd be glad to help you out."

Elliot gave me a smile that would melt butter. "You're good people, Lise. But I'll pass on a place. You ever hear of agoraphobia?"

"Sure. It's the fear of being outside."

"I got the opposite, whatever that's called. I can't stand being indoors for long."

I knelt next to him. "But you've gone inside a couple of times for me. Once at the library and that other time serving papers in that office building."

"Made my skin crawl." He shivered.

"Why didn't you tell me? I wouldn't have made you go in."

"I can take it in short bursts."

My respect for Elliot the Slim shot up tenfold. "You're employee of the month, Elliot."

"Really? Wow." He had a big smile. "Do I get a plaque?"

"You want one?"

"Not really. I got too much stuff to haul around as it is."

"How about I get one made and keep it on the wall at my office?"

"Awesome."

"Gotta run. Let me know if anything happens," I said, figuring nothing would and feeling frustrated at the snail's pace at which this case was moving.

When I got to my office, I dropped my cell phone on my desk, and a second later, the generic ringtone sounded.

I checked caller ID. "Uh-oh."

Baker was calling. The phone trilled again. All I could think was that he had filed a complaint and wanted to gloat. The ringtone went off again, and I could only stare at the phone like it was some cursed totem. Knowing the call would go to voicemail if I waited longer, I snatched up the phone and thumbed the answer button.

"Well, well, if it isn't my not-favorite detective."

"Listen, Norwood, Ortega and I want to sit down with you and discuss something."

"I thought you fired me."

"Well, I'm hiring you again," he said heatedly. After a beat, he said, "So? How about a get-together?"

"Damn it, Baker. Last time we spoke, you threatened my livelihood."

His volume rose a notch. "Only because you were interfering in my investigation. You know you weren't supposed to do that."

"Well, maybe."

"Look, Norwood, I didn't file a complaint, nor do I intend to file a complaint. And let's be honest here—you want to help us some more on this case. Right?"

I sighed. "I do."

I met them for lunch at Son of a Beach, a popular spot for the locals. Located next to the city's busiest beach ramp on Osprey Street off A1A, Son of a Beach was made of weathered wood planks decorated with hundreds of pieces of driftwood. We sat on the beachside deck under an umbrella, but it was still pretty hot. Baker and Ortega had removed their jackets and rolled up their sleeves. I was eating fish tacos, and the boys ordered burgers. Both foot and auto traffic to the beach was heavy, and I smiled at how Baker's attention got drawn to a group of young women in bikinis.

As if he could read my mind, Baker said, "I should have sat on that side of the table."

"Hard to concentrate?" I asked.

"You'd have to be dead, a priest, or gay not to notice the flesh today, and I'm not any of those."

"Don't drool, and we'll be fine," I said.

"I can't promise a thing," Baker said.

Wow, a non-sarcastic joke. Score one for the detective.

Ortega chuckled. "Just another day in paradise."

"So what'd you learn about Hurst?" I asked.

Baker wiped his mouth with a napkin, took a swallow of sweet tea, and said, "He was a player in Miami, rubbed elbows with celebrities, the uber-rich, artists, and the uppity-ups in organized crime. We called the district attorney's office and spoke to the prosecutor on his criminal case. Hurst was an out-of-control partier. Cocaine was his drug, and a party wasn't a party without him engaging in kinky sex."

Ortega referred to a small notebook. "That's how twenty-one-year-old Belinda Vasquez ended up in Hurst's bed. There'd been a drug-fueled group-grope the night before. Afterward, all the participants went to Hurst's pool for skinny-dipping. Belinda had passed out at that point. The prosecutor wanted to add sexual assault to his drug charge, but witnesses said Belinda was a more-than-willing participant."

I pictured the corpulent man, naked and rutting, but then quickly flushed it from my mind. *Not something to dwell on at lunch.* "Quite a stretch from being kinky to raping and killing."

"Yep. Anyway, his legal costs skyrocketed. They finally settled out of court, which cost Hurst his business and most of his money. He left Miami with his tail between his legs and ended up here in San Marco."

"So I did good?" I asked.

Baker grunted. "We'd have come across him sooner or later."

"Uh-huh," I uttered, like I didn't believe him.

"The point is"—Ortega cut in before Baker could respond—"we now have a suspect where we didn't have one before. We plan on talking to him, but before he knows the police are looking at him, we'd like to hire you as a consultant again. We want you to go in and talk to him while wearing a wire."

Wow! A bigger role in the biggest case of my life. Initially, I wanted to reply with, "Hell yeah, I'm in," but then again, pride dictated that I didn't sound too eager. "Really? You want me to go in and say, 'Hey, commit any sexually violent murders lately?'"

"No, we don't want you to ask that," Baker said loudly, ignoring the nearby diners who were gawking at us.

Ortega leaned in. "We want to utilize your expertise. Go in and chat with him. See if you can steer the conversation to classic sculptures, see what he says."

"Guys with raunchy appetites tend to open up more to an attractive woman," Baker said.

"Thanks."

"I'm not complimenting you," Baker said. "Use your sex, your gender, and your knowledge of art, particularly sculpture, and get this guy talking. Hell, flirt with him a little. We don't expect to learn much but want to see if we get anything before we go in and question him officially."

"I take it you guys will be nearby?" I asked.

"Sitting in a car right outside," Ortega said.

"Well, I don't know how much good I'll do." I turned to check out the bikini-clad body that had captured Baker's attention. "But I've always wanted to wear a wire."

We finished lunch, Ortega settled the tab, and we got into our cars. I followed them to Cadiz Street, and we parked half a block from the gallery. I got into their car, and Baker, as he put it, wired me up. His idea of a wire and mine were different. He called my cell phone, and we kept the line open, though he muted his mouthpiece. Baker would put his phone on speaker so the digital recorder he carried could record the call. It all seemed a step up from using two cans connected by string. I accused Baker of being the Barney Fife of the San Marco PD.

"Look, smartass," Baker said, "what we're doing isn't exactly on the up and up. You weren't paying attention in PI school if you don't know that you need a warrant in Florida if you're going to record a conversation without the other person knowing it."

"I know that. What I didn't know was that you didn't have a warrant."

Ortega said, "Takes time to get a warrant, and while we have learned some interesting things about Mr. Hurst, it's all circumstantial, so there's no guarantee a judge would sign off on one."

"Besides," Baker added, "we won't be using what we record today in any official capacity. We want to get a feel for the guy, that's all, see if anything interesting pops up. You got a problem with that?"

"No, because if it ever comes up, I'll say I assumed you had a warrant."

Granite faced, Baker stared at me via the rearview mirror and nodded. "And we won't say a thing to dissuade that assumption."

I got out and walked to the gallery, pausing between the kinetic sculptures. Thinking that I was about to have a one-on-one with a possible killer, I was surprisingly calm. I was, in fact, enjoying myself. I felt like a character from one of those old movies I loved so much, a tough dame like Lauren Bacall in *To Have and Have Not*. On a deeper level, the seriousness of what I was about to do struck me. This opportunity was in tune with what I wanted to do in my career—and in remembrance of my cousin.

I opened the door and stepped into the frigid air, wondering if he kept the gallery so cold because of his obesity.

"Well, hello," I heard with the same delivery I'd heard countless times from men on the prowl at bars and nightclubs.

I rolled my eyes while my back was to him, then I turned and flashed him a beauty-pageant smile. "Well, hello, yourself."

The big man I'd seen the previous day sat on a barstool at the cash register counter, though in front of it. He held a dwindling half of a sandwich, a Cuban, most likely. Smiling as he chewed, he placed the sandwich on a plate loaded with chips and a pickle then wiped at his lips with a napkin.

"You were in here the other day?" he asked.

"Yesterday, as a matter of fact."

"Ah, I never forget a pretty face."

"And I never forget a flatterer."

He chuckled, wiped his hands, and stood. "So how may I help you?"

I decided to lay it on thick. "I was killing time yesterday before an appointment, but I found your gallery so charming that I had to come back while I had more time."

"I'm glad you did." He moved toward me and held out his hand. "I'm Adolph Hurst."

"I'm Margaret Atwood," I told him, using my favorite alias.

His eyebrows rose. "Like the writer?"

"Uh-huh. Show me around your shop."

He held out his arm, and I took it. All business, he led me from room to room, filling me in on the artists and their histories. Several were artists from southern Florida; a couple had incredible talent. I figured he knew them back when he was a Miami dealer. The artwork in the front room averaged in the one-thousand-to-five-thousand-dollar range, steep prices for San Marco. It got even pricier in the room I hadn't gone into on my last visit. The least expensive there was seven thousand dollars, and a large painting of Henry Flagler's San Marco estate had a sixty-eight-thousand-dollar price tag.

"This room is a little steep for my pocketbook," I told him.

"Understandable." He led me to the room that held his work. "These are the more affordable pieces, under a thousand dollars."

He worked his way around the room, giving me the background of each artist, saving his work for last.

"I saw these yesterday," I said, indicating his paintings. "The artist has a wonderful sense of humor." I looked closely at the one with Marge Simpson's hairdo on Nefertiti. "Wait a minute. These are signed *A. Hurst*. That's you, isn't it?"

"Guilty." He put his hand on his chest and cast his eyes down in false modesty.

"They're wonderful."

"Thank you."

"Where'd you get the idea to combine cartoon elements with classic sculpture?"

He waved at air. "Where does anyone get any idea? Out of the ether, I suppose."

"Does it mean anything?" I asked.

"Not really. Oh, I suppose I could try to impress you and say it's a statement on contemporary pop culture juxtaposed upon mankind's great achievements."

"Well, that *is* impressive."

He smiled. "Sorry to say I just came up with the idea one day and liked the finished product. But please, if the other explanation holds me in higher esteem, pretend that's the answer."

For a moment, I found myself charmed by the portly man, but then I remembered Angela wired to the coquina stone at De Leon Park.

"You know, I studied a little art history at San Marco University," I said, and we wandered back to the front room.

"So, you have a keener eye than most?"

"Oh, probably not. At least not for paintings. I have a thing for classic sculpture, which is why I like your paintings."

"Greek and Roman?" he asked.

"Yes, but not limited to. I like everything from Da Vinci to Michelangelo to more modern stuff from Edvard Eriksen and H.R. Giger." I slipped in Edvard Eriksen's name and watched Hurst to see if the name of the sculptor of *The Little Mermaid* would get a reaction. It didn't, at least not that I recognized.

"Perhaps you have an appreciation of the three dimensionality that—" The young couple I'd seen Hurst talking with yesterday walked in and got his attention. "Excuse me. I'll be right back."

Damn, just as the ball got rolling. "Sure, take your time."

"Ah, James, Maris, welcome back." Hurst approached the couple. "I have your painting framed and wrapped in the back."

Hurst left the three of us in the front room. After nodding hello to me, the couple continued on into the room with the more expensive artwork, leaving me to assume they were loaded. I moved to the counter, where Hurst's lunch sat on the plate. He'd about finished half of his sandwich, but the other half sat untouched. The pickle, a large dill, had been sliced in half lengthwise. He'd taken one bite, leaving a perfect indentation of his bite pattern. My heartbeat picked up as I made sure I was still alone in the front room. I wrapped the pickle in his napkin and stuck it in my purse.

I went to the door he'd gone through and called, "Adolph, I have to leave. But I promise to drop in again."

He replied from a couple of rooms back, "Please do. I'd love to discuss sculpture with you."

Chapter 10

Just in case Hurst watched me leave, we arranged for me to drive my car to Winn-Dixie. We met there and stood between our parked cars.

"You did what?" Baker asked in a surly tone.

"I got you a pickle," I said, handing the napkin-wrapped item to Ortega. "You can run it against Michelangelo's bite pattern. Maybe you can get his DNA off of it."

"Can't you just do what we ask and stop improvising?" Baker said.

Control freak, I thought, trying to figure out Baker's unappealing disposition. *Misogynist maybe? Why did it piss him off that I snagged the pickle?* It's not like Hurst would notice. If he did, he would probably think he'd already finished eating it. And who cared if he knew I took it? Maybe I had a craving for a big dill and couldn't help myself.

I turned to Ortega. "What do you think? Will it work?"

Ortega unwrapped the pickle and looked at the bit end. "I think so. But we can't use it as evidence if there's a match."

"Why not?" I asked.

"Remember that little issue about not having a warrant?" Baker said.

"Ah, crap."

"Too late now," Ortega said.

"I'm so sorry."

Baker chewed on his lower lip, looking at me. "Remember Busby?"

"Yeah, the crime scene tech."

"He's a good guy. He'll compare the bite pattern on the pickle with those on the victims. At least we'll know if we're barking up the right tree."

"So I did good?" I asked.

"Don't get cocky. You did okay."

"You're welcome," I said to Baker then got in my car.

My Barry White ringtone sounded as I drove off. Ignoring safe-driving etiquette, I answered. "Hi, Nick."

"Hello, Lise. I had a wonderful time last night."

"Me too."

"I'm leaving tomorrow."

"Then we better get together again tonight."

"I concur. How about an early dinner and then we retire to my place and make enough love to last us the five months I'll be gone?"

"Five months' worth?" I whistled. "We better do some stretching first."

"Agreed. I've selected tonight's fare from the Kama Sutra."

"Kama Sutra," I said dismissively. "Rank amateurs compared to what I have planned."

"Where would you like to eat?"

"How about Razorback's?" As I said the name of the restaurant, I realized I picked it because it was near De Leon Park. Normally, for a romantic dinner, I wouldn't want to put myself close to a crime scene like Angela Lopez's murder. But I was thinking I might be able to combine business and pleasure.

"Good call, we'll need all the protein we can get. See you there at five?"

"Let's make it six. I have to follow my client's husband home. If he ends up heading elsewhere, I'll text you."

We ended the call, but before I could put the phone down, it rang again.

Elliot said, "Lise, he's on the move. He and that blond bimbo who works there went out and got in his car. I think they're leaving."

Ricky and yet another woman. "Damn. I just pulled out of the Winn-Dixie near Old Town. It'll take a few minutes. Stay on the line."

I wished I had a bogus police light to get the lackadaisical traffic out of my way. Retirees took their time, tourists never knew where they were going, and apparently, there were a lot of people who were clueless as to why the left lane was called the passing lane.

"He's heading south on US 1," Elliot said.

"And I'm just turning onto North US 1. Is he driving his Mustang?"

"Yeah."

Thank God. As if that car didn't stand out enough on its own, it was painted traffic-cone orange. "Why don't you go ahead and call it a day, Elliot."

"See you tomorrow, Lise."

I was half a block from San Pelayo Boulevard when I spotted the bright-orange Mustang. He turned left and was headed toward the beach.

"Gotcha now, playboy," I muttered, and after making a right, I settled in a few cars behind him.

After crossing the Pelayo Bridge, a high structure to allow vessels with tall masts to pass underneath, the Mustang made a right turn onto a dirt road that would take them down to the Lazy Sandbar, a tiny honky-tonk with a beachy vibe hidden under the east side of the bridge. I didn't want to pull in right behind him into the parking lot, so I blew by, made a U-turn about a mile down the road, and came back. There were only a handful of cars in the parking lot, and I parked a few spaces down from Ricky's Mustang.

I got out and stretched, taking in the Lazy Sandbar. Made from tabby, a rough concrete-like material, it was painted a faded teal. The place had been around since the fifties, and when I entered, it smelled of decades' worth of spilled beer. I blinked several times, trying to get my eyes adjusted to the dark. Finally able to see, I scanned the place, and it was dead. A few of the cars in the parking lot must have belonged to fishermen getting their lines wet in the Intracoastal. One old fellow sat at the bar, a bartender bent over and tinkered with the cash register, and Ricky and his friend sat in a booth to the left. I was behind and to the right of the woman, so I couldn't see her, but Ricky saw me and was giving me the up-and-down. He didn't know me or that his wife had hired me, but I still wished he hadn't seen me.

I had a choice to make. I could either sit in a nearby booth and attempt to eavesdrop on what they said, or I could sit at the bar and keep an eye on them. Opting for visual, I walked across the room to the bar and sat. The barkeep asked what I wanted. The trouble with little dives like the Lazy Sandbar was they didn't serve up craft beers. According to the taps, it was either Bud, Miller, or Coors.

"Coors," I told the bartender and got out my phone, pretending to pay attention to it while watching the booth. A minute later, he set down the beer. I gave him three bills and took a sip of barely cool brew.

Now I was at an angle where I could see only Ricky's left arm and leg, but I could see his midday date. Elliot the Slim had nailed the description with "blond bimbo." Her hair was full and bouncy, and coincidentally, so were her breasts. I'd seen her before at Jack Todd Ford. She wasn't a salesperson or a receptionist; they all worked at desks visible through the dealership's plate glass windows. She spent most of her time deeper in the building, and my guess was that she was in accounting. Ricky said something. Then she laughed, batting her eyes, and licked her lips. *Oh my, cheesy, sleazy romance at the Lazy Sandbar.*

Ricky went around the table to sit next to Blondie. A turn of his head, and he would know I was watching. I kept my focus on the phone and my thumbs moving like I was texting someone. I also hit the photo function and zoomed in enough so I could watch them on my phone's screen. After reaching into the inside pocket of his sport coat, he brought out a small box, maybe six inches long and two inches wide. A thin red ribbon was twisted around it and tied off in a bow. With a theatrical gasp, Blondie put a hand to her chest in mock surprise, then she snatched the box out of Ricky's hands. Making quick work of the ribbon, she pulled off the top.

"Oh, Ricky," I heard from clear across the room. The translation was clear, Ricky would be gettin' some.

She pulled out a necklace. I zoomed in further and saw a pendant with a ruby centerpiece about as big as the tip of my little finger ringed by a half-dozen smaller sapphires. It was one of the pieces of jewelry Shari listed as stolen in the burglary. Realizing my mouth was hanging open, I forced it closed. Shari's suspicions were right. Her lowlife husband had faked the robbery and taken everything of value. I heard Blondie squeal, and Ricky put the jewelry around her neck. Judging by the fact that he'd given that necklace to Blondie, he didn't realize the value of what he'd taken. *Dear God, please don't let him give* The Floating Ballerina *to some eager beaver he picks up on Tinder.*

Time to do some private-eye stuff. I zoomed out and rested my hands on the bar for stability and a decent picture. Feeling confident, like I could give gumshoe lessons to Sam Spade, I pressed the screen for the photo, and the dark bar was briefly illuminated by a flash of incandescence. *Shit!* Instinctively, I moved the phone enough that it appeared to be aimed at the bartender, and a second later, I looked up to see the old man at the bar, the bartender, Ricky, and his date all looking at me.

I spoke like I had a couple dozen fewer IQ points. "What? I like to post where I am on Facebook." To the bartender, I said, "You don't mind that I took your picture, right?" Before he could respond, I held my phone out to him. "Could you take my picture?"

He grumbled but took it anyway. By the time I'd primped, preened, and posed, the old man was staring down at his beer, and Ricky and Blondie were once again huddled together exchanging pheromones.

Acting like I was the queen of social media, I worked my thumbs over the phone. Instead of making vapid Facebook posts, I turned off the flash and got a few shots of the lovebirds admiring Shari's pendant. I took another sip of my beer and stood. When I said goodbye to the barkeep, he only grunted.

Back in my MINI Cooper, I brought up the photos. They were dark, but good enough. A second later, Ricky and Blondie left the Lazy Sandbar. Not paying any attention to me in my car, Ricky leaned her against his Mustang, and they locked lips and hips. After a minute, they sped off. My best guess was the happy couple would stop at her place or a nearby no-tell motel and have a quick taste of afternoon delight. Ricky would be too busy to unload *The Floating Ballerina* for the time being. I texted Shari and told her we needed to meet the following day.

Once home, I prepared for my date with Nick, as well as an evening romp that would prove a whole lot classier than what those two were getting into. I took a long shower. One should be squeaky clean for the kind of evening Nick and I had planned. Getting ready for our dates was always a kind of foreplay before the foreplay. I found myself mildly aroused as I dressed, selecting a pair of lacy pink panties. Tight jeans followed. While I didn't have huge boobs, I'd seen Nick's eyes when I went braless in a form-fitting blouse, so I knew my sleeveless silk white shirt should drive him bananas. I put on a pair of nice sandals, set my hair in a ponytail, and applied minimal makeup.

All during my preparation, I thought about that lover man of mine. Such a gentle and generous soul. His sense of humor rivaled a comedian's, and he had a skill for lovemaking that made temples of pleasure out of our beds. His intellect, particularly for his field of study and instruction, was off the charts, though he never bragged about it. He'd had so much going against him as a child that it was amazing he'd become the man he was. And it was no wonder that he'd focused on art. Growing up in the loveless house provided by his alcoholic aunt, he'd spent as much time away as possible. That was when he discovered the San Marco Public Library downtown.

Nick had relayed the tale of his savior librarian many times, and I enjoyed hearing it each time. Within that vast collection of books, he'd discovered classic art. One of the librarians had taken an interest in him and given him a library card. One night, a terrible thing happened. His aunt came home after a particularly long bender. For some reason, she took offense at his library books. He had checked out six books on art, and she tore the pages from each. With one drunken onslaught, his aunt had taken away his one happiness because he believed he could never return to the library again. The librarian had noticed his absence, and after several weeks, she had gone to his aunt's mobile home—luckily, when Aunt Pen wasn't there. The librarian had brought a gift for Nick—a one-year pass to the Benjamin Museum a few blocks from the library. He'd tearfully told her what his aunt had done, and she'd told him it didn't matter. What did matter, she'd said, was that he come back to the library because his smile lit up the place.

Ready for the date, I drove to De Leon Park and got there a little before five thirty, which would leave time to poke around and think about the Michelangelo case. I was a lowly consultant at best, and Baker had warned me not to stick my nose too far in to where it wasn't wanted, but I was too intrigued to stop. I hoped that if I spent enough time working it through my head before meeting Nick, then

I wouldn't think about it at all during our date. I wanted to concentrate on my boyfriend and send him off to Vienna properly sated.

I parked where I'd parked the morning that Angela's body had been discovered. It seemed like a different place now. There were no cop cars, no men in blue, and no lookie-loos. There were cars in the parking lot, and a group of joggers trotted by, taking the trail that would lead down to the fountain meadow. I followed at a leisurely pace, wondering how the killer had gotten Angela without any witnesses.

When I got to the meadow, I stopped. Baker was standing before the fountain. He looked rough, and his clothes appeared as if he'd worn them for several days straight. He stared at the fountain, transfixed, and I wondered if, in his mind's eye, he was seeing Angela Lopez. I was tempted to call out to him, but his lips moved like he was having a conversation with an invisible person. Unnerved, I headed back up the trail.

After a couple dozen steps, I heard Baker's voice. "What are you doing here?"

I stopped, waited a beat, and turned. "Came to think. How about you?"

As bad as he'd appeared at a distance, he was doubly so up close. He displayed none of the usual antagonism; he didn't seem to have the energy. "Same. I was on my way home and stopped in before I realized it."

"You live near here?" I asked.

He pointed west. "A couple of blocks over. By the way, sorry I yelled at you about the pickle." I smiled, and he gave a grin himself. There was something about the word *pickle*. In even the most serious conversation, it lightened the mood. "You saved us a lot of man hours."

"Not his bite pattern?" I asked.

"Nope."

"That sucks." I realized I was feeling frustration that my clandestine work was for naught. "So that's what it feels like for you cops to follow a lead, only to hit a brick wall."

Baker gave me a tired grin. "Welcome to the world of homicide. But you know what? Follow enough leads, and pretty soon, one of them is gonna stick. Anyway, we're still going to test the DNA against Michelangelo's." We started up the trail together. "We're getting pressure from the DA's office. Since Angela was one of their own, they're sticking their noses into all aspects of the case."

"Understandable."

"Commendable even, but it'd be a lot easier finding this creep without them buttin' in, demanding files, and trying to point us in a thousand different directions."

"Sorry to hear. Hey, since you live nearby, did you ever see Angela jogging in the park?"

"Nah. I'm a morning runner, and she jogged in the evening."

"You jog?" I asked.

"Gotta do something to stave off the middle-age spread," he said, patting his belly.

"So how did Michelangelo get her without anyone witnessing anything?" I asked.

"Looks like he got her at dusk, dragged her into the overgrowth, the Brazilian pepper tree, bound her, and gagged her with duct tape. We think he waited until it was good and dark before he started in on her. She died around two to three in the morning after briefly escaping him, or he let her run off for the sport of chasing her. Then he set to work mounting her on the fountain."

We got to the parking lot, and I stopped by my car and said, "This must be rougher than usual, a jogger killed in a park a couple of blocks from your home."

He didn't answer right away but continued to his car. He opened the door, and before he got in, he said, "I have a wife, a daughter. This going down in my backyard doesn't sit right with me. And it really gets me that I was at home, two blocks away, as he took his time raping and killing her." He slid into the driver's seat, closed the door, and sat for a moment, gazing straight ahead with a blank expression. After blinking several times, he glanced at me, started the car, and drove off.

As I drove to Razorback's, the last thing Baker had said replayed over and over in my mind. I understood his frustration and anger. I wasn't being egotistical in thinking I had brought a lot to the case with identifying the art that inspired the killer. But knowing Kristin was left as *The Dying Niobid* and Angela as *The Little Mermaid* didn't automatically lead to Michelangelo's identity. I wondered what more I could do to bring the murders to an end. I sat in my car after parking at Razorback's, trying to shift my mental state from the crimes to my lover and his pending departure. Putting on a smile that I hoped looked more sincere that it felt, I started for the restaurant.

I found Nick in the bar, and he was so sincerely happy to see me that the negativity I'd been carrying with me dissipated. With a couple of beers and a plate of smoked meat in front of me, I felt great.

"What can I do to make this a romantic bon voyage?" Nick asked as he cut into his beef brisket.

Razorback's Smokehouse was large, and I hated its cavernous dining room because of the echoing acoustics, so we always sat at one of the high-tops in the bar area. The bar had over twenty taps with mostly craft beers and an amazing selection of liquors.

Holding a baby back rib, I said, "You know that feeding me is the first step to making me a satisfied woman."

He waggled his eyebrows in Groucho Marx fashion. "It's the second step I'm most interested in."

"What can I say? I'm a simple woman." We laughed, and it hit me then that Nick was leaving for a long time. "Your raging libido is one of many things I'll miss."

Nick reached across the table and gave me a sad smile. "I will miss you. You do understand why I'm going?"

"Of course. But what're a few months in the grand scheme of things, right?"

"Normally, I'd agree, but being apart from you means time is going to slow down."

I took a sip of beer. "Yeah."

"And you can always visit me."

"Oh, that's definitely going to happen."

Nick grinned then gave me a serious look. "I ran into Gabe today. He said you told him about your cousin."

"I'd been thinking about her when he showed up. I did some research on that girl who'd been posed as *The Dying Niobid*. The newspaper had a photo of her. Kind of reminded me of Gracie."

Nick reached to put his hand over mine and give me a consoling smile.

After dinner, we went to his home, a late-nineteenth-century white-and-green Florida cracker house that had big windows and doors to allow the breeze through, a tin roof, and covered porches for shade. Once a farm, the surrounding land had been sold, though Nick still had five acres that mostly grew wild. It was private, with access by one gate barring the gravel driveway. Nick opened the door, and we stepped in, stopping to kiss next to his umbrella stand with his collection of antique canes and walking sticks. Nick took my hand, and we started up the stairs, my other hand grasping the bannister, which still wobbled even though Nick had worked on it several times. His home improvement skills were lackluster, at best, but a hardwood floor that buckled in places and a few visible drywall seams didn't lessen the pride he felt in the old house he was attempting to restore to its glory days. Nor did it diminish the love I had for the place.

We didn't come close to cramming five months of sex into one night, but it was fun to try. A creative and inventive lover, Nick sometimes planned extravagant scenarios, which I was surprised to learn I enjoyed. He was also masterful at dirty talk. Whenever other guys had talked dirty, it'd come across as silly. Not so with Nick—he could get me ready to roll with a few hot words whispered in my ear. That night, however, started with real romance that bloomed from the sadness that we would soon be parted. We took our time, holding one another tight, kissing and caressing, slowly working off each other's clothes. He kept on the skintight, long-sleeve black T-shirt I'd purchased for him at a Jeff Beck concert we'd seen at the San Marco Concert Hall.

"It was a gift from you. I want to wear it as we make love," he explained. It was such a sweet sentiment that I cried a little.

After our lovemaking, I lay still. He sat up and took in my nakedness. "You're so lovely, you could be a masterpiece."

I smiled and shut my eyes, but then I felt him get out of bed. "Where are you going?"

"I need to do a few things before the trip, not to mention packing. You go to sleep."

I opened my eyes to glance at the bedside clock. It was only a little after eleven. I thought to get up and help him, but our strenuous workout had worn me down. I went to sleep.

Chapter 11

T*he Artist*

He wandered aimlessly. The pursuit of art and love were often the same thing, and sometimes, one had to venture forth without a plan to find either or both. That was how he'd found his earlier models. He'd seen one waiting tables at the Italian restaurant where he'd been dining, and right away, he'd known she would be perfect. He'd waited outside the restaurant and followed her home. For over a week, he'd stalked her before she became *The Dying Niobid*. He'd been on a ramble through a park when he'd seen the runner. Then he'd returned each evening to watch her before finally striking up a conversation with her at the end of a run. They'd become friendly, saying hello or waving, until the night that it seemed right to take her and transform her into *The Little Mermaid*. He admired her spunk—how she'd fought and how she'd given him a wound that had yet to heal. Even though it was a warm night, he wore a long-sleeve shirt to hide the gauze wrapped around the bite on his forearm. He needed stitches, he knew, but that would have alerted authorities, so he just kept it wrapped.

His meandering led him to a large brick building. He took a deep breath and tentatively stepped through a glass door into a bar containing an amalgam of odors: smoke, stale beer, unclean restrooms, peanuts, and overcooked hot dogs. Someone sang on the jukebox, a country crooner from the sixties. A bar ran the length of the narrow space, which was reminiscent of a diner, and booths lined the opposite wall. The floor was hardwood and shiny, like a bowling lane. Numerous hanging bronze light fixtures hung over the tables, but the room was still dim, as a dive should be.

He gazed past the bar, over the shelves of liquor bottles, and except for his widening eyes, he froze as he stood before a cliché, a saloon stereotype—a full-size portrait of a reclining nude on the wall. She lay on her side, her head on her outstretched right arm, red hair spilling about. She gazed out as if she knew she was being watched and liked the attention. Her breasts were round and full. Her right leg was extended, the left bent at the knee. The skull of a steer had been strategically hung so that it covered her crotch. Waves of heat rolled through his body, and he pushed up his sleeves. He no longer cared if anyone saw the bandage on his arm; he was too hot. That reclining nude was not what he sought, but it was a gateway to that end.

"Hey! Quit eyeballin' my woman," a man shouted at him.

He twitched and saw several people at the bar chuckling and looking at him.

Sitting on a stool at the bar, the man smiled to show that he was just kidding around, adding a little barroom brevity. A heavy man, he wore a faded fish-camp T-shirt and cutoff shorts, a worn cap on his head. "I know she's purty, but she's mine."

What the man said sounded like gibberish.

"Excuse me?" the artist managed to say.

"Hell, she's your woman, Declan. She's always had a thing for me." The guy next to him laughed, gesturing at the painting. He wore Dickie work pants and a matching short-sleeve shirt. He was as thin as a pipe cleaner, just like the pipe cleaners the artist's father, also an artist, had used to clean his pipe. As a child, the artist bent and twisted them into human-like figures, often depicting scenes of violence. His own little wire sculptures.

Several empty stools sat on either side of them, and he was sitting next to the pipe cleaner. As the two men continued bantering, the artist decided that vying for the affections of the woman in the painting was a running joke among the regulars. His attention turned back to the portrait, and heat radiated from his cock, warming his entire body. He lost himself in the portrait's heavy breasts until somebody moved in front of him, blocking his view.

"What'll it be?" A bartender stood before him, a towel in hand.

The two men next to him each had a Bud bottle on the bar. He pointed to them and said, "I'll have the same."

The men tried to engage him in conversation, but he said he wasn't up to socializing and drank his beer while eyeing the painted nude. Turning on his stool, he saw two women hunched together in a booth, engaged in a serious conversation. The brunette was birdlike. *Her friends probably call her Birdie,* he decided. He focused on Birdie's companion and caught his breath, knowing he'd found another masterpiece. Her beauty and artistic potential caused him to moan aloud, almost the same sound he made during an orgasm. He looked around the room to make sure no one had heard him then returned his gaze to the woman.

She was a redhead, almost the same shade as the nude in the painting. As he stared at her, he calculated how to mix paint to get that exact color. Her complexion was pale yet enticing, and a collection of freckles started at one cheek and traveled over her nose to the other. He didn't think she was wearing makeup; she certainly didn't need it. Her lips were naturally pink, and he imagined her nipples would be as well. She wore faded denim overalls, which, oddly enough, seemed erotic. Then he remembered a girlfriend from long ago, a fragile blond artist whose name he'd forgotten—she'd liked wearing overalls. And he'd liked to hug her from behind and slide his hands in to cup her breasts.

Birdie noticed his attention first, then the redhead saw him. He knew they beheld a wild-eyed man perched on a stool, leaning toward them, staring at the ginger. Birdie's expression radiated a combination of fear and indignation. But the ginger was braver, showing no anxiety. Perhaps she knew that great things were afoot. He got up from the stool, threw a few bills on the bar, and strode to their booth.

He put on what he hoped was a sane smile. "Sorry I was staring, but I'm an artist."

Birdie glared at him with disdain, but the redhead's mien reflected curiosity.

He looked in her eyes. "You would make a marvelous model."

"Fuck off, Romeo," Birdie said.

He ignored her. She was insignificant, and if she got in his way, he would swat her down like a gnat.

"What kind of an artist?" the ginger asked.

"My focus is sculpture, but you, I think I'd like to paint." She didn't respond immediately, and he filled the silence with "In the nude. It's my specialty."

Cacophony erupted. Both of the young women shouted and cursed at him. Then the bartender grabbed the back of his neck and his left arm, pushing him out into the street. The artist laughed the entire time. He crossed the street, found a bench half a block down from the bar, and sat. Last call would be soon. He would wait for her outside and see where opportunity and inspiration led him.

Chapter 12

I woke after dreaming of my father. Not wanting to let go of the dream just yet, I kept my eyes closed. Pops had been a mechanic and an art lover, a dichotomy I was proud of. He'd run his own garage and had a faithful clientele. The poor man had tried to get me interested in engines when I was a child, but I couldn't grasp the simplest of mechanics. He had, however, inspired my love of art. Mom, too. A middle school social studies teacher, she was also an amateur painter. She'd have never been able to make a living at it, but she painted because she loved the process—and the slower, the better. She would take six months to complete a painting, usually a landscape, then give it to a friend or someone in the family.

On occasion, when finances were good, Pops would buy original artwork. Nothing higher than four figures. He'd called them investments that were beautiful to look at. Before I came along, he'd taken a chunk of money he inherited from his parents and bought his most valuable piece. It was a painting by twentieth-century Swiss-German master Paul Klee. *Tod un Wassar*, or *Death and Water*, was a small blue-and-green expressionist piece that Klee had painted before his better-known masterwork, which he'd titled *Death and Fire*.

Death and water. Death and fire. Death and death. Death of innocent young women. I sighed, ready to rid myself of the nostalgia I'd woken to.

I reached for Nick, but he was gone. Opening my eyes, I found a sweet love letter on his pillow. One page long, it said all the right things. *I am lucky, no not lucky, I am blessed to have you as both lover and best friend.* I laughed out loud when I read, *Yeah, I could say you're beautiful and a good person, but that's too easy. Other things I love about you include your sarcasm, your twisted sense of humor, your excellent taste in men.* And I actually said, "Aww," when I read, *I love you with all the love this simple man can muster, and I feel the solidity of this love, the permanence. In other words, Lise, I will always love you.*

I smiled as I got ready for the day.

An hour later, I sat in my car a half block down from the Stephenses' household, waiting for the lothario to head to work. Ricky came out of the house, whistling. He did a little half jog around his Mustang and got in, apparently still flying high from his hookup with Blondie yesterday. Shari had texted me back last night, saying she could meet me after Ricky left for work. He would have to drive straight to the dealership to make it to work at his usual time, so I wasn't worried about not following him there. Elliot the Slim would pick up surveillance once Ricky arrived at the dealership.

Shari and I sat in her kitchen. She lived in an older neighborhood with upper-middle-class homes dating back to the fifties and sixties. Hers was a mid-century modern home that had probably seemed futuristic when it was new. Its low roof peaked in the middle. It had high windows on the front wall and a lawn manicured to perfection. Her house was quiet since the kids had already left for school. She was dressed business casual because she had a meeting at her church after our little get-together. She was a volunteer on a board that raised funds for Saint Monica House, a place for young, single pregnant girls to live and receive an education and medical care. Shari sipped from an oversized mug that read, "Coffee in the morning, wine at night."

I filled her in on what I'd witnessed at the Lazy Sandbar. "At least we know for sure that Ricky faked that burglary. I'm really sorry, Shari. Are you okay?"

Shari scrunched her brows. "I'm not feeling much, Lise. After all I've been through, I'm just disappointed in Ricky. No surprise. No anger. No heartache. Just disappointment."

"We can go to the police. They might get *The Floating Ballerina* back for you."

Her voice sounded weary. "I'm not sure about that. Knowing Ricky, he wouldn't say a thing about where it is out of spite, and I'd never get it back."

I had the same worry. "Now that we're sure he took your stuff, can you act like you don't know, let everything go along as normal?"

"Why?"

"We can go ahead and bring the police in, but, like you said, that doesn't guarantee we get *The Floating Ballerina* back. He's hidden it somewhere and may decide to keep it hidden even if he's arrested. Think of it from his standpoint. He's arrested, he's facing a little jail time. What's in it for him to return the sketch? If he doesn't return it, then he'll have something he can sell for a big chunk of change when he gets out. I suggest we carry on as we have been, and hopefully, we find out where he's stashed it or at least catch him in possession of it or trying to sell it. But it's up to you. We'll proceed however you want."

"Makes sense. I'll pretend everything is hunky-dory." Shari gave a humorless laugh. "Acting and pretending is all I've been doing through most of our marriage." We were silent a moment, and she took a deep breath. "You're not married, are you, Lise?"

"Nope."

"Have a man in your life?"

"As a matter of fact, I do."

"Is he a good man?"

I thought of the note he'd left me. "He is."

"It must be nice," Shari said.

"I know things are crappy right now, but once everything's settled, maybe you'll find a good man too."

"Maybe, but I think I'd rather play the field for a while."

I laughed. "And then there's that."

Chapter 13

Nick had only been gone a couple of days, but it felt like weeks. I opened my bedside table and pulled out his beautiful note. He was so damn sweet. Perhaps he'd learned that kindness from the librarian of his childhood.

My thoughts went from the lovelorn to my work. I hadn't heard back from Baker or Ortega and figured my part in the Michelangelo case was done, which was frustrating but expected. A little before noon, I drove over to the stretch of US 1 where most of the new car dealerships were located. I passed Jack Todd Ford then made a U-turn into the strip mall parking lot. I parked at the end, under the shade of a tree, and walked to the overgrown lot next door, where Elliot the Slim was sitting on his blanket under a couple of live oaks and assorted foliage. He had a bottle of blue Gatorade in one hand and a humongous pair of military surplus binoculars in the other.

"How's the stakeout, Elliot?"

"It's going, man." Elliot the Slim was dressed in a dirty pair of gold corduroy britches and a faded T-shirt featuring a cartoon character I wasn't familiar with—a bug-eyed girl with a bow on her head. His old work boots were three sizes too big, but he'd taken them off and was giving his feet some air. Looking at his feral toenails, I understood why he needed oversized boots.

"Here." Elliot held out a scrap of paper with numbers and letters scribbled on it. "A couple of people came to talk to Stephens. I wrote down their plate numbers, though I think it was mainly car business."

"Thanks. He go anywhere?"

"Uh-uh."

"Take a lunch break." I handed him a ten and pointed back at the strip mall. "Sammy's has good lasagna, a good eggplant parm sandwich too."

I left him as he slid his feet back into his boots, and I crossed the parking lot to my car. I rolled down my windows to catch the cross breeze so I didn't have to run the car for AC. I opened the glove compartment and pulled out a pair of binoculars, which were much smaller than Elliot's. Judging from past surveillance, there was a fifty-fifty chance as to whether Stephens would go out to lunch or order something to be delivered. A few minutes later, one of the junior salespeople drove up and pulled a stack of pizza boxes from the passenger seat. *Guess ol' Ricky's eating in today.*

I'd been hoping to follow him to another licentious rendezvous. *Oh well.* I used my binoculars to look through the glass walls of the dealership and saw Stephens stroll into the break room and snag a slice. He flipped his tie up over his shoulder. Apparently, if there was a spill he preferred staining his shirt.

My phone rang, and I took a minute to sing along with Barry before I answered, "Hey, Nick, how's Vienna?"

"I find it very Austrian. What are you up to?"

"You caught me working."

"Work's good, brings in the bucks. Which case?"

"*The Floating Ballerina*, also known as the Case of the Asshole Thieving Husband."

Nick laughed, and good sensations ran through my body. Nick was quiet then said, "I miss you."

"I miss you too. So what's it like there?"

"Well, it's late afternoon. I'm at a café across from the Danube. It's really beautiful, Lise. I swear the sky is bluer here."

"Sounds romantic," I said.

"Anywhere is romantic as long as I can at least hear your voice," Nick said.

"That's smarmy, but I like it anyway."

"Where are you?" Nick asked.

"I'm sitting in my car, in the shade of a tree, across US 1 from Jack Todd Ford. Vienna sounds a lot nicer."

"What else is going on?" Nick asked.

"Not much. I don't think I'll hear from Baker and Ortega again on that murder case. Baker and I go together like caviar and feces. And for the record, I'm the caviar."

"Too bad," Nick said. "It was interesting."

Talking to Nick left me with a mishmash of emotions. There was love, melancholy, longing, and lust. *Wait, is lust an emotion? It should be.* I remembered one night that was spicier than most. Though not a great artist, Nick was a good one, and we'd played a little game where he was the master artist and I was the model posing nude for his sketch. It'd taken him forty-five minutes to finish, and the second he put down the pencil, we'd gotten right to it.

The rest of Elliot's lunch break passed with a feeling of immense loneliness. Phone calls to faraway loved ones were supposed to make people feel better, but in reality, it accentuated the distance and deepened the solitude. I cracked open a bottle of water and took a slug as I watched Ricky Stephens in the break room. He was telling a joke to a group of his salesmen.

Wait for it... Wait for it... and there it is. A brief pause before the punch line was followed up with forced laughter. Since he'd finished gracing his troops with his presence, he crossed the room like a hunter after prey and stopped to talk to a pretty brunette in business wear. The way he leaned on the table and smiled as they talked indicated some heavy flirtation. I doubted Blondie knew he was sniffing around another coworker. I focused in on the woman and snickered—her expression said he wasn't getting any. Ricky must have picked up on that, because he returned to the pizza, laid a slice on a paper plate, and disappeared through a door. My guess was he was taking it to someone who would be more receptive to his brand of sleaze, someone like Blondie.

Having seen enough of Stephens's charm, I lowered the binoculars and turned my deliberations to *The Floating Ballerina*. It seemed there should be some way to proceed besides watching Stephens and waiting for him to make a move. I got an idea, though I wasn't sure how good it was. Considering Adolph Hurst's past, there was a potential for danger. On the other hand, the pickle proved he had a different bite pattern than the killer. I decided it was worth the risk.

After another twenty minutes, Elliot the Slim leaned into my window. "I'll take it from here, Lise."

"I'll be back at five. Call me if it looks like he's leaving earlier."

Elliot tromped back to his observation post, and I drove to Cadiz Street, first stopping at Zayda's Deli to make a special purchase. Once on Cadiz, I had to circle around a couple of times to get a parking spot close to Delve Gallery. When I entered, Adolph Hurst was sitting at the counter, writing in an account book.

Without looking up, he said, "I'll be right with you."

I stood at the door and waited. He finally finished the entry, closed the book, and looked up with a smile. "Hello. It's you again. I'm sorry; I forgot your name."

"I told you my name was Margaret Atwood."

"Right. Like the writer."

"It's really Analise Norwood. Call me Lise."

He stared at me, lines showing on his brow. "You gave me a fake name?"

"If it makes it any better, Margaret Atwood is one of my favorite novelists." I walked to the counter and put a big jar of Kosher dills on it. "For you."

He glanced at it, to me, and back to the pickles. "Thank you? Why pickles?"

I was right—he hadn't even noticed the missing pickle. I sat on a stool at the counter and took a breath. "I was an art history major at San Marco University."

"Yes, I seem to remember you mentioning something about that."

"But now I'm a private investigator."

"Really? Like Mike Hammer?"

"But not as macho."

At this point his eyes had morphed from welcoming, to friendly, to confused, then to severe. He leapt from his stool and slammed one of his massive hands on the counter, causing everything on that flat surface to jump an inch. "If this has anything to do with Miami, I will lose my temper." He pointed his finger at me like a gun barrel. "And believe me, that is something you do not wish to experience."

Oh boy. I rushed the rest of the explanation. "Mr. Hurst, I came in under a false name as a consultant for the San Marco Police Department."

His body tensed.

"You were a person of interest in a case that they're working. And yes, you came to their attention because of your past as well as your art and the line of work you're in." I waited for a response, but all I got was silence and intense eyeballs. *Oh well, full disclosure.* "And you came to their attention because I told them about you." I glanced at his beefy hands, thinking they could sure make massive fists, and I readied myself to depart the premises.

"You brought me to the attention of the local police?" He said it in a soft monotone that I found more intimidating than if he'd shouted it.

I nodded.

His hands clenched into fists, he grunted and kept his gaze on me. I felt relief when he unclenched his big hands, grasped the pickle jar, and opened it.

The aroma got my mouth watering, so I had to swallow before saying, "Okay, I can't go into detail concerning the case I was consulting, other than to say there was an artistic quality to it. In fact, they refer to the criminal as Michelangelo. And they needed someone with knowledge of art history."

Adolph nodded, pulled out a pickle, and sniffed it like a cigar aficionado with a Cuban stogie.

I cleared my throat. "I came across one of your paintings, and there was a possibility that it was somehow tied to the crime committed." I paused as he bit into the pickle because I didn't want the crunch to drown me out. "Looking into your background, I learned about Miami. What happened down there kind of fit into what happened here, which made you, for a time, a person of interest."

I expected him to shout, rant, or threaten bodily harm. Instead, he pushed the big jar toward me. "Pickle?"

"God yes..." I dipped my fingers in and pulling out the daintiest near the top, which was still large enough to have come from the big-and-tall cucumber shop. I bit into it, and the crunch sounded like a firecracker in my head. The flavor was wonderfully Kosher and marvelously dill. I called to my chosen deity yet again. "God, that's good."

"Isn't it?" Adolph said. "Where'd you get them?"

"Zayda's Deli," I answered. "A couple of blocks up Minorca Avenue."

"I've seen it but never stopped in. Now I'll have to." We were chatting away like a couple of members of the local gardening club. "But you were explaining why you were invading my privacy and spying on me?"

I wished he hadn't put it that way. After taking another bite, I said, "So before the police questioned you, and thereby alerted you to the fact that you were a suspect, they wanted me to chat you up, get a feel for you, see if there was anything I could learn."

"Was this a violent crime?" he asked.

It wouldn't hurt to admit that much. "Yes, very much so."

"And they let you come in on your own? That's irresponsible—I mean, seeing as I was a suspect."

I pointed outside. "They were right out there. They could hear what was going on."

"You were wired?" A hoarseness colored his soft monotone, and I hoped that wasn't a bad sign.

"In the loosest sense. Anyway, you were eating lunch when I came in. I saw a pickle spear—well, it was actually a pickle half. You had taken a bite out of it and—"

Adolph gasped. "You took it for DNA matching!"

"Well, they might have done that, but I really took it to compare bite patterns."

"Bite?"

"I can't go into that. But your dental pattern is not a match, and since I stole your pickle, I brought you a gift," I said, indicating the jar. "You know? That's a phrase I never thought I'd use: *since I stole your pickle.*"

"It's a term I never thought I'd hear." He gazed past me as he finished the rest of his pickle. "I should be furious with you."

"And I'd totally understand."

"But it's also understandable how my past life might put me in a suspicious light. And I find you..." He seemed to be searching for an appropriate word. "Endearing." And with that, his eyes reset to friendly. "So I'm no longer a suspect?"

"As far as I know," I said. "I was only brought in short-term."

"Being a suspect is stressful. I learned in Miami how horrific it is to be under the microscope." He screwed the lid onto the pickle jar. "Since you've been honest with me, I'd like to return the favor and tell you what happened in Miami."

"You don't have to." Still, I was curious.

"But I will." Adolph came around the counter and sat on a stool next to mine. "I was an art dealer, quite successful. I was pompous, full of myself. I think the term *arrogant prick* is an apt description. I made a lot of money, which I spent on marketing, and by *marketing*, I mean parties where I could entertain wealthy clients. Looking at it in hindsight, I realize that though it was a PR move, I did it even more because I loved booze, women, and cocaine." He sighed. "Even though I'm not what you could call a studly man, I found women attracted to me, which, once again in hindsight, I now know they were attracted to my drugs, money, and spending habits. One of my new employees—"

"Belinda Vasquez," I said.

He nodded. "She was gorgeous and voluptuous, and I learned early on that her love for cocaine surpassed mine. Get a few lines in her, and she was up for anything. Well, you know where that led."

"Passing out and choking on her own vomit."

Adolph gazed past me with vacant eyes. "In my bed." He shook his head. "She was only twenty-one. Some twenty-one-year-olds are women; others are still girls." His voice remained calm and steady, yet I noted he was getting teary-eyed. "I told you she was gorgeous. With a couple of years of sobriety under my belt, an honest description would be that she was a pretty girl." Adolph blinked, and a tear started down his cheek until he brushed it away absentmindedly. "Voluptuous? She still had baby fat." He looked at me. "Did you know her father was a well-known attorney in Miami?"

"No."

"Yes. With one of the big firms. Several of his clients are violent men who make a living with criminal undertakings. He's the one who got the DA to go after me so intensely. When that failed, he brought his lawsuit. I settled, thinking it was over. Then one of his clients paid me a visit. This man is about as high up as you can get in organized crime. He told me I could leave Miami, or I could die. He'd leave the decision up to me."

"I think you made the right choice."

Adolph gazed at the floor. "I was a broken man, all injuries self-inflicted. I couldn't think straight. Was doing more coke and drinking more. I was a mess. One night, I was so messed up, I blacked out. This wasn't even a week after the mobster's visit. The first thing I remember was sitting in a pew at the Cathedral of Saint Mary in downtown Miami. I have no idea how I got there. There were only a couple of other people there praying. It was so quiet and peaceful." He smiled at me. "I wasn't raised in a religious family. Quite the opposite. As an atheist, I used to think I was smarter than anyone who was foolish enough to cross a church threshold. But that day, I got on my knees and said, 'God? Can you help me?'" He smiled, and his eyes sparkled. "All at once, it felt like the weight of the world had been lifted from my shoulders."

"Everything was all right after that?" I asked.

Adolph blew air through his lips. "Hardly. It's like this: I was a drunk addicted to cocaine and sex, and my excesses led me to ruin. But even worse, they led to poor Belinda's death. I can't forgive myself for what happened to her, but God has."

Those words hung in the air between us. I'd known people who'd turned their lives around through church and God. In this instance, however, it seemed like a minor miracle, and I felt inspired.

I took in his gallery and said, "Adolph, your excesses may have led you to ruin, but your resilience has led you to rebirth."

He smiled at me. "That's nice of you to say. This incarnation is certainly not as flashy, but I find that I'm happier than I've been in years. I no longer drink, except for wine with good meals. The thought of snorting up another line of cocaine makes me gag, and I no longer pursue women with the hunger I once did. All said and done, I hope we can be friends."

"To friends." I held out my hand. His massive mitt swallowed my hand as we shook. "Now that we got that out of the way, let me tell you why I'm here."

"There's more?"

I grinned. "Get us a couple of pickles while I find out if you're interested in helping me with another case I'm working."

While he opened the jar, I told him about *The Floating Ballerina*. When I told him who'd sketched it, he dropped his pickle.

Chapter 14

I checked my phone when I got to my car. Nick had called again and left a message. "I chickened out when we talked earlier, so I called back. I think we should talk about what we'd both like for the future, how to maybe—man, I hate this phrase—'take our relationship to the next level.' I also wanted to tell you that while you slept the night before I left, I carefully studied you, your face, and your naked body, so I could always bring you to mind while I'm away. I'm thinking of you now, and I really, really miss you for all kinds of reasons." And that was another reason I loved Nick. He could somehow combine "Aww, how sweet" with "If you were here right now, we'd bump uglies."

I sighed, started my car, and pulled into traffic. As much promise as *The Floating Ballerina* case had for intrigue, it was still a spy-on-a-spouse case. Even so, Adolph Hurst believed my idea held promise. When I'd told him how his name could be linked to the discovery of a sketch co-drawn by both Picasso and Dali, he was all for it and said he had a couple of people he would contact.

What I really wanted to do, however, was continue with the Michelangelo investigation. There was a developing serial killer on the loose who must have a fascination with classic sculpture. It could be someone who worked in San Marco's sizable arts community. It might even be someone I knew through my years of art study at the university. Or maybe it was someone who had little knowledge of the arts but found inspiration in statues. Whichever the case, I was confident the murderer was deeply affected by art. His whole being was taken over emotionally, mentally, and physically when confronting a piece of art that he connected with. In the case of Michelangelo, apparently statues and sculptures were the mediums that set him off. While I couldn't understand the sadism and violence, I'd found myself left in awe and reverence by a painting numerous times. In a couple of instances, they had so moved me that I cried.

I got to my office and saw I had forty-five minutes before I had to take over the stakeout from Elliot the Slim. I went through my mail first, which was a collection of bills and junk mail. Not a single check for services rendered.

My cell rang, and I checked the caller ID. "Oh, crap." With trepidation, I hit the answer button. "Analise Norwood Investigations."

"Who the hell do you think you are?" Ah, the dulcet tones of Detective Baker.

"I told you: Analise Norwood Investigations."

There was a heavy huff on his end. "We talked to Adolph Hurst, and apparently, that was just after you talked to him."

Hmm. I should have suggested to Adolph that he keep that whole being a suspect thing to himself. "I'll bet that was interesting."

"You talked with a person of interest about the case?"

"Didn't the pickle bite pattern clear him?"

Baker's voice got low and rumbly. "Just because the bite pattern didn't match doesn't mean he's not a person of interest. Stay out of it."

Like Baker had flipped a switch, I could feel my anger burn. "I'm not *in it*, Baker. That psycho-killer case is all yours. It's your responsibility to catch Michelangelo, not mine. However, I am on another case that has a piece of art at the center of it, and your person of interest has agreed to help me."

"If you're the art history expert, why do you need his expertise?" Baker asked.

"The man has contacts that could be important to my case."

"What kind of contacts?"

"Not that it's any of your business, but people with connections to art auctions and sales."

"Yeah? Don't you have your professor friends for that?"

"Art auctions and sales are different than art studies and education."

"La-de-dah. The only thing an art education is good for is wasting time and money."

I'd heard that same sentiment, worded in many different ways, during my days at San Marco University. When art majors gathered together, a common topic for bitch fests was what parents had to say about their chosen studies. "A waste of time and money" they called it, and they questioned how to turn a major in art into a career that paid well.

"Who told you that?"

"Told me what?"

"Art education being a waste of time and money?"

"My father," Baker said.

"Baker, were you an art student?"

The silence on the other end hung for a while.

"Were you?"

"This isn't an alumni call, Norwood. Stay out of the Michelangelo investigation, and stay away from the people who could be involved." Baker ended the call.

"Son of a bitch!" I shouted as I shut off my phone.

I looked up and noticed Gabe standing at the threshold of my office, with the door half open. Judging by his expression, my sign-off with Baker had been pretty intense.

"Are you all right?" Gabe asked.

I felt the tense expression on my face and noted how tightly I held my phone. I made myself relax, first my grip then my face. "Yeah I'm okay."

"What was that about?" Gabe asked.

"You caught that, huh?"

"Tail end of your conversation. Sounded…" It took him a couple of seconds to come up with the right word. "Harsh."

"Been having a bit of a rocky relationship with a certain homicide detective."

"Didn't they fire you?"

"They did. And then they brought me back, and judging from the tone of that call, I'm on the outs again." When Gabe remained standing on the outside of the half-open door, I added, "Come on in. My rage is cooling down."

When he opened the door fully, I saw he was carrying a cardboard tray with a couple of coffees from Starbucks. When he sat, he passed one of them to me. He wore jeans, deck shoes, and a sport coat over a T-shirt that showed a silhouette of Shaggy and Scooby-Doo being chased by Nosferatu. "I didn't mean to eavesdrop, but when I opened the door and heard your side of a testy exchange—well, it was like watching a car wreck. I couldn't turn away."

"It's all over now, no big deal."

"I actually popped in to see how you're faring as a young single woman on the mean streets of San Marco."

"I'm getting along fine. I figure as long as I stay busy, I won't miss him so much."

"Good."

"Ah, that's bullshit. I miss him like crazy."

Gabe laughed.

"Nick put a letter on a pillow the morning he left. A cheesy little love note that I've read about a hundred times."

"That, my dear, is true romance."

"I feel like a lovelorn middle school girl."

Gabe winked. "You'll be fine."

"I know. At least I have a really interesting case to keep me busy."

"That's good. Anything you can tell me about?"

I'd used Nick's expertise to justify my telling him about *The Floating Ballerina*. He'd said it looked like both artists' styles and signatures, though it should still be authenticated. And he'd given me a ballpark estimate of its potential market value, as well as its historical importance. I doubted Gabe could add anything more, and truly, I should take into account my client's confidentiality if I wanted to consider myself a professional. However, I didn't think there was a problem with giving him the barest of bones of the case.

"I can't go into too much detail, because it's still an active case, but I'm trying to recover what may very well be a stolen sketch that was a collaboration between Picasso and Dali."

Other than a slow blink of his eyes, Gabe sat without moving, mouth slightly agape.

"Can you believe it's been here in San Marco for decades, and no one has known of its existence?"

Gabe finally moved, leaning forward with an expression like that of a child who'd asked for a pony for Christmas and actually got one. Stunned, he swallowed. "And you've seen it?"

"A photo of it my client provided. I gave Nick a copy."

"What? He didn't say a thing."

"I made him promise not to say anything or show the photo to anyone," I explained.

"You're not going to show it to me?" Gabe was incredulous.

"I have a responsibility to my client that includes confidentiality. I needed to know a couple of things, and Nick served as my advisor."

"So you wouldn't have shown him otherwise?" Gabe asked, eyes narrow.

"No, Gabe. I wouldn't have." It was probably a bald-faced lie, but he didn't need to know that. He seemed so damn disappointed, I said, "Look, when I solve the case, I'll see if Shari will let me make some prints, and I'll give you your very own."

Gabe put a hand on my desk. "I'd like more than that, Lise. When it's recovered, will you please ask your client if I can study it, write a paper on it?"

Jeez, academics. I felt like a mother negotiating with her toddler at the toy store. But the longing on his face was so sincere. "Of course I'll put in a good word for you with Shari. I doubt she'd have a problem with it."

Gabe sighed and sat back.

"Nick thought there was a possibility that it could bring in millions in a legitimate auction."

"It very well could. Imagine, a Picasso and Dali collaboration."

"You imagine away. There's something I want to check." On my computer, I logged on to the university's site using Nick's username and password. I clicked here and there and finally found what I was looking for. "Baker did attend San Marco University, and I found his transcripts."

"What?" Gabe asked.

"That detective I was talking to. Something he said rang a bell." I squinted at the monitor. "He majored in art for a year. After that, he shifted into law, though he took at least one art class per semester. From what he said, I'll bet his parents made him shift his studies."

"Then why was he flummoxed about identifying the poses of the victims?"

I went through Baker's records. "Other than one intro class, no other classes in art history. He wanted to be an artist. His grades indicate he had some skill." I stared at the screen, and my heartbeat picked up. "Some of those classes were sculpture."

"What's going on in that pretty head of yours?"

My imagination hummed. "What's up with Baker, huh? If this was crime fiction, a TV show, or a book, I'd think that he was someone to look at."

Gabe shook his head. "Yeah, it'd work out great in fiction, but come on. Do you really think that the detective leading the investigation is the killer?"

I took a deep drink of black coffee. "In real life? No, I don't think he's the killer, but there's enough there that makes me want to at least check into it. I wish I could check and see if he has alibis for the murders."

"Good luck with that."

"I encountered him twice at the park, and both times, he seemed weird." I sat back in my chair and put my feet on my desk. "The first was shortly after Angela Lopez's body was found, and he'd looked exhausted, like he hadn't slept at all the night before."

"He's a cop and works odd hours."

"The second time was before meeting Nick for our final dinner. Baker seemed strange, like he was hypnotized, staring at the fountain like he could still see Angela's corpse. I swear he was talking to himself, and Gabe, he stared at the fountain with the same intensity as someone who is mesmerized by a masterpiece. You know what I mean?"

"Of course I do."

"The killer's hair is medium length and brown, the same as Baker's. Baker lives near the park where the second murder took place, and he jogs there like the second victim did. And why did he get so mad when I lifted the pickle from Delve Gallery?"

"Pickle?"

I gave Gabe the short version before saying, "If this were a whodunnit, Baker would have been mad because it cleared the smokescreen of a red herring."

"Some interesting coincidences, to be sure. On the other hand, I can imagine a number of reasons why he'd be mad about the pickle heist, which all come down to the possibility of you screwing up the investigation."

"He wanted to be an artist when he was young, and a sculptor at that." Something else occurred to me. "Baker said he and his wife liked to eat at Capello's Ristorante. That's where the first victim worked. If he's a regular, that gives him opportunity for the first girl. The park and locale give him opportunity for the second. Baker needs to be looked at."

"So what are you going to do?"

"I might call Ortega, Baker's partner."

"I don't think that's a good idea."

"If I can get Ortega the least bit suspicious, then I'm sure he'll find a way to check out Baker's alibis without him knowing about it."

"Lise, do me a favor." Gabe moved around to sit on my desk and took my hands. "Think about it before you act. Ortega is Baker's partner. You tell him, he'll tell his partner. I just witnessed your phone call. From what I could tell, he was only perturbed. Do you really want to see that man's anger in full bloom?"

"No. I imagine it isn't pretty."

"Think about it, okay?"

"Okay."

Gabe stayed long enough to finish his coffee. "I better go. But remember what I said. Think long and hard before you get in touch with Baker's partner."

And I did think about it—for a good two minutes. Mainly about how I could find out if Baker had alibis for the times of the murders. Frankly, the best and easiest way was to reach out to Ortega. I called him and said I had to meet him on the sly and told him not to tell anyone, not even Baker. He was reticent, claiming he was elbows deep in files, but he finally agreed to meet me at a small diner near the police station.

After I followed Ricky Stephens home, I drove to Rhonda's, a chrome-covered building thrown together in an art deco style. Rhonda and her staff had been slinging hash, burgers, and coffee to

San Marco for decades. Because it was so close to the station, the diner had a steady police clientele. I parked and went in to find Ortega at a far booth, doctoring a cup of coffee with sugar packets.

"Thanks for meeting me," I said, sliding into the booth.

The waitress stopped by, and though I didn't really want any, I ordered coffee as well. When she brought it, I took a sip, put it down, and slid the acidic concoction away.

"Okay, lay it on me," Ortega said.

Lay it on me? I felt like I was in a 70s police drama. "All right." I'd mentally planned what to say, though it didn't flow as smoothly off my tongue as I'd hoped. "I think you should look at Baker for the killings."

Ortega spewed out a mouthful of coffee. Suddenly, the '70s drama turned into a comedy.

Before he could recover and protest, I pulled a few napkins and cleaned the mess. "I know you think I'm nuts, but hear me out."

"You're right—I think you're nuts."

"The killer has medium-length brown hair, so does Baker."

"Well, golly gee, I'll jump right on this."

"The morning I went over to the crime scene at the park, Baker looked like he'd been up all night. Had you guys been working the night before?"

Ortega thought a moment. "No, but that doesn't mean anything,"

"I ran into him at the park after the murder. He stood staring at the fountain for a long time. It was like he was hypnotized."

"Detectives return to the crime scene all the time. It's part of the job."

"He was talking to himself."

Ortega shrugged.

"Baker lives a couple of blocks from De Leon Park, and he jogs there."

"I know where he lives, and I know he runs." Ortega drummed his fingers on the tabletop. "He runs at the park?"

"Yes. And here's why I called you. He majored in art his first semester at San Marco University."

"What?"

"He studied art," I told him. "Based on what he said, I think his parents made him switch his major, but he still took art classes. He wanted to be an artist. And he took a number of courses in sculpture."

Ortega stared down at the table.

"He said he likes eating at Capello's Ristorante, where Kristin Harmon worked. Look, I wouldn't bet on Baker being Michelangelo. But don't you think it would be best to at least consider the possibility?"

Ortega stared at me.

"At least clear him so we can concentrate on other things," I said.

"We?"

"Okay, you."

"I don't have to check anything. I know he's not Michelangelo." He leaned forward, angry, and pointed a finger at me. "I don't want you anywhere near this case again. Got it?"

Ortega stood and left. I thought he was angry because he was suspicious, at least a little. Maybe that would inspire him to check out his partner. And I hoped that suspicion-fed anger would keep him from saying anything to Baker about our conversation.

Chapter 15

T*he Artist*
Standing on the sidewalk outside her apartment, he could smell the nearby ocean. A two-block walk east would take him to where the shrimp boats came and went. The street was dark. The neighborhood was quiet, and there was little traffic. A sign hung out front, Raine or Shine Antiques. She had an apartment above the store.

The other night, he'd waited for her outside the bar where he'd first seen her. The redhead, accompanied by the friend he'd nicknamed Birdie, had stepped from the bar deep in conversation. He didn't get up from the bench near the bar, sure they would go into the parking lot, get in a car, and drive off. To his delight, they had continued down the sidewalk, past the parking area, and he'd followed. At one corner, Birdie had given the ginger a hug before they parted ways. The redhead continued on until she climbed an outside staircase attached to what had once been a gas station or garage and was now an antiques store. She had crossed a small balcony to a door and unlocked it.

Now he was back. He silently climbed the stairs to her apartment. He snuck across the balcony and peeked into the window to the left of the door. The room was dark, but a light was on in the hallway beyond it, so that he could see it was a small living room. A light flared in the window on the other side of the door, startling him. On his hands and knees, he crawled over, peeked inside, and gasped. She'd just entered a bedroom naked, toweling wet hair. He fumbled a cell phone from his pocket. It wasn't his everyday phone, but one he used when on the hunt for models. He took several photos of her.

He backed away from the window and went to sit in a patio chair located in a dark corner of the balcony, out of the sight line of the bedroom window. Looking at the photos, he wanted to get to work right away. But there were steps to follow with something like this, a protocol for both artist and model. Art was not a thing to be rushed. Now that he had pictures, he could study them and plan his looming creation. That reminded him of another picture that had to do with a future piece.

He felt as if he were floating as he descended the stairs and got back down to the street. After a block, he turned left and continued past a row of dark buildings. It was getting foggy, and the yellow pulse from a nearby traffic light carried in the mist. The flashing red in the cross directions added a dreamlike quality, but then his existence often seemed illusory. Poe came to mind: "Is all that we see or seem but a dream within a dream?"

To the artist, the answer was yes. It was his philosophy on existence. If he struggled to stay in reality, the end result would be insanity. Or perhaps he was already within madness, and it would drive him to a total breakdown, so that his body would be a bag of meat and organs, and his brain, a three-pound mass of congealed pudding. He giggled at the idea of pudding for brains. As for being insane, he liked the idea. He skipped down the road for half a block then stopped, thinking it was one thing to be insane and another to look it.

Hearing the hum of rubber rolling on pavement, he looked to see a taxi approaching. He raised his hand. The fact that the cab showed up right then, at that instant, cemented that he was on the right path. He gave the driver a street name. Twenty minutes later, he walked down that dark neighborhood street in the fog. He strolled past houses, all of them dark, a few with porch lights on, until he came to one that stood on legs.

"Where's the picture?" he asked himself and reached into his back pocket to pull out a small photo.

He moved to the driveway of the stilted house then walked up close enough that he had to crane his head up to see it. A vehicle was parked in the carport under the house, so he knew she was home. He felt the stirrings of an erection as he ascended the staircase. He tried the door, but it was locked. Around the side, a window was open, and he used a knife to cut through the screen. He climbed in and immersed himself in the beachy décor and feminine spirit. He felt sexually charged, and the ache of his erection encased in denim inspired him to remove his clothes.

After carefully folding them, he placed them on the sofa then walked through the home. It felt more like floating, and he returned time and again to the beautiful woman who slept soundly in her bed. After placing the photo on the pillow beside her, he bent over her to lightly kiss her lips. If she woke, then it was fate proclaiming his need to create then and there. But she didn't wake, and as his lips touched hers, he ejaculated. The preparation for this piece was intense enough to bring him to orgasm. He'd caught the mess in his hand and used a paper towel from her kitchen to clean himself. Back in the living room, he put on his clothes, tucked the towel in his pocket, and crept down the hall to peek in on her one more time. Then he left through the door, locking it behind him.

Chapter 16

I woke in darkness after dreaming of my mother. Even in my dream, she suffered late-stage Alzheimer's. But something had changed. Mom's mental acumen had vastly improved. Impossibly, she was recovering.

I descended a staircase in my childhood home while she ascended it. Not only could she maneuver stairs, but she also carried an armload of folded laundry.

We met at the midpoint, and I said, "You want me to take those?"

"Would you?" The two words were spoken clearly. After I took the laundry, she put her hands to my cheeks, kissed my forehead, and said, "You're a good daughter."

I was so happy that I woke near tears. I lay still, allowing the sadness to run its course. Then I heard a noise, a furtive sound like the sole of a foot brushing the floor or a hand grazing the wall. No longer a grown woman, I was a frightened child under the covers, listening for things that go bump in the night. Like a smell triggering a memory, my fear brought back the boogeymen of my childhood—two headless mannequins that wandered my childhood nightmares. I had named one Eng and the other Ang, and they could be differentiated only by one thick black hair that grew from the center of Eng's neck. And like a child in the thrall of terror, I lay on my right side, unable to move, as my breath came and went in shallow bursts. My eyes opened and flicked this way and that, seeing nothing in the darkness. Another sound came from a place in the hall where my wood floor creaked when stepped on. I needed to move, a motion to carry my body over to my left side, where I could reach the small biometric gun safe mounted on my bedside table. Once I placed my index finger on the reader, I would have access to my Ruger SR9. I envisioned it in my mind, then I was moving, rolling in bed. Once on my left side, I glanced at the door and the equally dark hallway beyond it. Though nothing was visible, I sensed a presence. I turned to the safe and, in an instant, had the Ruger in hand.

Keeping the pistol aimed at the door, I considered turning on my bedside lamp, but decided not to alert the intruder to my presence. A soft click came from the front of the house. I kicked free from the sheets and was on my feet, instinctively crouched, gripping my gun with both hands the way my instructor had taught. Pausing at my bedroom door, I listened.

My house, a rental, was a small blue stilt home a few blocks from the beach. There was a second bedroom across the hall and a bathroom to the right. Farther down the hall, the kitchen and dining area were to the left and the living room to the right, all in an open floor plan. Parking was under the elevated house. There were two access points to the deck and the outside stairs down: the kitchen door and a set of French doors between the kitchen and living room.

I stepped into the hall, armed and ready. I reached for the hall light with my left hand and switched it on. Crouching, gun aimed down the hall, I took a few moments to listen before slowly making my way down the hallway. I took my time clearing the house. Once I finished a general search, I allowed myself to breathe normally. Two subtle noises, probably the house settling or a breeze against a window, had brought me close to panicking. No wonder—the Michelangelo case was the stuff of nightmares.

I stopped at the refrigerator for a big slug of orange juice straight from the bottle. I did sense a presence earlier, and it seemed so real. Now it seemed as if I was alone, but still, I went through the house again, more carefully, closets included. There was nobody behind the couch or the shower curtains in the bathroom. I dropped to my knees in the guest bedroom and made sure no under-the-bed lurker lingered there. I checked my bedroom closet then did a pushup to check under my bed. I put my Ruger back in the safe and locked it.

Straightening the sheets, I stopped when something resting on the pillow on the far side of my bed caught my eye. A small photograph. I forced myself to walk around the bed, and knowing I shouldn't touch it, I picked up the picture anyway. It was about the size of an old polaroid photo and looked as if it had been made with a home printer on a sheet of glossy paper. The picture showed the sculpture of a nude woman on a sarcophagus; her right hand was by her head, and her right elbow rested on her left thigh. An owl stood under her bent left knee, and a bearded mask sat under the nude's left shoulder. I knew the statue, which was part of the Medici Chapel. And I knew the significance of that picture on my pillow. It had been sculpted in the sixteenth century by Michelangelo.

Chapter 17

The interval between calling 9-1-1 and the police arriving passed in a blur. It wasn't fast, but more like a moment taken out of time to exist on its own. I stood behind my kitchen counter, Ruger at the ready.

To come under the scrutiny of a killer was an odd thing. I'd watched psycho killer movies and was always amazed by the bad choices the victims made. *Not me.* I planted myself in the kitchen and stayed there, because it afforded me a clear view all around and no chance that Michelangelo could sneak up on me. I was also sure I would vomit, so I wanted to be close to the sink. I hadn't yet, but the nauseated feeling lingered. I saw the police car turn in and went to lock the gun in the safe, as police tended to be nervous about civilians with guns in hand. I put on my robe and let them in. As I explained what had happened, I noticed that the officers, Dunn and Brees, were a couple of fine-looking men, so as they looked around the house and property, I ducked into the bathroom to brush my hair and teeth. Apparently, one could face the threat of a madman and be shallow at the same time.

Brees told me, "Looks like your visitor gained access through one of your living room windows. He cut the screen."

"I like to sleep with the windows open. The sea breeze is nice."

"I'd recommend you lock them and use the AC."

"You don't have to tell me twice."

Dunn put in a call to either Baker or Ortega, who told the officers to stay with me until they arrived. That sounded like a party, so I started a pot of coffee. I thought about Baker being at my house.

Yes, there were several things about him that should be checked out, things that Ortega had said were circumstantial at best. I asked myself, *Do I really think that Baker is Michelangelo?* The answer was no. Still, even though Dunn and Brees were here, and Ortega would be shortly, I was a little apprehensive.

The coffee pot burped, gurgled, and hissed, indicating it was about done. As I waited for it to push out its final drop of black gold, my mind turned to Michelangelo's work. I'd seen Angela Lopez wired to the rock in De Leon Park, and I'd seen the crime scene photos from Kristin Harmon's apartment. Those women had been brutally raped before he murdered them. Had the assault been so bad that their deaths had come as a relief? If he came at me, Michelangelo would find that I wouldn't die easily. I would fight with everything I had, every ounce of strength, and every weapon available to me. And though I meant it, I was also sure that if Kristin and Angela had known what Michelangelo had planned, they would have said the same. And as evidence showed, Angela had fought for her life and lost the battle.

"Screw Michelangelo," I muttered and got three jumbo mugs out of the cabinet. "Coffee's on, boys," I called.

Dunn, Brees, and I sat at the dining table, where we drank coffee, ate Doritos out of a bowl, and armchair quarterbacked the Jacksonville Jaguars into the next playoffs. A half hour later, Baker announced their arrival with a growl-like "Comfortable, gentlemen?"

His voice raised goosebumps on my arms. Dunn and Brees stood. Brees gave a brief report, then Ortega dismissed them to keep vigil outside the house.

"All right," Baker said, "what happened?"

For a split second, I had a mental image of Baker moving silently through my house while I slept. *It's not Baker,* I reiterated to myself, then took a breath. "I woke up and heard someone in the house."

"What did you hear exactly?" Ortega asked.

"I'm not sure what it was that woke me, but right away, I could hear movement, subtle movement."

"Uh-huh," Baker said.

"I heard when Michelangelo stepped on a squeaky board in the hall. By the time I had my gun and was up, I heard one of the doors closing."

"Gun?" Baker said.

"Ruger SR9, licensed and locked away."

"What makes you think it was Michelangelo?" Ortega asked.

"He left me a gift."

"The picture Brees mentioned?" Ortega asked.

"Yes."

Baker asked, "A picture of what?"

I motioned for them to follow me into the bedroom and took them to the pillow that held the picture. Pointing at it, I admitted, "I picked it up before I thought better of it."

Ortega slid it into a clear plastic evidence bag and handed it to Baker, who held it up. I studied his face as he studied it, looking for any sign that he was the one who'd put it there.

"Shit," Baker grumbled. "What is it?"

"Part of the Medici Chapel, that statue represents night." I waited for a three count so I could get the appropriate reaction. "*Night* was sculpted by Michelangelo." Wanting to reiterate the suspicions I had to Ortega, I said, "You know what I think?"

"What?" Baker asked.

I looked Ortega in the eyes. "Seeing that it's the police who use the nickname, I think Michelangelo might be a cop."

Ortega narrowed his eyes and shook his head subtly.

"It doesn't mean Michelangelo is a cop," Baker said.

"If it's only cops who use the nickname, if it hasn't been in any of the media, then that's probably a damn good sign it is," I argued.

"Look, cops talk, to wives, friends, family," Ortega said, glancing from Baker to me. Still, I could see the doubt in Ortega's eyes and the suspicion, which was growing. "Word gets around. No telling where the psycho learned that we use Michelangelo."

"Maybe it's coincidence," Baker said. "Maybe that's what he thinks of himself, not knowing we use Michelangelo too. Or maybe it's a coincidence that he used a photo of a Michelangelo sculpture."

I snorted my disbelief, which set Baker's eyes to burning.

"Maybe it's not only cops who talk," Baker said, voice low. "Who have you told? Your professor friend?"

"Yeah, I told Nick, but you came to him before asking me to be a consultant. And seeing as he's in Vienna, he's not the one to worry about."

Baker crossed his arms. "Oh, yeah? What'd you tell that fat slob that runs the gallery?"

I inhaled deeply so I could unleash a proper retort, but instead emitted a squeaky sigh. "Oh, yeah."

"Oh, yeah," Baker repeated sarcastically.

"We know you told him he was a suspect, but you actually told him we call the killer Michelangelo?" Ortega asked.

"Well, I had to explain because I needed his help on something else. I figured since he was cleared by the pickle—"

"Cleared by the pickle!" Baker exploded.

I yelled back, "The bite pattern, whatever the hell you want to call it!"

Maintaining his volume, Baker answered, "I told you that just because the bite pattern didn't match doesn't mean he's not a person of interest. Hell, it may not have been him who took the bite of the damn pickle—did you ever think of that?"

Tired of talking loudly, I calmly replied, "I talked to him. I didn't get the feeling that he was some psycho killer."

"Well, if you don't feel it," Baker muttered sarcastically. "We talked to him, too, and I'm not gonna start calling him Saint Adolph anytime soon."

"Lise, he's got a past of questionable sexual appetites," Ortega said.

"And I talked about that with Adolph. He's cleaned up his act. People change."

And voila, Baker's voice shook the roof again, "People change?"

"Baker." Ortega spoke softly, but it did the trick.

Baker looked from Ortega to me, shook his head, and left the house.

"Coffee?" I asked Ortega.

"Yeah." He watched me pour and took the cup. "You know it's not Baker."

"I don't know that at all, and the fact that Michelangelo broke in and left me that photo, knowing what police are calling him, only makes me more suspicious."

Ortega took a sip. "Maybe it wasn't even Michelangelo. Might be a prank."

"Yeah, real funny one. Who'd be stupid enough to risk getting shot for a prank?"

"I don't know. But I was the one who got the call from the uniforms, and I called Baker, waking him from a deep sleep."

"Or he was pretending."

"He was home," Ortega said.

"Did you call his cell or a land line?" I asked.

Ortega chose not to answer.

"Yeah, cell, huh? You going to check his alibis now?" I asked.

He sighed. "Maybe. Yeah, I'll get around to it."

"You'll probably be right and can take great pleasure in calling me an idiot."

"I wouldn't call you an idiot." Ortega sipped then grinned. "Maybe naïve."

"Baker's married, right? So give his wife a call tomorrow. Pretend you're looking for Baker and can't find him. Ask if your call tonight woke her up. If she said it did, then Baker *was* at home, and you're right."

"Maybe."

"Hey, it'll put your mind to rest as well."

"Maybe," he repeated a bit more sternly.

Cops and their loyalty, I thought, but said, "Consider it."

Ortega opened his wallet, thumbed through it, and extracted a business card. "Here's something I want you to consider." He passed the card to me. *Buddy Reid Security: security systems for home and business*. Ortega reached out and flipped the card over. The name G. Fitzgerald was scribbled in ink on the back. "That's a friend of mine, an ex-cop who works as a consultant for Buddy. Get in touch with him, tell him you had an intruder and that I suggested you get a security system installed as soon as possible."

I stared down at the card. "Yeah, that's a great idea. Thanks."

Dunn and Brees stuck around, sitting in their unit until the sun rose, but apparently being scared shitless could make a person tired, because by then, I was back in the land of Nod. My phone rang, and I struggled from sleep like a dinosaur in a tar pit. Cracking open an eye, I tried focusing on the alarm clock until I saw it was almost time to get up.

I mumbled something into my cell phone that vaguely resembled "Analise Norwood Investigations."

"We've got a lead." It was Ortega, and he sounded excited.

"You got in touch with Baker's wife?" I asked.

"Would've been a waste of time. This is promising. We've got a sexual predator who moved to San Marco a couple of weeks before Kristin Harmon was killed."

"Oh?"

"Earl Banner, creep from Worcester, Massachusetts. He left there without telling his parole officer, and there's a warrant for his arrest up in the Bay State. Needless to say, he didn't file any of the required paperwork for predators when he arrived."

"And he's good for being Michelangelo?" I asked.

I could hear the smile on Ortega's face when he said, "Oh, yeah, he got himself a small apartment a couple of blocks from Kristin Harmon's place."

"Any connection to Angela Lopez?"

"Not that we know of yet. One step at a time."

"Did Banner do things like Michelangelo?" I asked.

Ortega became grim as he said, "Banner liked to abduct young women and bring them blindfolded and bound to his house and chain them in his basement. He'd take his time assaulting them, and when he was done, he'd drive them out to the country and let them go, always naked."

"But he let them go," I pointed out.

"After abusing and beating them."

"Anything connected to art?"

"Not that we know of yet." He was starting to sound aggravated.

"And since he let them go, there wasn't any kind of body posing."

"Almost all sexual killers have a period of escalation. Maybe he's reaching his pinnacle here in San Marco."

"Lucky us," I grumbled. "How would he know about me and the nickname?"

"Those are things we'll find out when we nab his ass."

"When's that happening?" I asked.

"Soon."

"Let me know how it goes, okay?"

"You bet."

Chapter 18

Even with all that had happened the night before, I still had things to do, and I started with a shower. Twice, I thought I heard a noise over the running water and shut off the shower to listen. Both times, my house was silent, but I couldn't shake the image of Michelangelo sneaking up behind my shower curtain like Norman Bates, butcher knife in hand.

I felt better once I got out in the Florida sun. I drove over to the Stephenses' house then followed Ricky to the dealership. While I waited for Elliot the Slim in the strip mall across the street, I called to see if Buddy Reid Security was open. Buddy himself answered and told me Ortega's friend wasn't there. I related to Buddy what Ortega told me, and Buddy said he would meet me at home later that afternoon. I hung up and saw I'd missed a call from Adolph Hurst while talking with the security company. I carefully considered the warning that Baker and Ortega gave me concerning Adolph. Call me old-fashioned, but if a pickle demonstrates a man's innocence, I'm not going to argue. So I returned his call.

"Delve Gallery," Adolph said when he answered.

"You would have saved me some grief if you hadn't told San Marco Homicide I blabbed that you were a person of interest," I said.

"It didn't occur to me until after I spoke that I might have made things troublesome for you. Sorry about that."

"Don't sweat it. If I can't raise Baker's blood pressure to dangerous levels, then I'm not doing my job. You called?"

"I have something I'd like to tell you over lunch. Your treat, to make up for the pickle you absconded with."

I almost pointed out that I'd already given him a whole jar but changed my mind. "Sounds intriguing. Give me a place and time."

After some gym time, I spent the rest of the morning on paperwork. A little before noon, I stopped by Elliot the Slim's observation post across from Jack Todd Ford, bringing a pizza and a six-pack of Cokes. I asked if he could cover his usual lunch break. He had no problem, especially since I'd brought him a pie loaded with jalapeños and anchovies.

With Elliot covering my usual lunch surveillance, I drove to my lunch date, and after turning onto Ninth Street from Cadiz, I found a parking spot right away. My mind drifted back to the gift Michelangelo had left. I gripped the steering wheel tightly as my body seemed to get cold enough that I shivered. I wondered if I was experiencing some sort of shock or the aftereffects of shock. I threw open the door, and a passing car honked as it swerved to miss it.

"Shit," I mumbled and got out. The sun felt delicious, thawing away my anxiety, along with my chill. I locked the car since I now carried my Glock 19 in the glove box. As for the Ruger SR9, it was safely stowed in my pocketbook. *Concealed carry is a wonderful thing when a psycho killer takes an interest in you.*

The Butterfly Nine Café was at the corner of Cadiz and Ninth, a block and a half down from Adolph's gallery. It sat back far enough from the sidewalk that several wrought-iron tables and chairs could fit for outdoor dining. The stucco walls were painted bright purple with an electric-teal trim. Hippie-dippie dining at its finest. I went in and spotted Adolph sitting in a booth. As I crossed the café, I breathed in the aroma of their food—lots of cumin, curry, and garlic—and took in the sixties and seventies rock concert posters framed in reclaimed wood and hung over almost every inch of wall space. Adolph stood and gave me a chaste kiss on the cheek. He may have been an insufferable whoredog down in Miami, but in San Marco, he was a gentleman. Sometimes the harder the life lessons, the better a person emerged.

A dreadlocked waitress soaked in patchouli and wearing a tie-dyed sundress took our order. Her hemp bracelets shook as she wrote down Adolph's buffalo chicken panini. At his suggestion, I asked for the goat cheese salad with datil pepper dressing.

Normally a teetotaler until the magical five-o'clock hour, I saw they had Duke's Brown Ale on tap and ordered one of those. Adolph ordered a sauvignon blanc with a name that danced off his tongue like poetry. When the waitress returned with our drinks, I watched Adolph twirl his glass, sniff it, twirl it again, and sip. I gulped my beer and burped.

We traded some pleasantries and Adolph asked, "So how did young Analise Norwood get so into art that she majored in its history?"

"That can probably be traced back to my parents."

"Artists?"

"My mother was, to a degree. Not in your league, but she loved to paint landscapes."

"And your father?"

"Pops was into the history, knew all the masters from each century, studied books on art, even owned a Klee," I said.

"Was he in academia?"

I laughed. "Pops was a mechanic. Both he and Mom supported my art history pursuit, though they advised me to look for unique ways to make a career in the field."

"But a private investigator?"

"Yeah, that's kind of out of left field. No one saw that coming, including me."

"Are your parents still with us?" Adolph asked.

"Mom is, sort of. She is in the late stages of Alzheimer's."

"I'm so sorry."

"Dad passed a few years ago from a fast-moving cancer."

"Again, my condolences." He hesitated, thinking, and said, "So you're now the proud owner of a Paul Klee?" That seemed harsh, and I guessed my expression reflected it. "I'm sorry, Lise. I guess it's the art dealer in me."

"That's all right. And no, I don't own the Klee. When Mom was diagnosed with Alzheimer's, Pops kept her home as long as possible. I don't know how much you know about the disease, but it can be pretty rough on the loved ones of those suffering. Though it broke his heart, he finally had to put her in an Alzheimer's facility."

"I can't even begin to imagine."

"But it turned out to be a good thing. Pops had been so exhausted caring for her that it was affecting his health. He finally got rest, got his strength back, and saw that Mom was no worse off at San Marco Eldercare. In fact, she seemed to do a little better with some of their treatment. She'd been out of the house for about nine months when Pops was diagnosed with his disease. There was little chance of survival, and worrying about Mom, Pops sold the Klee and put the money into a trust to help pay for her care, at least what insurance doesn't cover."

Adolph reached for my hand. "A good man, your father."

"Amen to that," I said, and we lifted our drinks in an unspoken toast to Pops.

"You still see your mother?"

"Yeah. It's funny, but I still go to her for advice, bounce things off of her."

"Does it help?" Adolph asked.

"Kind of. In my mind, I can hear what advice she'd give me if she hadn't gotten sick."

Adolph lifted his wineglass. "To mothers, and the advice they dispense with love."

"To mothers," I said, and we drained our glasses.

Adolph signaled the waitress, and she brought us full glasses.

"Shall we get down to business?" I suggested.

"Yes. But I was wondering if, perhaps, you had a picture of the sketch?"

I considered bringing up the photo on my phone but changed my mind. "For now, while the sketch is missing, I'm keeping a lot of the case close to my chest. You're only the second person I've told about it. When it's solved, you can see it for yourself. I promise."

"Good enough." Adolph sat back, his wine held before him. "I have planted a few seeds."

"Have you now?"

"Whether they will grow to fruition, I cannot say."

I leaned forward. "We're not really talking about gardening, are we?"

He smiled. "I've put out word to a couple of *seedier* acquaintances in South Miami."

"Seedier." I chuckled.

"I told them that I've expanded into the realm of hard-to-get art."

"By that, you mean stolen?"

"Basically. These men have been known to procure and sell high-priced art to private collectors with no scruples about how said art is obtained."

"What did you tell them?" I asked.

"That I have a client who collects twentieth-century masters and price is no object. And though most of his collection has been built through legal sales, he's now looking into other avenues for his private collection."

"Good," I said. "If *The Floating Ballerina* goes on the black market, word will probably get to Miami."

"Even more good news," Adolph said. "Through one of my connections I got the name of a man in Jacksonville who also provides a similar service. His name is Alden Whitt, and as far as my connection knows, he is the only person in Jacksonville to handle such transactions at the level of expense we're talking about."

"Have you contacted him?" I asked.

"My south Florida contact gave him an introductory call, and then I phoned him." Adolph picked up his glass, swirled the remaining wine, sniffed it, then drank it. "When we spoke, I asked how best to introduce him to the wealthy tycoon's art acquirer. That would be you."

"It's good work if you can get it," I said.

"My connection told me a couple of things about Whitt. One works against us, and the other is to our benefit. The first is that he's a suspicious man. If he senses anything awry, he'll bolt."

"What's to our benefit?" I asked.

"Alden Whitt has a weakness for beautiful women. Anyway, Whitt, when I told him about you, said he'd rather work through me. I told him that after my troubles in Miami, I was keeping myself at arm's length from the actual transactions. Whitt was on the verge of turning me down, but I told him it would be a shame that he wouldn't get to meet the stunning agent for my buyer. He said—"

The waitress arrived with our lunch.

After she placed everything on the table and left, I asked, "He said?"

Adolph pushed a folded square of paper across the table. "Here's his phone number. Call and set up a meet. And I figured you'd prefer an alias, so I told him you were Margaret Atwood."

"You remembered my fake name. How sweet."

Chapter 19

The Artist

He made a mug of Earl Grey tea. As it steeped, he picked up the wadded paper towel he'd used to wipe his hands at Lise's house. He held it under his nose and imagined he could smell the scent of her home as he relived his late-night visit. The memory was not as sexually charged as actually being there. Still, he was firmly erect as he put the towel on the counter, sipped his tea, and studied the nude photos he'd taken of his next masterpiece.

He noticed blood seeping through the gauze covering the bite wound on his forearm. He banged his wrist against the kitchen counter, and pain flared from the wound. He laughed, feeling charged by the sting. A true artist embraces the pain of creation and is inspired by it. And that model was a true inspiration. He let the wound bleed freely through the gauze, and he hoped it would never heal. The blessed agony took him back to when she'd bitten him, and he moaned appreciatively.

He felt motivated and returned to the model at hand. Three pictures of the redhead were particularly fetching. He settled on one that showed only a small portion of her face and texted the photo.

Chapter 20

After lunch, I arrived home just as Buddy Reid pulled up in his company van. He was a tall, thin, serious man who moved with deliberate grace. We were chatting in the driveway when my next-door neighbor, Dottie Bell, approached. She was the quintessential nosy neighbor. With her brows firmly cemented in concern mode, she asked what had happened last night. I lied and told her I'd seen a prowler and called the police.

Dottie nodded, eyeing the van. "It's a good thing you're having a security system installed, living on your own and all. Maybe it's time you and that professor get married." She sounded like my mom in her better days.

"Thanks for checking up on me, Dottie. I better show him around," I said, indicating Buddy. Waving goodbye to Dottie, I led Buddy into the house and gave him a quick tour while telling him that the intruder was more than a prowler. He was a violent killer who might return.

"We got some options," Buddy said, speaking in a low voice. He listed various systems, cameras, sensors, monitors, motion detectors and their prices. I asked which would be best, and surprisingly, it wasn't the most expensive. It was a wireless monitored system with a backup power supply in the event of an outage, door and window sensors, and a glass-break detector. If all that failed, a motion sensor would trigger the system. "And since you're a friend of Detective Ortega, I'll knock off another ten percent."

"Thanks," I said.

"However, if you're also a friend of Baker's, I'm gonna tack on another twenty percent."

"Totally understandable."

"Ten off, it is," he said.

The combination of little sleep and beers at lunch had left me logy. I went into my room to change into a sundress. When I opened my closet and looked in, goosebumps rose on my arms. I wondered if Michelangelo had been in my closet, hiding like the boogeyman. A harsh truth struck me then. It was obvious, but I'd avoided it since the incident. Michelangelo could have killed me if he'd so chosen. He hadn't. Maybe he'd played a similar game with his earlier victims. If he'd made a late-night house call, I was already a victim too.

Something happened to me. I was no longer brave, confident Lise Norwood, PI. My heart pounded to the point that my chest felt bruised. My breathing fast and shallow, I grasped the closet door for support then lowered myself to the floor, afraid I would pass out. Trembling started, and I shook all over, violently. Tears followed.

It lasted about five minutes, then I told myself I couldn't allow fear to take control; that would be handing a victory of sorts to Michelangelo, so I grabbed the knob on the closet door and pulled myself up. I picked out an old sweatshirt I no longer wore, wiped the tears and snot from my face, found a sundress, and put it on.

"Damn you." I muttered the curse at Michelangelo, wherever he was.

I got a glass of water, the latest Virgil Flowers mystery, and shouted at Buddy that I would be in my backyard. It was my favorite part of home, and it would soothe me. Stately live oaks twisted their gnarled limbs high overhead, providing shade. I had a few palms scattered about, along with a variety of native plants. Everything encircled a brick firepit. The area was furnished with antique outdoor furniture and a couple of hammocks that swung with the breeze.

I got in one of the hammocks. I didn't want to think about Michelangelo's nocturnal visit, especially after my panic attack, but my mind often wandered where I didn't want it to. Though it was breezy in the shade, the day was still hot. Even so, I shivered because that man had been in my house. There were two opportunities for him to leave the photo on my pillow. One was while I slept, and I shivered again. The other was that he'd hidden somewhere then put it there while I searched the house. *Screw this line of thought.*

I opened my John Sanford novel. While I appreciated his Lucas Davenport books, I was in love with Virgil Flowers. If he lived in San Marco, he would be a surfer. In the midst of reading, my emotions shifted gears, and all the stress of the past few days mounted until I cried yet again.

"Damn it," I muttered.

I wasn't lost to an all-out boo-hooing; it was more of a quiet cry. Maybe it was an aftershock of my panic attack, but I knew it was also because I didn't have the one person to talk to who could make me feel better. I called Nick.

"Lise. Hey." With those two words, his voice chased away the aftereffects of the boogeyman's visit.

I wiped off the tears and put on a happy voice. "Hi, Nick. Damn, I miss you."

"I miss you too. How's everything going?"

I started to tell him about Michelangelo being in my house, but I stopped myself. If I did that, Nick would come charging back to San Marco to protect me, Vienna be damned.

"Lise?"

Not only that, but, in all seriousness, I didn't think Nick could offer up much in the way of protection. No offense to my man, but he was the traditional lover, not a fighter.

"Lise, are you there?"

Maybe later, if something else happened, I would tell him. But I wouldn't distract him from this golden opportunity. It was too good for his career.

"Sorry, phone was breaking up," I said.

We talked about Vienna, about San Marco, and about missing and loving each other. When we ended the call, I felt sad but good. His voice was a balm against the craziness of a madman. I gazed up at the live oak branches overhead and the blue sky beyond. After a half-minute, my phone buzzed, signaling a text. Hoping it was another message from Nick, I was disappointed at seeing an unfamiliar number. Sighing, I opened the text message. It was a photo of a nude woman standing just in the doorway of a room. She was drying her red hair with a towel, as if she'd just emerged from a shower. Her face was angled down. She had a good figure with pretty breasts, and her complexion was pale and freckled.

The sender had added one sentence to the text. *A lovely model. -M*

Chapter 21

Ortega stared at my phone as he sat across from me in a back booth at Rhonda's Diner. He sent the text to his phone then wrote down the number it was sent from.

"He didn't even block the number. You and I both know it's going to be a burner," Ortega said.

It was just us. I'd called him, and as before, I'd asked to meet with him alone, without Baker knowing about it.

"Yeah."

Ortega checked his phone, making sure the picture came through. "Is this pose anything?"

I looked at my phone. "I don't think so. Michelangelo is showing us the model, not the finished work." It was obvious that she was being spied on, unaware her photo was being taken. Not much of the woman's face was visible, and there were few clues as to where the photo had been taken, other than through a window and in a bedroom. I couldn't think of a single way to identify her or her location. "How much time do you think she has?"

Ortega shook his head. "I don't know. Not enough. I'll see what I can get from the photo, and though it's an exercise in futility, I'll run down the number." Ortega cleared his throat and stared down at his coffee cup. "The predator from Massachusetts, Earl Banner? He had alibis for the Angela Lopez murder and for last night, so he wasn't your gentleman caller."

"Where is he now?"

"Locked up. He'll soon be on his way back to Worcester, where he'll get another stretch in prison."

"I'm sorry, Ortega." I wasn't surprised. From what he'd told me, the suspect didn't sound much like Michelangelo.

"Yeah. Look, when you work with a partner day in and day out, you know their history, particularly work related. Baker's first law enforcement job was with the Saint John's County Sheriff's Department. He'd told me before about a unique bust, so I did some checking, and in 1992, there were two murders in Saint Augustine while he was there. Both were surfer girls. One was nineteen, the other twenty-two."

I rubbed my arms and felt goose bumps. "Same kind of murders?"

"There wasn't any art aspect to the killings, at least that we know of, but they were bound, raped, and killed."

"Let me guess," I said. "The murders were never solved."

"They were. An ex-con rapist was convicted for the crimes, but it was a deputy who pulled over the man, saw his record, searched his car, and found evidence."

"What'd he find?"

"A locket from the first victim was hanging from the rearview mirror and a lock of hair from the second in his glove box." Ortega sipped his coffee and made a face like he was drinking toxic sludge. "The rapist said that the deputy planted the evidence and stuck to his claim all through the trial."

"The deputy was Baker?"

He didn't have to answer, so we sat in uneasy silence. I started to ask what he had planned next, but a large figure in wrinkled clothes appeared beside our booth, dark circles under his eyes.

"Well, ain't this all cozy," Baker said. "So, why wasn't I invited to the party?"

I pulled my purse closer. With my earlier suspicions and what Ortega was now revealing, I think I subconsciously wanted to keep my gun close. I couldn't work up the nerve to look up at him, worried that my expression would reveal that we'd been discussing him, so I gazed at the tabletop.

Ortega said, "Lise was contacted by Michelangelo."

Baker pushed into the booth next to Ortega. "Why didn't you tell me?"

"I didn't know where you were," Ortega said. "I was going to call, but you've saved me the trouble."

"Yeah, yeah, yeah," Baker grumbled. "What's the message?"

Ortega showed him his phone with the forwarded text.

Baker gazed at it with the intensity of a fortune teller looking into a crystal ball. He banged his fist on the table. "Damn it. He does this girl, and we can kiss our case goodbye. Fuckin' gift wrap the whole thing and hand it over to the FBI with a pretty bow on top."

I wanted to tell him his priorities were screwed up, but I was so unsettled by his presence, I stayed silent.

Ortega asked, "Any ideas?"

"Yeah," Baker said. "Time to go to the media."

Ortega sat back with wide eyes. "Really? You think the captain will go for it?"

"We'll convince him. Look, we can crop the girl's picture, from just above her nipples on up. Get it on this evening's news." He checked his watch. "By the eleven o'clock news, anyway. And in tomorrow's paper. Let them know the girl is in trouble and could be the target of a person of interest in the murders of Kristin Harmon and Angela Lopez."

Ortega studied the photo. "Can't see much of her face."

"No, but maybe enough that someone close to her would recognize her, and if she saw it she definitely would. I'm gonna get the wheels rolling," Baker said and was gone.

Ortega and I stared at one another over the Formica tabletop.

"Doesn't seem very serial killer-ish, does he?" I asked.

"I'll keep an eye on him and figure out a way to check his alibis. In the meantime, you keep your head down and let me know if you hear from Michelangelo again, and I mean right away."

I nodded.

WHEN I GOT HOME, BUDDY had finished the security system installation. He showed me the control panels: one near the front door and one up in my bedroom.

"I installed two alarms. One is the usual screamer that you hear throughout the house if someone tries to get in. If that happens, and you're pretty sure it's the guy, hit the big red button that says P. That's the panic button—my own design—and it'll sound like a World War II air-raid siren all up and down the street."

I laughed. "Thanks."

Buddy kept a serious expression. "Lotta my clients like me putting out signs that say the house has a security system because it'll dissuade burglars from targeting their homes. But in this case, if this guy is targeting you specifically, maybe that's not such a good idea. He might find ways to get around the system."

"Good point," I said. "Thank you for coming out so soon."

"Yeah, no problem."

Bedtime came earlier than normal, and for pajamas I grabbed a too-large concert T-shirt that belonged to Nick. He'd picked it up when Mumford and Sons headlined a music festival in Saint Augustine. I brushed my teeth and washed my face. While I looked in the bathroom mirror, I contemplated taking some melatonin, but then I figured with last night's activities, I would sleep fine. Hopefully worries about another nocturnal nutjob visit wouldn't keep me up. I went around the house, making sure everything was locked and the security system was armed like Buddy Reid had shown me. It did make me feel safer. I went ahead and opened the gun safe by my bed. I liked the idea of a couple of seconds quicker access.

In bed, I grabbed the TV remote and turned on the flat screen. Two of the local stations ran their news at ten o'clock, and I wanted to see if Baker and Ortega would get the photo of the woman on. It headlined the news on one of the channels. They rehashed the earlier murders and tied it to a woman-in-jeopardy story. Next, they flashed the cropped photo of the redhead. They reported that police believed the woman shown might be in danger then asked that if anyone knew her to call a number they put onscreen. I switched to the other station offering early news and caught the wrap-up to their story, which sounded about the same. I could call Ortega in the morning and see if the news produced any results. I considered calling Alden Whitt, the black-market arts dealer, in the morning as well but decided that since Adolph had said he was a very careful man, I would wait. I didn't want to seem too eager. It would also give me time to come up with a plausible backstory.

Chapter 22

I sat back against a couple of pillows and cracked open my Virgil Flowers novel. I woke up a little before midnight, the book still open in my hands and on my belly. Disappointed that the part of the book where Virgil had walked up to me in slow motion and bent down to plant one on my lips had been a dream, I switched off the light. Approaching sleep again, my brain did a one-eighty, and all of sudden, Michelangelo popped into my head. Security system or not, I felt uneasy. So I tossed and turned until my bladder insisted it needed a bathroom visit. Afterward, I decided to put myself at ease by checking the house. All was normal, the windows and doors were locked, and the security system was armed. I shut off the kitchen light and wandered to the French doors to look out at my neighborhood.

Across the street and about half a block to the left, the houses abutted marshland. I had a limited view, but what I could see was illuminated by a streetlight, and it was beautiful. Wisps of fog hung over the marsh, reminding me of a similar night years earlier. I'd been eight or nine, and my family was visiting Gracie's for Christmas.

Their home had been right on a marsh, and she and I had spent hours on their back deck. That night, there was a low fog over the wetlands, but none overhead, as we lay on our backs looking up at the stars, hoping to see Santa's sleigh pass overhead. We'd talked about the future, who we would marry, what we would be when we grew up… that kind of thing. I couldn't remember what I'd said, but I remembered Gracie saying she wanted to be a veterinarian because seeing sick and hurt animals was so sad.

I rested my forehead against the window and shifted my attention to the right. A dark sedan was parked across the street in front of a yard catty-corner to my property and facing my backyard. The car was way too similar to the unmarked Crown Victoria I'd seen Baker driving, so I rushed back to my bedroom and shut off the light. I pulled my Ruger from the safe and picked up my phone and made my way back to the front of the house. I watched the car for a long time then got an idea about how I could find out for sure. I scrolled through my cell phone contacts and called Baker. It rang once, twice, and on the third time, I could see a little bit of light illuminate the interior of the car outside, not enough to see the person sitting behind the steering wheel, but enough to know the car's occupant was using a cell phone.

"Baker," he answered. "What do you want, Lise?"

My mouth moved as I tried to come up with a plausible reply. My mind was blank, and I thumbed to end the call and next called Ortega. He answered after a few rings, and from his voice, I could tell that he'd been sleeping.

"Your partner is sitting in front of my house," I said in a shaky whisper as if Baker might hear me from out on the street. "Do you know anything about that?"

Ortega suddenly sounded wide awake when he answered, "Stay in and make sure your doors are locked. I'll get someone there right away."

My hands trembled as I ended the call. I pulled up a stool where I could get a better view then sat in the dark house, watching the car. The driver's-side door opened, and Baker stepped out, peering up the street then the other way. A moment later, he reached back in the car and came out with a flashlight. I watched, my pulse quickening, as he walked to my house, his flashlight aimed down at the pavement. Baker got to the base of my driveway and raised his flashlight, tracing the beam along the outside staircase, and played it along the front of the house, then I was awash with light. He knew I was watching him.

I almost ran to hit the panic button, but then I saw approaching headlights. They caught Baker's attention a second before the colored light bar of a police cruiser flashed on. I watched from the comfort of my own home as Baker reached for his badge and the policemen exited their car with guns out, ordering him to the ground. They shouted at one another, and finally, he went down. They cuffed him as another car arrived. It was Ortega. An explosive argument between the two ensued, and finally, Ortega pointed toward the police car. Two uniforms took Baker away, but not before he gazed up and gave my house a hard stare. Though I still sat in the dark, it seemed as if he was looking straight at me. A couple more police cars arrived, and I stepped out onto my deck as Ortega climbed the stairs.

"You all right?" he asked.

"I am now."

"He says he was watching your house to see if Michelangelo came back. When you called and didn't say anything, he worried that you were in trouble."

"What do you think?" I asked.

"He's my partner. I think he's telling the truth."

"Yet you sure got over here in a hurry," I said then waited for a response. When none came, I asked, "Did he tell you he'd be here?"

Ortega glanced at the ground. "No."

"Isn't that something a partner should share?"

"Look, I spoke with the captain. He doesn't think it's Baker, either, but he's no fan of the man. So we're going to lock him up, and I'll check his alibis."

"Like I suggested?" I said.

"Like you suggested. But now I don't have to worry about doing it on the sly." Worry crossed Ortega's face. "This doesn't mean it's him."

"Not to you maybe. But I'll sleep better knowing he's in custody."

Chapter 23

T*he Artist*
His passionate quest to create had opened his eyes to so many things, including his theory that paintings and sculptures were actually doorways to other realities. The keys to opening these doors were faith, acceptance, creation, and implementation. He dreamed that he'd accomplished it and was traveling from painting to painting. Existence felt of canvas and the smooth, hard coolness of marble and bronze. Reality smelled of paint and the fine dust a chisel brought from stone. And he saw the colors, so many shades and hues. And yet, he had discovered something on the journeys that his art unlocked. Red was the only true primary color.

He woke to the common world. The clock read a little after five in the morning. He was on a bed, leaning against the headboard. Naked and coated with that primary color, he swung his legs off the bed and stretched, undoing knots of stiffness in his back and shoulders. As he turned his head far to the right, something in his neck popped. He plodded into the adjoining bathroom and stepped into the shower. When he scrubbed the scabbed wound on his forearm, he remembered the energy of *The Little Mermaid* model. Out of the shower, he brushed his teeth with an unfamiliar toothbrush, spit out toothpaste, chastely wrapped a towel about his waist, and returned to the bedroom.

He stared in fascination at his painting on the wall above the headboard. The life-size nude was on her side, her head rested on her outstretched right arm, red hair covering her biceps and much of her forearm. She gazed out blankly. Her full breasts were affected by gravity, and her right leg was extended, the left slightly bent. Gasping shallowly, he approached the bed with one short step after another. He climbed onto the mattress and stood, putting his face inches from the face in the portrait. Her expression was slack, the tip of a tongue showing between her lips. He reached to touch her breasts, then her thighs, but they were two-dimensional and felt of canvas. He made a choking sound and jumped down.

For a long, indeterminable time, he stared at his latest piece. Sometimes when he created, there were tears, and other times, he laughed. This time, he smiled contentedly. A warm glow filled his chest. Sooner or later, others would come to see this nude, and that was good. Art should be shared. Before any admirers arrived, he had to prepare. Leaving the room, he found the kitchen, checked under the sink, and retrieved a bleach-based cleaner, rubber gloves, and several rags. Whistling, he felt a great sense of accomplishment as he began the arduous chore of cleaning every surface he'd touched.

Chapter 24

Though it'd been another night of interrupted sleep, I got up early, feeling refreshed. Maybe it was the fact that Baker was in custody. My morning ritual of following Ricky Stephens to Jack Todd Ford took more time than usual because Elliot the Slim was late. From there, I hit the gym then went to my office. I worked on the story I would use when I called to set up a meeting with Alden Whitt, the unscrupulous art dealer. I would claim my fictional client, a stinking-rich collector, wished to remain anonymous for obvious reasons. I was sure Whitt could appreciate that, and I would make it clear there would be more business coming Whitt's way. I would have to come up with a creative way of telling him what my fictional boss was looking for so Whitt would let me know if he got wind of *The Floating Ballerina*.

That afternoon as I sat at my desk, I heard a low chuckle from my door and looked up to a sight that froze me.

Baker leaned against the jamb, sunglasses hiding his eyes. "Guess who got released, sweetheart?"

My first instinct was to grab the phone and call 9-1-1, but like a confrontation with a rattlesnake, I didn't want to move suddenly. "You're out?"

"A stupid question. And one even stupider is, do you really think I'm Michelangelo?" He wasn't angry with his question but sounded like he'd pity me if I answered *yes*.

"I think..." I paused, figuring how to express it. "There are things that indicate that you needed to be—vetted."

"Vetted, huh? Well, there are some things you should know," he said, stepping inside.

"What kind of things?"

"That Ortega found alibis for me."

"Well, that's good," I said, not sure I believed him.

"And there's one more tidbit that proves my innocence."

"What's that?"

Baker used a finger to lower the sunglasses down his nose so he could peer at me over them. "Michelangelo killed again while I was in lockup."

Ortega walked in behind Baker.

"Is that true?" I asked Ortega. "Michelangelo killed again?"

"It's true. I came to get you." Ortega looked from me to Baker. "And to tell you about—well—Baker gave you the good news."

Baker crossed the room and leaned onto my desk. "I go to your house and spend hours watching it, waiting to see if Michelangelo shows up again, and all the while, you think I'm the psycho. Then you get my partner thinking it's me—"

"I didn't think it was you," Ortega said in a way that told me they'd been down this road before. "But some things indicated—"

"Yeah, well, fuck you." Baker started for the door then stopped long enough to add, "Fuck both of you."

I got up and pulled aside drapes from the window, and we watched him stride through the parking lot, get in a car, and drive off.

"Where's he going?" I asked.

"It's best we investigate separately for a while. He's going to check out a bar our victim was at a few nights ago."

Ortega invited me to ride with him over to the latest crime scene, and he gave me the lowdown as he drove to San Marco's little shipping district made up of docks, warehouses, processing centers, and shipping businesses.

"Should I apologize to Baker?" I asked.

"Only if you want a *fuck you* in return," Ortega said.

"So, is the redhead in the photo the victim?"

"Looks like it. Beverly Raine, in her twenties, owns Raine or Shine Antiques."

"Shit. Any idea as to what happened?"

"We may have gotten lucky. The other night, she met a girlfriend for drinks at a little neighborhood dive called Coyote Lick. Her friend had recently separated from her husband, and they were out commiserating over the rotten state of crappy-ass men."

"That's what she said?"

"That's my translation. Anyway, a half hour or so before last call, she says they were harassed by a crazy guy claiming to be an artist who wanted to paint Beverly in the nude."

"No shit," I said.

"They got into it with the guy, and the bartender threw him out. That's the last they saw him. I'm thinking he waited for them outside the bar and followed Beverly home, which happens to be a little apartment over her antiques shop. It's an old converted gas station. Her friend saw the photo Michelangelo texted you on the morning news shows, thought it resembled her friend, went to her apartment, and found her body."

"Did she give you a description of the man?"

Ortega shrugged. "They'd been drinking, the lighting was low, so not a great one. Average build, though in good shape. Brown hair. Crazy eyes. Guy was older than them, but she couldn't say by how much. She's going to work with a sketch artist. We'll see if that helps."

"Was the victim—Beverly, was she posed?" I asked.

"Apparently. I haven't been there yet, but I've been warned to prepare myself. Guess that goes for you too."

We got to the industrial area near the shipping docks, and Ortega maneuvered through the warehouses to a corner lot and Raine or Shine Antiques. The old gas station building had been painted in bright pastels. What looked like a hanging sign from an old English pub had been repainted with the name of the business. The shop was surrounded by all the marked cars and vans that indicate a crime scene.

Ortega parked, and we went around the corner to a staircase that led up to her apartment. At the top of the stairs, we ran into Reuben Busby, the crime scene guy.

"Ah, hello, Ms. Norwood." He smiled like he'd run into me at the supermarket, not at a murder scene.

"Mr. Busby."

"What do we have?" Ortega asked.

"Definitely Michelangelo. But maybe it's best that you see it for yourself. I'll fill you in on what I know later." Busby pointed down a short dark hallway to an open door.

I followed Ortega, and when he stopped at the door and muttered something in Spanish, I reconsidered going in. He disappeared across the threshold, and I followed.

"My God," I whispered.

The victim was displayed to look as if she were lying on her right side. In reality, she'd been mounted like a hunting trophy on the wall above the headboard of the bed. Long nails and spikes held her in place. Her head rested on her right arm as it extended out, pinned in place by nails through her palm, wrist, and forearm near her elbow. Her red hair collected on the left side of her head and neck, bunched on her right arm, and hung down in places. Her open eyes stared dully. Her mouth was half open, and her tongue protruded an inch. I could see where Michelangelo had bitten her breast and thigh.

A spike hammered through her left shoulder helped to hold her against the wall. Her stomach and sternum were impaled by two spikes. The flesh around them sagged as gravity worked against the hardware. Four more pierced her biceps and each thigh. Her skin puckered in around each spike, dried blood lined down from each. Her feet were nailed in place. No matter where I looked, my gaze always ventured back to Beverly's dead eyes. His masterpiece was framed with lengths of two-by-fours. A nail-gun on the floor by the bed, a hammer next to it. Coils of long nails lay unwound on both sides of the bed, along with more than a dozen long metal spikes.

"Excuse me," I mumbled and left the room. In the hallway, I rested my forehead against the wall, shutting my eyes.

A couple of minutes later, Ortega followed me out. "We think he got the wood and tools from a backroom downstairs." He pointed into the doorway. "That mess in there, it mean anything to you?"

I swallowed and shook my head. "I don't recognize it as any sculpture or statue. That doesn't mean it's not. Considering that rudimentary frame around the body, he may have found his inspiration with a painting. If you give me a ride back to my office, I'll go online and see if I can find the piece Michelangelo was replicating."

"I have to stay, but I'll get a uniform to run you back."

I sighed. "Yeah, but I better get a photo for comparison." I stepped back into the doorway and felt like a ghoul as I used my phone to photograph Beverly Raine. Because of my shaking hands, it took several attempts to get a clear picture.

The police officer who drove me was a rookie. I felt sorry for him. He'd seen the body and was ready to barf. I talked to him, trying to take his mind off what he'd seen. He caught on pretty quickly, and we chatted about a number of things, none of which had to do with murder.

I got out and went around to the driver's-side window. "Thanks for the lift."

"No problem." A second later, he looked sick again. "Guess I better get back to the crime scene."

I went into my office, logged on, and searched for a sculptural match to the supine pose Michelangelo had created with Beverly

Raine. Thinking about the frame around the corpse, I expanded my search to include paintings. Still, nothing was close, so I googled "art reclining nude woman" and came up with plenty of paintings and photos. After some time without a match, I switched up and utilized the word "masterpiece" in my parameters. From there, I went through various centuries, as well as art styles. There was no shortage of reclining naked women, but none matched the pose on the wall.

I was so focused on my laptop monitor that I was startled at the sound of the door opening. "Norwood."

I groaned. "Hello, Detective Baker."

I didn't like his grin. Ortega followed him in, looking as though he'd been at the receiving end of a verbal lashing.

Baker leaned on my desk. "You"—he pointed at me—"and you"—he pointed at Ortega—"are still a couple of assholes. But I have to work with him. I no longer have to work with you." His finger came my way again. "But I came by to gloat. While you're hard at work trying to find the artwork that Michelangelo based his latest killing on, I have already found it."

"Really? What is it?"

"I'm not going to tell you. However, I'll show you."

"For Christ's sake," Ortega said. "Just tell her. The painting is over the—"

"Shut the fuck up," Baker said. "You want to come and see it with your own eyes, or not?"

"Yeah." I closed my laptop and followed them outdoors.

I didn't want to close myself up in a car with a pissed-off Baker, so I said I would follow them. When I realized we were heading in the direction of the shipping district, I thought we were returning to Beverly Raine's apartment, but Ortega's car turned right at one intersection with a blinking traffic light where we should have made a left to get to the crime scene. About a block from one of the big dock facilities, he pulled into the parking lot of Coyote Lick—the bar where

Beverly and her friend had been. It was a small place set in the first floor of a much larger building.

After parking, I walked up to Baker and Ortega. "Didn't you say the FBI would take over after the third murder?"

"And that's gonna happen any minute," Baker said. "So let's not waste time."

I almost pointed out that his gloating was wasting time, but considering his current temperament, I kept quiet. He led us through twin glass doors covered on the inside with thick purple curtains. The bar smells were strong. Underneath the scent of beer and bar snacks, I caught a whiff that indicated plumbing issues. A dozen or so people were scattered along the bar and sitting in booths. David Allan Coe was belting, "You Never Even Called Me by My Name," from an old jukebox. The bar itself was long, but the painting behind it caught my attention.

"Ohhh," I said.

"Damn straight," Baker said.

The life-sized nude painting was definitely not a classic, but in the pinup art genre. The painter had been talented and laid the subject horizontally in the position that had inspired Michelangelo. I brought up the photo of Beverly Raine on her wall. Beverly and the nude were the same pose, except no cow skull was blocking Beverly's crotch.

"His attention to detail is impressive," I said.

Both detectives looked at me as if waiting for me to continue.

"The way her right arm extends and how the hand bends, it's as close to a perfect match as possible. How the left leg is bent with that knee above the right knee. He couldn't do anything about gravity when it came to her hair, but even that's close."

"Yeah, well, that's a 'come fuck me' expression." Baker pointed at the painting. He planted his index finger on the screen of my phone. "That expression says, 'I'm dead.'"

"The detail is still amazing," I said.

"He could have photographed it and studied it at the crime scene," Ortega said.

"Anyone here see anything?" I asked.

"Yeah, we've got some witnesses," Ortega said. "You can sit in while we question the bartender."

"Not that you're actively involved in the case or anything," Baker grumbled.

We each sat on a barstool, and Baker rapped the bar with his knuckles, getting the bartender's attention.

He ambled over.

Baker referred to a small notepad then asked, "Lucky?"

The bartender shrugged. "That's what they call me."

"Lucky the bartender," Baker said. "That's almost as original as Lou the bartender or Sal the bartender."

"I've already answered questions for two other cops," Lucky said.

"Good, then you're nice and polished and won't have trouble answering ours," Baker said.

Lucky sneered and started to say something, but Ortega interrupted. "Don't. It won't do anything other than escalate a pissing match, and no matter how far it goes, we'll win. So if you don't want us dragging you to the station, play nice."

After a few seconds, Lucky nodded. "Sorry. Beverly was a regular. A nice person."

Baker still wore his asshole expression, and Ortega didn't say anything, so I said, "We're sorry too. But these two gentlemen are the lead detectives on the case and are the best chance of catching your friend's killer." *Until the FBI gets involved.*

Lucky nodded, and Ortega referred to a small notebook of his own. "So Beverly Raine came in with her friend Tonya Abraham."

"Yeah. It was sometime after eleven."

"There was a problem with a guy. What time did the guy come in?" Baker asked.

"An hour or so later, I guess."

"Drunk?" Baker asked.

"Nah, I can recognize drunk. He might have been on something, though." He motioned over his shoulder with a thumb at the painting. "I mean, he came in and stared at that, eyes wide, mouth open, without moving for a good two or three minutes. It was weird, like he was hypnotized. Anyway, he drank most of a beer then stared at Beverly and Tonya. I mean, turned on the barstool and stared, nothing subtle about it, ya know? He went over to them, and I knew there'd be trouble. He said something crude, they started shouting, and I threw his ass out."

"Ever see him before?" Baker asked.

"Nope."

"Give me a description," Baker said.

"Good-looking if you were a lady. Smaller than me, so I guess a medium build."

"And?" Baker said.

"And I don't know. When I'm back here, I'm working, not studying what people look like."

"What was he wearing?"

"Jeans, I think. Long-sleeve shirt. That's about all I got."

"Anything about him stand out?" Ortega asked.

Lucky considered the question. "Had a bandage on his right arm, a little up from his wrist."

"Thought you said he wore a long-sleeved shirt?" Baker said.

"Yeah, but the sleeves were rolled up."

"A bandage? Like a Band-Aid?" Baker asked.

"No. It was that gauze stuff, wrapped around his arm." Lucky pointed at his forearm. "Could see a little bit of blood coming through."

"You noticed him staring at the painting," Ortega said.

"That was just weird. Couldn't help but notice."

"You threw him out."

"I grabbed him and shoved him out the door. I wasn't memorizing his looks."

"How about his hair?" I asked.

"Dark brown, I think, but lights in here are low."

"Age?" Baker asked.

Lucky worked at a smudge on the bar top with a towel. "Hard to say. If I had to guess, I'd say in his forties or fifties."

"Forties or fifties," Baker said, like it wasn't any help at all.

"Could've been older." Lucky pursed his lips. "Could've been younger."

"When did the women leave?" Ortega asked.

"Last call."

"Notice anything out of the ordinary after they left?" I asked.

"Hang on." Lucky got fresh beer for patrons down the bar, poured a draft for a newcomer, then came back. "No, nothing out of the ordinary."

The interview was winding down, so I asked, "I'm curious. Why is the bar called Coyote Lick?"

"Because of what it is," Lucky answered.

"What's a coyote lick?"

"His balls, mostly." Lucky shrugged. "It's funny under other circumstances."

Ortega said, "We'd like to get an artist in here and help you come up with a sketch of the guy. That all right?"

"Sure, anything to catch the bastard."

Lucky left to serve patrons, and we sat silently. I studied the painting of the nude.

"What's running through your head?" Baker asked.

I kept my gaze on the painting. "That Michelangelo is branching out into new mediums."

"Meaning that using an MO to nab him is just about impossible," Baker said.

I nodded. "It also means that he'll be eager to find new models."

Chapter 25

We stepped out of Coyote Lick, and Ortega promised, "We'll make sure there are regular patrols by your house."

"Why?" Baker asked. "She didn't like it when I was outside her house waitin' on Michelangelo."

"Come on. I'm sorry," I told him.

"Good. You ought to be sorry," he said.

When I grinned, he gave me a stern look and asked, "What the hell you so happy about?"

I just shook my head, not bothering to explain that Ortega had told me to expect a *fuck you* if I apologized. What I got was a lot nicer.

The promise of regular patrols did the trick, and I slept surprisingly well. After following Ricky Stephens to work and hitting the gym, I decided a little sun was needed, so my next stop was the beach instead of the office. At my house, I stripped down, put on my sunflower-yellow bikini, and threw on a sleeveless San Marco University tee over that. I put the Virgil Flowers book in my beach bag, filled a water bottle, and stepped out my door to find myself face-to-face with a woman. She wore a dark-gray suit with slacks, dark sunglasses, and a tie. Her hair was cut short with precision, like her stylist had measured each single hair with a ruler. One second, her arms were at her side. In the next, she held up a billfold that displayed an ID on one side and an FBI badge on the other. I figured she practiced that move in front of a mirror.

"Special Agent Janet Davis," she said in a deep, clipped voice.

"Beach-bound Lise Norwood," I answered.

"Analise Norwood?" she questioned, as if Lise and Analise were worlds apart.

"Uh-huh, that's still me."

In one quick movement, her billfold disappeared into her suit. "We understand that you've been assisting the San Marco PD in the recent murders?"

I put down my beach bag. "As a consultant. I have an arts history background."

"We know."

"And as the killer left his victims in poses replicating famous sculptures, they used me to tell them which ones. Except for that last one—her body was based on a painting."

The special agent's left eyebrow rose in an arc over the top of her sunglasses.

"Which you already know."

Special Agent Janet Davis reached up to resituate her sunglasses, which might have slipped a whole micro-millimeter. "We've taken over the case, and your services will no longer be needed. However, since you have been given two photos by the person responsible, we consider that a direct threat and will have an agent watching you at all times."

It was instinctual for me to reply with a smartass zinger. However, I admitted to Davis, "Thanks, I'll feel better having you around. Though I'm bummed about not working the case anymore. If something comes up and you need my—"

Davis shook her head. "Not a possibility. May I see your phone?"

After fishing it out of my beach bag, I handed it to her.

As she tapped in a number, she said, "If anything at all happens, hit this number, and it'll go right to my phone." She gave my phone back, and I saw she'd put it as my number one contact. "The others on your surveillance team will provide their numbers during their initial shifts." She slid her sunglasses down her nose and looked over them with remarkably clear blue eyes. "Let me reiterate, however, that you are no longer doing anything for the case. In any capacity."

"Okeydokey."

She stared at me like I'd spoken Greek. "Do you understand?"

Trying to speak in her lingo, I answered, "That's affirmative, Special Agent Janet Davis."

As I watched her descend my stairs, I wondered if her time at Quantico had wrung every ounce of humor out of her. It wasn't until she got in the car at the curb that I realized she was to be the first agent to watch over me.

At the beach, I took off my T-shirt, spread out a towel, and lay on it, closing my eyes. The smell of the salt air and the sound of the surf were intoxicating. I always preferred coming in the morning because it wasn't as crowded. It might have been early, but it was already a scorcher.

I thought about those murdered girls and my murdered cousin. I was no longer connected to the current investigation, not even as a lowly consultant, and I was only connected to Gracie's by being a member of the victim's family. An idea came to me. I wondered if I could get copies of Gracie's case file since I was related to her. The Panama City PD might have relegated it to cold-case status, but I wondered how far I could get if I took a run at it. My aunt and uncle were still alive, and I knew they were still distraught their daughter's killer had never been brought to justice.

Even if I did go ahead with it, I would have to wait until I was finished with *The Floating Ballerina* case. I was eager to call Alden Whitt, the black-market art dealer Adolph had contacted, but I worried that if I seemed impatient, it would make him doubly suspicious. On the other hand, I didn't want to wait too long in case information about the sketch was already in the pipeline. It was a balancing act, but my gut feeling told me to wait another few days then call him.

Still, Michelangelo kept coming to mind, and I was thankful the FBI was watching over me. However, I was sorry that the first special agent I'd met had a stick so firmly embedded up her backside that her burps smelled like pine. I sat up and waved back toward the dunes, where Davis sat in the sand, suit jacket off, tie pulled down, and sleeves rolled up. It was hard to tell with her sunglasses on, but her mood didn't seem to be a happy one. *Must suck being so hot*, I thought as I rolled over and got the Virgil Flowers book out of my beach bag.

THE TIME I PUT IN TRAILING Ricky Stephens was long, but Special Agent Janet Davis worked in shifts with two other agents, Mark Carter and Kyle Teague, each taking eight hours. While I had enjoyed making Davis sweat at the beach, I didn't go out of my way to make things difficult for them for the next few days. When at my house, they stayed in their car at the curb. At my office, they stayed in the parking lot. I brought them the occasional coffee and snack.

That morning, I'd picked up a coffee cake at Genelle's, a bakery and coffee shop that was on the way to my office. I ran a piece out to Teague, and while we chatted, I found out he was from Columbus, Ohio, where his father and mother both taught at Ohio State. A proud Buckeye, he loathed the Florida Gators, loved the beaches, and tolerated the heat and humidity. He could have been the poster boy for an FBI recruitment ad. He was tall—I guessed six two—in optimum condition without bulking out, and had a strong jaw and coffee-dark eyes. My favorite of his features was a lock of his near-black hair that fell over his forehead. I could tell it bothered him; he was constantly brushing it back in place with his hand.

My phone rang, and I told him, "Duty calls," then headed back in. "Morning, Baker."

"Those feds still breathing down your neck?"

I liked two out of three of the agents and stuck up for them. "They're not breathing down my neck."

"Parked in front of your office?" Baker asked.

"Uh-huh."

"Okay, good. Come out your back door. We want to talk to you."

"You're here?" I asked, but Baker had hung up.

I went down the hallway that led out the back door. Sure enough, Baker and Ortega sat in a dark unmarked car. I opened a backdoor and climbed in. "If I'd known you were dropping by, I'd have picked up more coffee cake."

"The feds tell you anything about the case?" Baker asked.

"Other than to stay out of it, they've been tight-lipped."

Baker chuckled. "When did you start listening to anyone when they tell you what to do?"

"It's kind of hard when they have people watching over me."

"We're still working it," Ortega said.

"Officially?"

"Unofficially," Baker said. "And it's nice without having everyone from the mayor to the captain to the DA's office trying to micromanage us. Now the DA can be a pain in the butt to the feds."

"What's your boss have to say about that?"

"The key word is *unofficially*."

"We work the cases assigned us and squeeze in working Michelangelo where we can," Ortega said.

"Good for you," I said and meant it. "How's it going?"

Baker said, "There's been another murder."

"What? When?"

"Sometime last night," Ortega said. "She was found early this morning at her place of employment. We're not supposed to know a thing about it."

"Another pose?" I asked.

"Yeah," Baker said, "but this time, it's not a sculpture or a painting he's copying."

"What then?" I asked.

Baker brought up a photo on his cell phone and passed it back to me. The brunette corpse had been forced into a pose I was all too familiar with.

"A sketch," Ortega said.

She'd been posed exactly like *The Floating Ballerina*.

Chapter 26

"Think they'll notice you're gone?" Ortega asked.

We sat in a booth at Rhonda's. Ortega and I had coffee while Baker chewed his way through a patty melt. I borrowed Baker's phone again for another look at the latest murder victim, though I hadn't yet been able to stomach more than a quick glance.

"Only if they need a bathroom break, and from what I've noticed, the FBI must teach them urine retention. They pretty much stay outside unless I invite them in. How'd you get the crime scene picture?" I asked.

"We have connections," Baker mumbled around a mouthful.

"Cryptic," I said.

"The feds are using some of our techs," Ortega said. "Reuben Busby may be taking orders from them, but he's still rooting for the home team."

"Go team," I mumbled, trying to work up the nerve to give the photo my attention.

"Busby sent a couple dozen pics from the crime scene. Swipe through them," Ortega said then went on to tell me the victim's name was Amanda Kellogg and that she was found in the back room of the hip, upscale clothing store she managed. I'd stopped in once, but the styles weren't to my liking, and the prices were out of my humble budget.

"It's a small business," Ortega said. "Amanda was working alone yesterday and was supposed to go out with some girlfriends after work. Her boyfriend woke up at four this morning, and she still hadn't come home, so he phoned one of her friends. She said that

Amanda had never shown up, and they figured she had to work late. He found her car at the store and broke a glass pane to gain entrance through the back door. That set off a silent alarm. The responding uniforms found him collapsed on the floor under her body. They said he was near comatose."

"Silent alarm? Do they have security cameras?" I asked.

"Only in the front of the store, to catch shoplifters. Apparently, she was taken from the back of the store. Nothing on camera," Ortega said.

"Used wires and rope again," Baker said.

I took a deep breath and forced myself to study the crime scene pictures, swiping from one to the next. Michelangelo had positioned her in mid-leap four feet off the ground, her body twisting in air as if dancing without gravity. To keep her in that position, Michelangelo had used rope and thick wire to suspend her from wooden beams that ran under the ceiling. Some of the wire he had pushed through her shoulders, the two bones in each wrist, and through her calves.

"Our killer changed things up again," Ortega said.

"You mean besides copying a sketch?"

"Busby said that even though she was posed there, he killed her somewhere else."

"Well, he did the same at the park," I pointed out. "Raped Angela Lopez in the bushes, killed her in the grass, and carried her to the fountain."

"But it was all in the park," Ortega said. "They haven't found where Michelangelo killed Amanda."

I wanted to make sure I had a grasp of the facts and mumbled, "So he took her at the shop. He takes her elsewhere for torture, rape, and murder."

"And then brought her body back to the shop and worked hours posing her," Ortega said.

"That's it," Baker said, leaving a small portion of his patty melt on the plate. "As if it isn't risky enough to kill and pose them in the same location, he's really taking chances with this one."

"Any connections with other victims?" I asked.

Baker shrugged. "Haven't gotten that far along. Might leave that avenue to the feds."

My attention went back to one of the photos. "I can't tell from the picture, did he bite her?"

"Busby says once on her calf and again on her right buttock," Baker said. "Here's the thing. We saw that pose in the picture at your boyfriend's office. You didn't like us looking at it and stuck it in a folder. So fill us in."

I gulped the rest of my coffee. "It's from a case I'm working. That sketch was drawn on a linen napkin in Barcelona, Spain in the thirties. It's a collaboration between Picasso and Dali."

Baker raised his eyebrows, appreciating the importance.

"It belongs to my client, has been in her family for a couple of generations, and it was stolen. She thinks her husband, her soon-to-be *ex*-husband, stole it in a staged burglary, and she wants me to get it back."

"Must be worth a fortune," Baker said.

"My client considers it a family heirloom. I don't think she realizes its significance. It's unknown to the art world. It's worth some serious bucks. Nick, Professor Weldon, said he wouldn't be surprised if it went in the seven figures, even eight."

Baker whistled. "None too shabby for a sketch."

"On a napkin," Ortega added.

"The value has more to do with the uniqueness, what it represents, and its history. More so than the quality of the art. Frankly, I could imagine how a museum curator could devote rooms to the works of Picasso and Dali and use *The Floating Ballerina* as its centerpiece."

"That's all well and good, Lise. But if it's an unknown in the art world, then how does Michelangelo know about it?" Ortega asked.

"That's the big question," I said.

"Answer it and crack the case," Baker said.

I grabbed a French fry off Baker's plate. "Yeah. It has to be someone who has seen the sketch, has had time to study it."

Baker pushed his plate toward me, offering the rest of his fries. "We have to compile a list of people who have seen the sketch."

"The only person I showed was Nick, and he's off in Vienna."

"He show it to anyone?" Ortega asked.

"No. I told him not to."

Baker's eyes narrowed. "Uh-huh. You sure he wouldn't get so excited that he'd have to share it with someone else?"

"Pretty much."

"Give him a call. Ask him about that."

"Now?"

"Good a time as any," Baker said.

I got out my phone, hit Nick's number, but it went to voicemail. "Hi, Nick. Got a question for you. I'll try again later. Miss you." I ended the call then pointed out, "Actually, I know of two other people who've seen it."

"Who?" Ortega asked.

"You two, when you came to his office."

"I'm gonna get pissed if you blame me again," Baker said.

"You have an alibi," I said. "How about you, Ortega?" I said it half-jokingly and half with an interest to see how he'd take it.

"He's clean. I checked him out," Baker said.

"I'm—wait—you checked me out?" Ortega asked.

"Well, I was pissed at you two for thinking I might be the nutjob. Then I thought, well, if I was a suspect, that means Ortega should be as well. So, yeah, I checked you out. Tit for tat. You got alibis."

Ortega looked offended, then he smiled and laughed.

"What about your artist friend? Hurst?" Baker asked. "There's something about him I still don't like."

"I told him about it, but I didn't show him the picture. Whoever killed Amanda Kellogg had to have seen it in order to replicate it in such detail."

Baker nodded. "What's this Ricky Stephens like?"

"Not a likable guy. A philanderer, but I haven't seen anything to indicate violent sex. Frankly, I get the feeling that even though Michelangelo is nuts, he's smart, really smart. Ricky's not an intelligent man."

"You think he's still in possession of the sketch?" Ortega asked.

"I do. Unless he got rid of it immediately after stealing it. I've had him under pretty tight surveillance."

"We're going to have to talk to your client and her husband," Baker said.

"Yeah, I know." I wasn't happy about the prospect. Right now, Ricky's ignorance was my bliss when it came to my investigation. "Look. I know this case trumps mine, but there's a way you could help me out when you talk to my client and her family."

"What's that?" Baker asked suspiciously.

"Ricky is probably ignorant to the fact he could well be a multi-million-dollar art thief. If, when questioning him, you act as if he's not a suspect in the theft, it would be much appreciated."

"We can do that," Baker said.

"I was hoping for more," I said. "Can you say something that puts pressure on him to get rid of it? I have some people with their ears to the black-market pipeline. If he panics and tries to sell it, I'll hear about it."

"We can do that too," Ortega said.

Chapter 27

On the way back from Rhonda's, I had Baker and Ortega stop by Radio Shack so I could pick up a burner phone. At my office, I snuck through the back door and went to peek out the front. Teague sat in his car, oblivious to my absence. We exchanged a wave, and I went to my desk and tinkered with my new phone so it would show Margaret Atwood on the shady art dealer's caller ID. Figuring I should contact Whitt before Baker and Ortega visited Shari and Ricky Stephens, I got the piece of paper Adolph had given me and called the number scribbled there. I put it on speaker phone and hit the red button on the little digital recorder I keep in my desk.

There was a click, a good five seconds of silence, then a voice said, "Yes?"

"Hi, I'm trying to reach Alden Whitt. My name is Margaret Atwood."

"Like the writer?"

"You're a reader, Mr. Whitt?" I asked.

"I've never read one of her books, but I did try to find something about you. All I got was Margaret Atwood, the writer."

"I suppose that could be a problem sharing a name with someone famous," I said. "But sometimes I find it better to fly under the radar."

"I understand what you mean."

"Our mutual friend, Adolph Hurst, said I should meet you."

"Ah, Adolph. He said he knew you in Miami," Whitt said.

I almost answered in the affirmative, but then I realized he was testing me. Adolph hadn't told me what he said to Whitt about our relationship. Going with a gut feeling, I said, "No, I've only become acquainted with Mr. Hurst since he's been in San Marco, which is a shame. I hear he threw some grand parties back in the day."

"So I understand," Whitt said.

Figuring he would have hung up if I'd responded incorrectly, I knew I'd passed one test and would have to be wary of more.

"Mr. Whitt, I represent a man of means who is hoping to expand his private collection. For the sake of intrigue, I'll call him Mr. X. Until now, Mr. X has acquired his art through galleries and auctions, all above board. Realizing that there are many more valuable and rare pieces to be obtained through other channels, Mr. X has instructed me to explore this possibility. Mr. Hurst gave me some of his contacts in south Florida, but up here in northeast Florida, he said you were the man I should talk to."

"That is true. You'll find that between Atlanta and Orlando, for certain kinds of acquisitions, I am the man to know."

"Excellent. I assume that you'd like to meet in person to discuss the details. We could split the difference and meet in Saint Augustine," I suggested.

"For business I prefer to stick closer to home. Can we meet in Jacksonville?" Though he phrased it as a question, I knew it was a demand.

An hour and a half to get there. "Is this evening too soon?"

"Tonight will be fine. Might I suggest we meet at the bar at Blue Bamboo. It's located on Southside Boulevard."

"Sounds Asian."

"It is, at least an upscale version, and one of my favorite restaurants. I'm sorry to say I won't be able to dine with you as I have an appointment later. But the bar has creative cocktails, and if you like spicy cuisine, we can split their calamari, which comes with a wasabi and sriracha dipping sauce."

"You certainly know how to tantalize a woman, Mr. Whitt," I said suggestively.

"In more ways than you can imagine, Ms. Atwood."

And a braggart to boot, I thought. "I look forward to seeing you this evening."

"Oh, one last thing."

I didn't like the sound of that. "What's that, Mr. Whitt?"

"I will need to speak with your employer before we conduct business."

"But—"

"I know he wishes to remain an unknown entity, and that's fine. Still, I wish to talk with him either via phone or in person."

"Why?" I asked.

"I want his assurances that if you and I agree to a deal, that he'll stand by that deal."

"I can assure you—"

"It's his assurances I'm concerned with."

I took a few seconds to think. "I understand." I wasn't sure how I was going to pull this part of it off.

"I want to feel comfortable with Mr. X. My trust in buyers and sellers is key to why I've been in business so long."

"When would you like to speak with him?" I asked.

"When we meet tonight, of course. Goodbye, Ms. Atwood." He hung up.

Tonight? Nothing ever comes easy. I got an idea and left the office, pausing to lock the door. I shouted to Teague, "I'm heading to the university."

Teague followed me over. I called Gabe en route, and he agreed to see me between a class and a meeting. I had a half hour to kill when I got there, so I took Teague to the cafeteria and bought him a soft-serve cone. We ran into Gabe as we wandered to his office. I started to explain why Teague was with me, but halfway through the tale, Gabe lost it.

"Good God, Lise! Last time we talked, you were simply helping with the case. Now the killer's broken into your house? He knows about you?" Gabe stared at me openmouthed.

"And he texted me," I pointed out.

Gabe made a strangled noise of exasperation and gripped me by my shoulders. "This isn't *The Maltese Falcon* or *Kiss Me Deadly*. This is serious, Lise. It's real. I advise you—no—I *strongly* advise you to stop working with the police on this."

"Too late, Gabe. Since the FBI is involved, I've been given the boot. Until they solve it, I'll have the best federal protection money can buy." I patted Teague on the back. His lock of hair had fallen to his forehead again, making him resemble Superman. That made me feel even safer with him around.

Gabe looked from me to Teague and sighed. "I'm glad to hear it. You take good care of our girl, here."

Teague gave a single nod. "I'm on it."

We got to Gabe's office, and Teague waited outside.

Gabe sat in his office chair, and I sat in one on the other side of his desk. He opened the bottom drawer and pulled out a bottle of Jameson and two small glasses. He poured a swallow in each, passed one across the desktop, and sat back with the other.

He held up a hand. "Look. I'm shaking. I can't believe the psycho was prowling around your house while you were asleep." He emptied his glass and poured another finger of whiskey.

I almost told him about the latest victim, Amanda Kellog, but he was upset enough as it was. If I pointed out that I had another connection with the killer, he would really freak. Hoping to change the subject, I said, "I like your sport coat. Pink?"

"Rose. So they can see me coming." Then he turned the topic right back to Michelangelo. "So have you told Nick what happened?"

I took a sip, and despite what we were discussing, I took a moment to enjoy the burn. "No. I was worried that he'd abandon his fellowship and come back. And even if he didn't, all it would do is worry him."

"I'm not sure that keeping secrets, even for his benefit, is a good idea."

"Maybe not. I'll figure it out the next time we talk." I gazed out his office window onto a lawn of fresh-cut Saint Augustine grass. "Up until the point I became of interest to Michelangelo, I was thrilled to be part of the investigation, even peripherally. Why does Michelangelo leave his victims in poses that mimic art? Is he a sculptor or in the art world? How did he select these women? Why does he leave DNA splashed all over the crime scenes but clean up his prints?"

"Intriguing to be sure. But I, for one, am glad you're out of it. Cheers to that." Gabe hefted his glass before finishing his Jameson. "Now, what did you want to see me about?"

"How would you like to help me solve another case?"

Gabe raised an eyebrow. "What case?"

I grinned. "The one with the Picasso-Dali sketch."

He smiled back. "What do I have to do?"

"I want you to talk to someone on the phone. All they'll know about you is that you're the mysterious Mr. X." I filled him in on my plan and how he should play his part, and he was all for it.

Leaving the office, I took Teague's arm, and we went to our respective cars in the parking lot. An hour later, I was at the house, showered, and pondering what to wear. Since I was meeting Alden Whitt at a restaurant featuring Asian fare, I chose a white sundress with a blue hibiscus flower print. It was short and displayed cleavage. I figured that if my boobage got Alden Whitt's carnal attention, he would let down his guard. I added a single-strand pearl choker that was one of the few pieces of expensive jewelry I owned, a hand-me-down from my grandmother. I put on my counterfeit Rolex watch with a pink face that I'd bought from a street vendor in New York. I added blue pumps. When I looked in the full-length mirror, I knew that I would have Alden Whitt eating out of my hand.

I left the house and walked to Teague's car.

"You look like a million bucks," he said as he rolled his window down.

"Thanks. I've got to meet someone in Jacksonville. It's for a case I'm working. I don't suppose I could talk you into cutting me free for a few hours?"

"Not a chance."

"I thought so. I'm meeting him at a restaurant bar up in Jacksonville. The Blue Bamboo on Southside. Make sure he doesn't see you," I said.

"I'll be like a ghost."

"Great. Does the ghost need to use the potty first?"

He did, then we were off. I first met Elliot the Slim and followed Ricky Stephens home from work. From there, I drove to the interstate and headed north. Teague was good. I only saw him behind me a couple of times, and that was because I knew what kind of car he drove.

Almost an hour into the trip, my cell phone rang. Being a good driver, I didn't check caller ID. "Analise Norwood Investigations."

"Lise, hi. It's Shari," she whispered.

"Crap, don't tell me Ricky is going out."

"He is. He said he's going to meet some friends at a bar. Is that a problem?"

"I'm on my way to Jacksonville to meet someone who'll get wind of *The Floating Ballerina* if it goes on the market."

"Oh. Do you want me to follow Ricky?" she asked.

"No. He'd probably spot you, and that could be messy. Let me think about it. When's he leaving?"

"Half hour, forty-five minutes. He's in the shower. There's another reason I called. A couple of detectives were here, asking questions about the burglary and especially about the sketch."

"Baker and Ortega?" I asked.

"That was them. I made them a preliminary list of people who've seen the sketch, and they want us to work on a more thorough one."

"Did they show any suspicion that Ricky is the thief?"

"No, but I think they made him nervous," she said.

"Why?"

"They said something about how statistics show that the longer the burglar hangs on to stolen art, the more likely they are to be caught. I saw his expression when they said it, he was concerned."

"Good, maybe he'll make a move soon." *But not too soon. Oh no, maybe that's why he was going out.* "Did he say he was going out before or after the visit from the detectives?"

"Before. He told me when he got home. I haven't had a chance to call until now."

"Okay, that's good. Don't worry about tonight. I'll see what I can come up with."

It was definitely more productive that I meet with Whitt. Besides, I wouldn't get to San Marco in time to follow Ricky Stephens. I could call Baker and Ortega and see if they would trail him, but I got an idea and called Adolph Hurst instead.

"Really?" he said after I told him what I wanted. "You want me to follow the man you suspect stole the sketch?"

"You don't want to?"

"Are you kidding? I've always wanted to play spy."

Relieved, I said, "Are you sure?"

"This will be fun, and I don't have any plans this evening, most evenings, for that matter."

I gave him the Stephenses' address, and he agreed to leave *posthaste*. I grinned, thinking he was probably the only man I knew who would use a term like that.

Twenty minutes later, I pulled into the parking lot for Blue Bamboo, a yellow-and-blue pagoda building with box containers of bamboo growing out front. I walked through double doors, each with a large half-circle of glass, and paused to let my eyes adjust to the darker surroundings. The foyer had dark tiles with gold letters on the floor that spelled out the restaurant's name. I told the hostess I was meeting someone at the bar, and she pointed the way. The restaurant was full of diners enjoying Asian cuisine at tables with black tablecloths, white linen, and woven green placemats. As busy as the restaurant was, there was only one man sitting at the dark wooden bar, his back to me.

I sidled up on the barstool next to him. "Dr. Livingston, I presume?"

His eyes lit up as he looked me up and down. "Adolph said you were attractive, but I see that was an understatement."

"Flattery will get you interesting places, Mr. Whitt."

"Call me Alden."

"If you call me Meg." I figured a shortened version of Margaret would add to the believability of my undercover persona.

Probably in his early forties, Alden was an attractive man who would have been at home on the cover of *GQ Magazine*. His gray suit was tailored and expensive. A red tie added just enough color. There was no hint of gray in his dark hair. By reflex, I compared him to the sparse description of Michelangelo that Coyote Lick's bartender had given us. He could fit.

Judging by the liquid in the glass in front of him, I pegged him for a Scotch drinker. "So what are you drinking?"

"Laphroaig single malt. Here, why don't you select something?" He handed me a drink menu.

Based on the menu's description, I settled on a Cucumber Smash, and the bartender finished making it at the same time the calamari arrived. Whitt and I chatted like we were on a first date as we nibbled the calamari, which tasted amazing, and the wasabi and sriracha dipping sauce was a delight to the palate. He ordered another round for us then checked his watch. Unlike mine, it was an authentic Rolex.

"Before we proceed further, I would like to speak to the mysterious Mr. X," Whitt said.

I smiled like it was no big deal, got out the burner phone I'd called Whitt with, and brought up the only other number I'd programmed into it.

"Hello, Margaret," Gabe answered. We'd talked about him speaking loudly and me turning up the volume so that Whitt could hear some of our interaction, so Gabe used my alias.

"Hello, sir."

"How is your meeting?"

"So far, so good. We're just getting down to brass tacks, and we figured it was a good time for you to speak with Mr. Whitt."

"Put him on."

I passed the phone to Whitt.

He stood from the barstool, held out a hand to me as if he were instructing a dog to stay, and wandered toward the end of the bar. All I caught was Whitt saying, "Good evening, Mr. X. My name is Alden Whitt." Two minutes later, he returned and passed me my phone. He believed my little scenario. "Your employer seems to think the world of you and says you may speak on his behalf on all matters concerning future purchases."

I raised an eyebrow to make a face that translated into "That's what I told you," then took a sip of my drink.

"Why don't you tell me specifically what your employer wants?" Whitt asked.

"There aren't specifics. More along the lines of parameters. He wants to build his collection of twentieth-century masters. Cezanne, Duchamp, Picasso, Monet, Gaugin, Pollock, and Dali. But really, he's open to any of the major artists of the past century."

"I see," Whitt said. "And his price range?"

"It really depends on the piece, doesn't it? Let me assure you that he wouldn't balk at six figures for the right painting, perhaps even seven. But I should warn you that he won't be taken advantage of. He knows art and value, as do I, and the adjusted value of art that is purchased in, shall we say, a nontraditional manner."

Whitt placed a hot hand on my wrist. "And let me assure you that I got where I am by being a scrupulous businessman in an unscrupulous business."

"That's good to hear." I let his hand linger as if I enjoyed the contact.

"I don't usually work with go-betweens, but in this case, I'm glad to."

I patted his hand, and we broke contact as I took a sip of my cocktail. "Don't think of me as a go-between. Think of me as Mr. X's aide-de-camp." Frankly, I didn't know if there was any difference between the two. It just sounded cool.

"Have you discussed with Mr. X how our business will be conducted?"

"Yes. Because we are all aware of counterfeits and authenticity issues, Mr. X would like to know if this would be acceptable to you. Payment on acquisition, yet you hold that payment for three days while authenticity is verified. If there's ever any question as to authenticity, we return the painting in question, and you refund the money."

"And who authenticates for Mr. X?" Whitt asked.

"Very reliable experts."

He sounded a little perturbed when he said, "I, too, have reliable sources."

"Then there shouldn't be any issues," I said.

"Right. Should I put out feelers right away?" he asked.

"Yes. I think the sooner we can conduct a transaction, the better for us to get to know one another," I said with the right amount of seductive suggestion.

"There have been rumors of something unique and exceptional coming on the market," he said.

"Oh? Do tell."

"I don't want to say right now. But if it proves to be more than rumor, it'll be an excellent piece with which to begin our relationship." He winked at me. "And you'll be the first person I call." He turned serious. "On the other hand, it may come through another broker. If that happens…"

Whitt left it hanging, so I said, "My employer will see to it that you get a generous finder's fee."

"Excellent." Whitt checked his watch again. "Perhaps I should reschedule my next appointment so we can continue our evening together."

I gave him a smile that could melt ice. "I have no qualms combining business and pleasure, Alden. How about this? Upon completing our first transaction, you and I will celebrate in grand fashion."

"Then I better get the wheels turning." He stood and kissed me on the cheek.

Chapter 28

Night had fallen by the time I got to my car. Right away, I opened the glove compartment, got out a wet wipe, and scrubbed my cheek where Whitt kissed me. Yes, he was handsome and fit, but also repugnant. *Smarmy* was the word Mom would have used. But all in all, I felt optimistic that our meeting would produce results.

At one of the red lights heading out of town, Teague pulled up beside me and waved. When the light turned green, we headed for the interstate. Once I was riding 95 southbound, I called Gabe.

"Hi, Lise. I hope I did good."

"Apparently. We're in business. He stepped away, so I didn't hear any of your conversation. What did he ask?"

"He wanted to feel me out. I acted like a bored billionaire, and he bought it. He also asked how quickly I could come up with the money to make expensive buys. I told him twenty-four to seventy-two hours, depending on how high the price. I hope that was okay."

"I never considered that," I said. "What else?"

"He wanted to know how much I trusted you, and then he wanted to know if you were single. I think he has more than profit on his mind."

"He's a whoredog."

"Be careful, Lise."

"I will," I said then called Adolph.

Music was playing in the background when he answered. "Hi, Lise. I'm still on the job."

"Where are you? It sounds like a party," I said.

"Sitting at the end of the bar at the Hunker Down Tavern, watching our man make an ass of himself."

The Hunker Down, located near Old City, was where people went to get drunk. The bar didn't serve food, people could still smoke in the bar, and an evening at the Hunker Down meant waking the next morning smelling like an ashtray.

"The Hunker Down? I'll owe you big for this," I said.

"Oh, it's quite entertaining. He's been hitting on anything with breasts."

"Is he having any luck?"

"Quasimodo would have luck in this place. I fear getting an STD from my barstool."

"Gross. I'm heading back and will relieve you when I get back to town."

"I'll be here."

Since I had my phone in hand, I tried calling Nick, but it went to voicemail. I left him an impassioned message. When I finished, my phone rang. It was Baker.

"Be still, my beating heart."

"Put a sock in it, Norwood."

"I heard you paid a visit to the Stephenses. What do you think?"

"Well, we forgot to mention we were from homicide and told them we were investigating their recent burglary, particularly the theft of the sketch."

"Shari said you got a preliminary list of people who've seen the sketch," I said.

"Yeah, damn long list. Anybody who's been in their house over the past few decades. Family for holidays, friends for parties, that kind of thing. We'll be talking to them."

"Are you going to alert the FBI about the latest victim's connection to *The Floating Ballerina*?"

Baker sighed. "Damn feds should do their own work. But yeah, after we talk to a few people, they'll probably get an anonymous tip. I swear you gotta lead some of these feds by their nose hair. And they still think they're smarter than Einstein."

"What did you think of Ricky Stephens?"

"Ortega and I agree with you: the guy's a loser."

"What are the chances that he's Michelangelo?" I asked.

"He doesn't have the brains to do what happened to those girls and get away with it. We'll have to tip off the feebs pretty soon, but we want to give him time to try to move the sketch."

"Thanks."

"We told them that we're confident they'll get the sketch back, that statistically speaking, the longer a thief hangs onto stolen art, the greater the odds of recovery and arrest. The art that's hard to recover is the art that is sold to a fence soon after the theft," Baker said.

"Any of that true?"

"Hell if I know. I work homicide."

"Anything else?"

"That about covers it."

"Thanks again, and sorry I thought you were a homicidal maniac."

"Happens all the time," Baker said and hung up. His sense of humor was drier than unbuttered toast.

I'd intended to head straight for the Hunker Down Tavern and relieve Adolph, but he called before I got close to San Marco. Ricky Stephens had left, and they were going in the general direction of his home.

"I owe you a favor or a dinner or a hundred bucks," I told him. "Your choice."

"I'll take the dinner."

"It's a date. Well, not a date date."

Adolph laughed. "A not-a-date date it is."

"Where are you now?"

"Still heading in the direction of the Stephenses' house."

"Anything noteworthy take place?" I asked.

"He engaged in hilarious repartee with the guys and made the women swoon, at least in his own mind. And then he started making phone calls."

"Oh?"

"Right after I talked to you, he checked his watch and made a call. There was no answer on the other end, or it went to messages and he didn't want to leave one, so he bantered with the boys for another fifteen minutes and tried again. Still nothing. This time he looked perturbed and moved from beer to whiskey. He tried five minutes later and was no longer jovial after that failed call. He tried again a couple of minutes later and finally got through to whomever he was trying to contact. They talked for about ten minutes, and then he said goodnight to his compatriots and started for what I assume is home since we just turned onto his street."

I switched on my blinker and pulled into the left lane to get around a convoy of three tractor-trailers. "Anything about the phone call? Did you overhear anything, notice his demeanor?"

Adolph said, "I was across the room, so no, I didn't hear anything. As for his demeanor, I'd say anxious, moved to angry—"

"Angry?"

"Not shouting angry, but I could tell he wasn't happy by the way he shook his head a few times and made that 'now listen here' gesture with his index finger. Then his mood changed again, and he was smiling after that. And he's turning in to his driveway."

"My guess is he's in for the night. Thanks, Adolph. I'll talk to you soon."

When I got home, I said goodnight to Teague then patted myself on the back for a job well done. The evening had gone well, laying the groundwork for recovering *The Floating Ballerina*. It sure beat surveillance, for which I was going to owe Elliot the Slim a small fortune. Ricky Stephens's phone call in the bar was interesting. It made sense that if he did have *The Floating Ballerina*, and if Baker and Ortega had rattled his cage, that he would be looking to move it sooner rather than later. I figured there was a good chance that he would been talking to a connection in the art-world black market. It would be a hoot if he was talking directly to Alden Whitt.

Chapter 29

My alarm was set early enough that I could get in my morning routine and tail Ricky Stephens from home to work. Yet a phone call woke me ten minutes before that. I answered groggily, but no one spoke. When the phone rang again, I realized it was my burner still in my purse. I stumbled from bed and got it before it went to message. The caller ID listed Alden Whitt's number.

"Alden," I answered. "Glad this isn't Skype. I have a hideous case of bed head."

"Bed head I hope to soon witness myself."

"Smooth talker. Can you make morning breath seem romantic?" I asked.

He chuckled. "There are limits to my abilities."

"Why the call at the crack of an obscene hour?"

By the sound of his voice, I could imagine his face aglow, a wide smile in place. "That object of art I spoke of..."

"Yes?"

"It goes on the market tomorrow afternoon," Whitt said.

"You're taking bids?"

"Of course."

"You said my employer would have first dibs," I made sure my voice carried the right amount of annoyance.

"And I have made that arrangement. If your Mr. X pays a premium well above the starting black-market bid, then he may purchase the piece outright tomorrow morning."

I nearly cooed, "Thank you, Alden. Who will be managing the sale?"

"If we come to terms, I've arranged it all so that I'll take delivery of the piece and turn it over directly to you, at which time you will pay me."

"I'm excited already, and I don't even know what it is."

"If you're excited now, expect a near-orgasmic thrill, Meg. This piece is a heretofore-unknown sketch by two masters working in collaboration."

And there it is. I was well onto solving one of the most interesting cases in my short PI career. "I'm intrigued."

"Admittedly, its value lies more in its historical importance than its medium, which happens to be ink on linen."

"Ink on linen? I'm not sure I like what I'm hearing," I said, figuring lack of enthusiasm would go a long way in reinforcing my cover.

Whitt laughed. "Would you change your opinion if the sketch was made by both Picasso and Dali?"

I did a silent slow count to five so he would think he'd rendered me speechless. "Picasso *and* Dali?"

"Ah, I've regained your interest."

"Hell, yes. Give me some details."

"The two masters sat at a small café and collaborated on a sketch of a dancer on a linen napkin, which they both signed. A piece unknown in the art world."

"And it's been authenticated?"

"Yes, and though I wasn't involved, I know the expert who looked it over. I'm satisfied it's the real deal. And with our arrangement, if Mr. X is doubtful, he can give it back for a full refund."

Alden had unknowingly done me a favor by authenticating it through his experts, but still, I'd suggest Shari do the same, when I got it back, but with a bona fide appraiser. "Okay, here's the big question: how much to buy the piece outright?"

"The starting bid will be five hundred thousand dollars, with confidence that it will fetch at least a million and a quarter. However, if you can meet me tomorrow morning with a million dollars with an added ten percent finder's fee for me, then the sketch goes to your employer."

I whistled at the price. "Oh, sorry. Hope I didn't rupture your eardrums." Stolen art is sold at a percentage of its potential value on the legal market. A million for a sketch would be extremely high were it not for the collaborative nature of the piece. Yeah, it's not like I really planned to buy it, but I needed to barter to make it sound real. "I tell you what, Alden—since I like you, my employer will pay six hundred and fifty thousand, and a ten percent finder's fee."

Whitt was quiet a moment. "Shouldn't you check with your employer first?"

"Alden"—I put ice in my voice—"you spoke with my employer and have his guarantee that I have the authority for these negotiations."

"Very well, Meg. And since I like you, I feel confident that I can arrange for the sketch from Mr. Picasso and Mr. Dali for three quarters of a million, plus my seventy-five-thousand-dollar fee."

I went quiet again, making it seem as if I were considering his offer. Finally, I said, "With that finder's fee, I hope our celebration will be lavish."

"So it's a deal, then?"

"Yes, Alden, it's a deal, an expensive deal. But I'm sure my employer—"

"Mr. X."

I laughed. "Yes, Mr. X, will agree."

"Here's some good news for you, Meg. As things are, it will work out for us to conduct our business in San Marco."

"Sounds good. As I'm sure you'll have some security nearby, I will as well. But as it is our first buy, and I'll have so much money, I'd like the deal to take place somewhere public," I told him.

"Fine with me, though I hope our festivities afterward will be a little more private."

"I was thinking that after I deliver the sketch to Mr. X, and you handle your financial affairs, we meet for an early dinner, and then we'll see what happens from there."

"Lovely. Do you have any suggestions for where to make the sale?" Whitt asked.

"Most definitely. Do you bowl, Alden?"

Chapter 30

After hanging up with Whitt, I called to see if Baker and Ortega would like to do the actual arresting when I showed up for the sketch.

Baker said, "Might as well. There's only so much we can do on Michelangelo with federal agents gumming up the works. Why don't you come by, and we'll work out a plan?"

I told Special Agent Davis that I would be going to the police station, but I didn't tell her who I would be working with. She might get suspicious that with Baker and Ortega, we were still poking around the Michelangelo case.

She asked, "For how long?"

"Couple of hours, I expect," I said.

"I can do with a break," she said. "Since you'll be at the police station, I'll follow you over and cut loose. Teague will meet you there."

Once I pulled into the parking lot, Davis sped off.

I felt like a real detective hanging out at the police department, part of a complex housing police headquarters, county jail, and courthouse. Storefront bail bondsmen and low-budget lawyers' offices circled the legal center like stationary vultures.

I met Baker and Ortega at their desks, which were each facing the other. Ortega's was neat and pristine. Baker's looked like a garbage truck had backed up to it and dumped a load of paper, empty coffee cups, food wrappers, and office supplies on it. Since we were dealing with stolen property, they'd brought in someone from robbery to take charge. Detective Eve Ramirez was drop-dead gorgeous. Her long black hair actually shone, and it was all I could do to keep from reaching out to touch it. I have the same problem with late-term pregnant women. I'll be talking to them, and the next thing you know, my hand will be resting on their belly. My life is filled with awkward moments, but thankfully, I did resist touching Detective Ramirez. With her dark complexion and nearly-black eyes, she could have been cast as an exotic spy in a 1940s movie. She wore tight jeans, boots, and a violet V-neck blouse with a beige sport coat.

"You met my boyfriend a while back," I told her. "Nick Weldon."

"Rings a bell."

"A professor at the university. He helped with some stolen artwork you recovered."

"Oh, yeah. Funny guy. How's he doing?"

Interesting. I felt a little stab of jealousy that she remembered him. "He's on a fellowship in Vienna."

"Nice. Though it sounds lonely for you."

"It is," I admitted.

My friend from high school, Jillian Caine, owned San Marco Bowling Lanes located on the beach road. I called her and arranged to have the easternmost bowling lane because there were glass doors there. Baker and Ortega could hide behind the shed and foliage just outside, until it was time to make the bust. Eve's partner, Herman Banks, was a handsome black man as tall as a pro basketball player. He would be with Baker and Ortega, and a squad car with two uniforms hidden nearby would act as backup. Eve would play my security, and if it came up, we would be vague, but hint at a military and mercenary background. We decided on her instead of one of the guys because we felt that two attractive women would be doubly distracting to Alden Whitt, though in my estimation, standing next to Eve would lower my hotness rating from attractive to old maid.

"We'll need money," Eve said.

"Why? We're not really buying the sketch," I said.

Baker blew out some air and mumbled, "Rookies."

"This is a buy bust," Eve explained, "and it could go down different ways, but experience shows that Whitt will keep the sketch at a remote location, check the money, and then have it brought to us. We need some cash to show him."

"Where are we going to get that kind of money?" I asked.

"We don't need all of it, just enough to look like it," Eve said. "I might be able to squeeze two or three grand out of investigative funds, but we'd need more than that."

"How much to make it believable?" I asked.

Ortega said, "Enough to bundle it in banded stacks in a bag of some sort, gym bag or duffel bag. In the bottom of the bag, we'll put in banded stacks of one-dollar bills with hundred-dollar bills on each side. At the top, we'll have several that are all one-hundred-dollar bills in case he wants to riffle a stack."

"That's still a lot of money," I said.

Eve grabbed a yellow sticky note and pencil from Ortega's desk. She wrote down some numbers, did some math, and said, "It'd be nice if we had fifty to sixty grand."

I had an idea. "Hang on a minute." I called Shari Stephens and explained what was going on, how we were on the verge of getting the sketch back for her, but that we needed to borrow the cash.

"You're just borrowing it?" Shari asked.

"We're just borrowing it, right?" I asked Eve.

"If the cash actually changes hands, we'll have to keep it in evidence until after a trial."

"Oh."

Baker spoke up. "But if it's flash money, she can get it right back when we're done."

"What's flash money?"

"Money we show to the seller," Herman said. "But it never really changes hands."

I explained it to Shari, who agreed, then asked, "Can someone meet Shari at the Ameris Bank on US1 to get the cash?"

"Before we take that step, I have the unpleasant task of asking for the Pope's blessing," Eve said. She saw my confusion and added, "Have to run it by the captain."

I told Shari I would call her back when we got the go-ahead, then we all squeezed into Captain Briggs's office. The robbery officer seemed to embrace every gruff, antisocial captain stereotype from every cop show on TV. A short heavyset man with more hair growing from his ears than on his head, he sat glowering behind his desk. When I was introduced to him, he'd scowled when learning my profession. The more Eve pleaded her case, the more he frowned. When she finished, he sat back and looked at the ceiling for a long time.

Expecting the worst, I was surprised when he said, "Go for it." He pointed at me. "Get your client down here. I'm going to have some papers drawn up stating that she willingly supplies the money and that we aren't responsible if her cash is lost."

Shari sounded wary that the San Marco PD wouldn't be held responsible if the cash was lost. "It just seems like a double loss to lose the sketch and then lose its value in money."

"That's just a fraction of its value, Shari." I went on to explain how much Whitt and Ricky thought we were paying and how we would be bundling up the money to fool them into thinking it was the full amount.

"Three quarters of a million?" Shari asked, a little breathless.

"That's black market. If you were to put it up for auction, a legitimate auction, you would probably get a whole lot more than that."

"Oh my God. I never had a clue. Yes, okay, I'll get the money and sign whatever paperwork."

Eve and Herman went to meet Shari at the bank, then escorted her to the police station, along with her sixty thousand dollars in ones and hundreds. At the bank, they picked up a bunch of ten-thousand-dollar bands. Shari stuck around to help as we spent the afternoon bundling it up. We made four authentic bundles with ten thousand dollars in each. Those we would put at the top of a gym bag we found in evidence. Then we bundled the singles between authentic bills until we had enough to fill the bag. It wasn't the right number of bundles, but they weren't going to have the opportunity to count them. Hopefully, opening the bag and showing the money would be enough.

When we were finished, Shari drove home, promising that she could act natural in front of Ricky on this eve of what promised to be his big bust. Later that afternoon, I didn't follow Ricky Stephens, though Special Agent Teague followed me as I showed up across from the dealership to let Elliot the Slim know that the case would be closing.

"I did good?" Elliot asked.

"You did great." I paid him what he was owed, added a generous bonus, and told him to keep the burner phone.

Wanting to be refreshed for the fun to come, I went to bed by ten, but my mind was racing a mile a minute, so around eleven-thirty, I got up and took some melatonin. Twenty minutes later, I was in la-la land.

In the morning, I explained to Davis what I had going, and she had no problem ducking out again once I got to the police station, though I would have to phone her when I no longer had cops around me. All of us good guys got together in a police station conference room in the morning a couple of hours before the eleven o'clock meeting to go over everything. Baker, Ortega, and Eve's partner, Herman, needed to know when to come in and make the bust. We considered having me wear a wire, but if Whitt checked for one, things would go bad, so we decided to do what we'd done the first time I talked with Adolph Hurst. I would call Baker's phone from mine, and he would mute his and leave the call open. We decided on a phrase to signal Baker, Ortega, and Herman to make their move: *This is it. This is really the sketch.*

I phoned my friend Jillian to make sure everything was still a go at the bowling lanes, and she was excited to see everything go down. It was a slow time of day for bowlers, but she would make sure that anyone else would be given lanes down at the other end of the building. Baker, Ortega, and Herman left before us, wanting to get in place before the bad guys showed up. Next, Eve sent the backup patrol car to park out of the way and near the lanes.

It was almost time to leave, and I felt as nervous as a middle schooler at her first school dance. I kept repeating the phrase, *This is it. This is really the sketch*, so I wouldn't screw it up when it came time to call in the troops. I called Baker on my phone, and we got our poor-man's wire set up, then we went over everything one more time. There were variables we couldn't count on when it came to what Alden Whitt would do, but we covered most of the possibilities, and the likely possibility that his security, if not Whitt himself, would be armed.

We got to the bowling alley twenty minutes before our arranged time. There were two other lanes in use at the far side of the building. I'd told Jillian to pretend not to know me when I showed up, and she pulled it off like a pro. She gave us lane number one and rented us our burgundy-and-tan bowling shoes. Eve carried the gym bag and went to sit at our lane. I could sit and get nervous all over again, or I could keep busy and roll a few balls. I put on my shoes and found a black ball with blue swirls that fit my fingers. Eve shrugged, put on her shoes, got a ball, and joined me. I was not a great bowler, but Nick and I came to bowl from time to time, like we did with putt-putt and the zipline through the trees above San Marco Gatorland Zoo. My first ball knocked down three pins, and I missed all seven on my next attempt. Eve got in place, lifted her ball, and froze for ten seconds before she started for the lane. When she released it, the ball headed for the gutter, and as I was about to wish her better luck next time, the ball arced back toward the center of the lane and hit the pins with an explosion that knocked them all down.

"I take it you've done this before," I said.

She grinned, which made her all the more beautiful. "Twice a week. I'm in a league."

"Should have met Whitt at the putt-putt course," I mumbled.

When she didn't roll a strike, she would roll a spare. She gave me tips, and my game picked up. We got so into bowling that it wasn't until I picked up a split and Alden Whitt applauded, that we realized he'd arrived.

"Meg Atwood, you have so many talents." Whitt smiled widely, yet the joviality did not make it to his eyes. I could sense his intensity now that we'd moved into the cash-for-art part of the deal. His gravitas was further reflected by his dark suit with subtle pinstriping.

"Alden, you have no idea as to the depths of my skills." I was happy my voice didn't tremble.

Eve's whole demeanor changed upon Whitt's arrival. With an expression that said, *"Look but don't touch,"* she picked up the gym bag and moved to my side. Halfway between us and the front door, Ricky Stephens stood, a red box under his arm. Next to him was a man dressed much like Eve, in a dark golf shirt, slacks, and a sports coat.

"So who's your friend?" Whitt asked, eyes roaming over Eve's body.

"She's Mr. X's version of that guy," I said, pointing to the man standing with Stephens.

"But so much easier on the eyes."

"Don't" was all Eve said.

"We call her Evil Eve," I warned Whitt. "You really don't want to know her."

"Okay," he said, "but I'm still hoping to get to know *you* better."

I flashed him a smile. "Business today. Pleasure tonight."

"Of course. You have the money?"

"Right there," I said, nodding to the gym bag in Eve's grip. "You have the sketch?"

Whitt gestured at the two men standing at a distance. "The man with my security is the seller; he has it with him."

"Really, Alden? You brought an amateur to a transaction?" I made sure to sound plenty disappointed.

"I know what you mean, but he wouldn't have it any other way."

Still working the con, I was silent for long seconds, wanting him to think I was considering calling it off.

"Meg, come on. He's harmless. Come on, check it out."

I focused in on the box in red wrapping paper that Ricky carried. "Let's see it."

Whitt smiled like I'd said something silly. "By all means—after I've seen the money."

I returned a sarcastic smile. "By all means."

Eve, moving her eyes back and forth between Whitt and his muscle, slowly unzipped the gym bag. She held it open for him to see, and without taking her eyes from him, she moved it so that I could reach in. I was as cool as a cucumber on the outside, but inside, I was praying like mad that I'd picked a bundle of all hundreds. I surprised myself with a steady hand and grabbed a stack from the top. Using both hands, I held out the stack to Whitt and riffled it like a magician showing a deck of cards. I'd picked a good stack. Whitt stepped forward and reached for the bag. Eve, as quick as a snake, gripped Whitt around the wrist.

"Show us the sketch, and you get the rest," Eve said then growled, "Not until then." Damn, she even scared me.

It took Whitt a couple of tugs to free himself, and he held out a calming hand to his security guy. I noticed the bodyguard had moved his hand into his jacket.

"Quite the grip you have there, Evil Eve," Whitt said, massaging his wrist.

"She's a badass," I said.

Whitt did that "come here" gesture with two fingers, and Ricky Stephens approached with the security guy. When they got to us, Whitt said, "Ms. Buyer, I'd like you to meet Mr. Seller and Mr. Security."

"Charmed," I said sarcastically, noticing that Ricky was sweating freely.

"They have the money?" Ricky asked.

Whitt gestured to the gym bag Eve gripped.

I took it from her, put back the banded stack, and patted it. "Seventy-five bundles plus Mr. Whitt's fee safely tucked inside."

Ricky studied me. "Do I know you?"

Shit. I hoped he didn't remember me from when I'd spied on him and Blondie at the Lazy Sandbar. "I doubt it."

"Who are you working for?" Ricky asked.

I acted offended. "Alden, you are on thin ice here."

"Don't mind Mr. Seller, he's a little nervous," Whitt said and took the wrapped package from Ricky. "Look, he brought you a present." He handed me the package, which was the size a dress shirt might come in.

As Ricky continued staring, I handed the bag with money back to Eve, put the box on the computerized scoring console and carefully removed the wrapping paper to reveal a white gift box. Eve kept her eyes firmly on Mr. Security, who returned the favor. I lifted the lid, removed some crepe paper, and there was *The Floating Ballerina* in a simple black frame. I'd seen a photo of it, but to see it in person, to realize what it represented, to know who had touched and drawn on that bit of linen, took my breath away.

"Amazing, isn't it?" Whitt said.

I smiled.

Ricky jerked like he'd been hit with a jolt of electricity. He glared at me with recognition. "Wait a minute."

Now! I had to say the words that would bring Baker, Ortega, and Banks, "*This is—*" *Oh crap!* My mind went blank.

"This is what?" Whitt asked.

Ricky said, "I saw you at the Lazy Sandbar the other day."

"What? Me? No, not—This is it, this—uh…"

Eve stared at me wide-eyed. Suddenly, I was back in my middle school production of *Annie*, and as Miss Hannigan, my mind had blanked on one of the big lines. "This is it. This…"

The entire cast had stared at me just like Eve was doing now.

"Meg?" Whitt reached for the sketch.

Ricky pointed a finger at me. "You were taking pictures of us."

It was like a lightbulb over my head clicked on to a million watts, and I remembered. I screamed, "This is it! This is really the sketch!"

Everything happened in an instant, and I felt like I was in a movie progressing in fast-forward. Whitt grabbed the box with the sketch at the same instant Mr. Security seized one of the money bag's handles. It was like a new Olympics competition, synchronized snatching. I had a firm grasp on the other side of the box holding the sketch. With his other hand, Mr. Security reached into his jacket. Eve moved so fast, it was almost a blur, and she had her gun out and up under Mr. Security's jaw before he could free his. By then, the three detectives had rushed through the glass doors by our bowling lane. Mr. Security left his gun in his holster, released the money bag, and raised both hands.

Whitt gave one more tremendous tug on the sketch box, pulling me off balance. Stumbling toward him while trying to regain my equilibrium while maintaining my hold on the sketch, my body fell into his. He made a high-pitched squeal, and I realized I'd inadvertently driven my right knee into his testicles. He released the box and fell to the floor, both hands holding his injury.

There were shouts of "freeze" and "police," and Ricky bolted. Herman ran after him. Ortega took control of Mr. Security from Eve. She holstered her gun, passed the money bag to me, grabbed her bowling ball, ran a few steps, and rolled it hard. Instead of the wooden lane, it sped down the carpet and past racks of stationary balls, curved by Herman, and smashed into Ricky's feet. He fell hard.

Eve cuffed Ricky, Ortega put his pair on Mr. Security, and Baker helped Whitt up into a kneeling position and cuffed him. Whitt looked up at me with raging eyes and a beet-red face.

"Sorry about the knee to the—it wasn't intentional," I said.

As Baker got him to his feet, Whitt continued to stare in silence. Maybe he didn't say anything for fear he would still be speaking in upper registers. Baker took him away.

I went up to Eve and asked, "You're a superhero, aren't you?"

Chapter 31

Everyone had something to say about me kneeing Whitt in the crotch.

"Dirty pool." Baker eyed me like he wasn't sure who I was.

"That was harsh, Lise," Ortega said.

Herman shook his head. "That was cold, girl. Ice cold."

Eve grinned. "I thought it was funny."

"It was an accident," I repeated for the umpteenth time.

Baker held the bag of money, and Eve had the box with *The Floating Ballerina* as we headed for the front exit. I went to Baker and quietly asked him a question.

He answered, "Not gonna happen."

So I moved on to Ortega, who gave a tamer version. "That's against procedure."

Luckily, Eve was riding with me, and I put it to her when we got in the car.

She said, "Sure, no problem. But just for a few minutes, and then we secure it at the station."

Fifteen minutes later, we were on the doorstep of the Stephenses' house in Wilson Shores. I rang the bell. One of the kids opened the door, a boy on the younger end of the teen spectrum. He wore a smirk like it was the latest fashion. When I sent him on a quest to get his mother, he moved at the pace of a sloth.

Shari eventually came to the door. "Lise, hi. What's up?"

I introduced her to Eve and asked if we could speak, and we ended up at the kitchen table sipping lemonade.

Shari said, "The FBI was here earlier."

Baker must have made his anonymous tip.

"What'd they want?" I asked.

"The sketch is tied to a violent crime. Do you know anything about that?"

"Yeah, but I can't say anything, especially now that the feds are involved. I imagine they got a list similar to what Baker and Ortega picked up."

"Yes, and they didn't seem happy to know about Baker and Ortega stopping by."

I grimaced. "You told them?"

"Shouldn't I have?"

"Baker and Ortega were investigating on their own time, and the FBI frowns on that. Anyway, the reason we're here—we have some good news, bad news, and news of subjective status."

"Since that's new to me, I'll pick news of subjective status," Shari said, a bit confused.

"Subjective," I said, "because it depends on whether you consider it good or bad that your husband has just been busted."

It took her a moment to get the meaning. "Wait, does this mean the good news is..."

Eve put the gift box on the table, opened it, and displayed *The Floating Ballerina*.

Shari gasped. "Oh, Lise, you got it back." Her eyes welled.

"With Eve's help."

"Oh, that's wonderful, and Ricky had it?"

"We nabbed him as he was trying to sell it to..." Eve held out her hand to indicate me.

Shari laughed then sniffed. She got up for a tissue. When she sat back down, she asked, "Wait a minute. What's the bad news? Because Ricky in hot water is definitely good in my book."

"We brought the sketch by for you to see, but not keep," I told her.

"It's evidence of a crime. We have to hang on to it for a while before we can release it back to you," Eve said.

"That's fine. At least I know where it is." Shari took a drink of lemonade. "How much trouble is he in?"

"That's a tough one," Eve said. "Yes, he did steal the sketch and other valuables, but he is your husband, and this is his home. His lawyer will play on that. On the other hand, he faked a burglary and called in the police under false pretenses. This will be a tricky one, though I think he'll be in a fairly rough patch when it gets to court."

"Good," Shari said. "All these years, he's been playing me for a fool. Thinking he can get away with anything." She started to cry. "He stole from me."

I took her hand and squeezed. "Now's the time to call your lawyer and tell him that you want to move along with the divorce, ASAP. Tell him you need make sure he doesn't have access to your money. Tell him that after all that's occurred, you don't want Ricky in the house or around your kids."

"I will, as soon as you leave." Shari nodded. "The only thing I'm truly worried about is how to break it to the kids."

"My advice is to simply tell the truth," Eve said.

Shari walked us to the door, and I held up the sketch. "You need to get this appraised, insured, and if not auctioned, put somewhere safe. The news about it is going to come out. To the art world, it's a big deal. You have to consider how unsafe it would be on your wall. Consider loaning it to a museum until you figure it out."

Shari nodded. "Yeah, I'll see what my lawyer advises."

Eve made arrangements with Shari to meet up to sign some paperwork to get her money back, then I drove to the police station. Eve and I promised to get together for a girl's night of margaritas and bowling. I called Special Agent Davis and waited for her in the police station parking lot.

Davis followed me to my office, where I started thinking about closing *The Floating Ballerina* case. I should be happy, ecstatic even, but something bothered me. Not the case itself, but how the image was copied using a corpse. I wondered where Michelangelo had seen the sketch. But then the answer would depend on who Michelangelo was. If it was someone tied to the Stephenses, then the FBI would, in all likelihood, have the best chance of catching the killer. They would also be looking at Ricky Stephens now that he was sitting in jail for staging the burglary, but I really had a hard time seeing him as anything other than a sleazeball. I still suspected Michelangelo was tied to the police, even if it wasn't Baker. The fact that the killer knew the nickname the police used, which had yet to be publicized, certainly indicated a strong possibility of a cop or someone connected to the police.

The killer knew about, and had seen, *The Floating Ballerina*. Outside of the Stephenses' connections, few people had seen the sketch. Before it was recovered, it was limited to me and Nick, then Ortega and Baker glanced at it in Nick's office. I wasn't Michelangelo. We'd learned it wasn't Baker or Ortega. It certainly couldn't have been Nick because he was in Vienna. He'd promised me he wouldn't tell anyone about it, and I hoped he hadn't broken that promise. I needed to find out for sure. I got out my phone. However, before I called, a funny thought entered my mind, like a bird zipping by, then because it was so ludicrous, it flew on, leaving me to giggle.

"Nick, a killer?" I snorted more laughter and decided to put my mind at ease. I called Nick. He answered, and I said, "Hi, Nick. Miss you like crazy."

"Ditto. Got your message. Sorry I haven't gotten back to you yet. Been kind of busy."

I held a pencil with my free hand and doodled on a Post-it. "I told you I had a question." There really wasn't any way to word it so that it didn't sound like I didn't trust him. "Did you show the photo of *The Floating Ballerina* to anybody?"

"You told me not to."

"And you didn't?"

"No, Lise. I'm surprised you have to ask."

"Did you say anything about it to anyone?"

"No." The tone of his voice told me that he was getting a little peeved. "Why are you asking?"

Gabe had told me not to keep secrets from Nick, so I went ahead and told him about my night visitor and the text. I told him I was asking about the photo because the killer's latest victim was posed like *The Floating Ballerina*. When I finished, several seconds of silence followed.

"Good God, Lise. You're only just telling me this now?" I detected shock, panic, and anger.

"I didn't want you to worry."

"Didn't want me to—I'm coming back."

"No, Nick, don't. Don't mess up your fellowship."

"You're in danger, Lise." His voice rose a notch. "What kind of boyfriend would I be if I didn't come home to protect you?"

"You don't have to protect me. I'm being protected by the best security a person can get, the FBI."

"Really?" The relief in his voice was palpable. "The FBI?"

"Round the clock. Twenty-four, seven. Three agents, each on eight hours a day."

"No shit? Is that weird? Having them around all the time?"

"Not bad. They mainly stay in their cars, though I invite them in from time to time. Teague's my favorite; we hit it off pretty well. The other guy is nice too. The woman, Special Agent Davis, could be a poster girl for Anal Retentive Anonymous."

"Oooh, bet you two don't get along."

I tapped my stapler so that it bounced up and down like a diving board. "I watch my mouth around her. Not that I'm scared of her, but she's keeping me safe, and I appreciate that."

"Yeah, I appreciate that too."

"So I'm not in imminent danger, and you can continue on with your fellowship."

Nick was silent a minute. "Yeah, okay."

"What is it?"

"Oh nothing," he said dismissively. "It'll be all right. I'm just worried it's not going to be what I expected."

"Well, give it time."

"I will."

I leaned forward and put both elbows on my desk. "Hey! I have some good news. The case of *The Floating Ballerina* is officially closed."

"You got the sketch? Awesome, Lise." Nick's tone indicated he had a big grin. "Tell me all about it."

I opened my mouth to start but changed my mind. "You know what? Next time we're together, be it here or in Vienna, let's sip some bourbon, and I'll tell you the story. It's really a great story and one you'll enjoy more face-to-face."

"Well, okay."

"I will tell you that Gabe played a role in my getting it back."

"Gabe?" Nick laughed in amazement. "How? Oh wait. A story best told in person."

"I guarantee you'll laugh long and hard."

"I can't wait. Man, I wish I was there to help you celebrate," he said.

"Me too."

We were quiet a moment, then Nick said, "Hey, why don't you call Gabe and celebrate with him?"

"Good idea."

"I can't wait to hear this story."

We talked a bit more then said our goodbyes. Satisfied my boyfriend hadn't shown the photo to anyone, I brought up the invoice template on my laptop. After invoicing Shari Stephens, I would get to work on a report that she could give to her lawyer. I would, no doubt, be called to testify if their divorce made it to court.

Oops... There it was again, a piddling little something that fit in somewhere between doubt and suspicion. Say the killer had been inspired by the photo I gave Nick, but Nick hadn't shown it to anyone. That would mean that Nick—*Nope.* I hated when these random thoughts popped into my head, especially when I was trying to do something else. My brain wouldn't stop pestering me, saying things like, *How do you really know Nick is in Vienna?* He could've been in the next room talking to me on his cell for all I knew. *Shut up, stupid brain!*

Finally, I decided to do what I'd pestered Ortega to do when I'd suspected Baker. I would check alibis and look at the dates and times of all the killings to see if I was with Nick during any of them.

"Fine," I mumbled to my brain. "I'll check, there'll be an alibi, and then I'll tease you for being so stupid."

For the third and fourth killings, Nick was in Vienna—supposedly. *Of course he was.* That should be enough to get my brain to shut up, but I went ahead and looked at the date and time of Kristin Harmon's death. *Wait. Ha! Got it.* That was the night Nick and I went to try the new tapas place in Old City. I remembered it specifically because the first two times we'd tried to get reservations, we couldn't. Finally, we'd picked a date two weeks out and made our reservation. And though I didn't use my day planner to remember dates with Nick, I did put this date on there because of the rigmarole we'd gone through to get reservations.

I got my phone and scrolled through the calendar. "Crap."

I'd remembered wrong. We'd gone to the restaurant the night before Kristin's murder. And though I couldn't be sure, I didn't think we'd spent the following night together. I went through the file for information on the Angela Lopez killing but stopped. That was when I'd been pissed at Nick for not telling me about his fellowship. I'd stayed home alone that night. I would need to approach it from another angle. I compared Nick to what we knew about Michelangelo: Both had knowledge of art, and both had seen *The Floating Ballerina*. That was it. Well, except that they both had medium-length brown hair.

"He's in Vienna!" I shouted, hoping it would sink into my brain. I couldn't understand why I was so antsy about this. My stomach grumbled, and a solution came to mind. "Gordo's Grande."

I left the office, waved at Special Agent Janet Davis, got in my car, and headed for Dicky's Surf Shop, where Gordo's food truck was parked. Davis pulled in after me, and I walked over and offered to buy her a late lunch, which she declined. She was the kind of person I pegged as subsisting on kale salads and other gluten-free, fat-free, taste-free fare. Luckily, the lunch crowd had already come and gone, so my gastronomic nirvana wrapped in a flour tortilla was prepared quickly. I sat at a picnic table with an icy Diet Coke, a small pile of napkins, and a bottle of datil pepper salsa then went to work. After one particularly big bite, I saluted Davis in her car with my burrito. The revulsion on her face was priceless.

The Grande did the trick, and I returned to my office and finished my paperwork.

Later that night, I woke up and was unable to get back to sleep. And no, it wasn't due to intestinal distress, but rather a cold realization that Nick had something else in common with a madman. Michelangelo had left me a photo on a pillow beside me as I slept; Nick had done the same with his love letter on the morning he left. In the bright light of day, that might have seemed like a coincidence, but at that moment, it seemed near damning. Finally, I got up and went to make myself tea. I sat in the kitchen, thinking. It was a little after three in the morning, which would put it a little after nine in Vienna.

"Screw it." I was going to do something I would never do under any other circumstances. I would check up on my boyfriend and make sure he was really where he said he was. It wasn't like I was being the jealous type and checking because I doubted his fidelity. I needed to put my mind to rest that he wasn't a killer. I got my computer and looked up information for Vienna's Academy of Fine Arts. I stopped and put both hands on my desk. If I went through with this, I was admitting that I didn't trust Nick. But this was so much more than looking for a girlfriend on the side. This was life and death, and as selfish as it sounded, I needed my peace of mind. After finding what I hoped was the correct number, I called. A woman answered, but the only word I understood was something similar to *academy*.

"Hi, I'm calling from the United States. Do you speak English?" I asked.

In response, I heard a lot of guttural consonants.

"I'm sorry. Does anyone there speak English?"

"Was?" In the manner of how it was spoken, I believed she asked, "What?"

I googled "translator" on my computer, mumbling, "Hang on," in the process. I was sure I butchered the language when I asked, "*Hat jemand da speak English?*"

There came another batch of words along with a name, Professor Gildersleeve, and I was put on hold. Hoping for the best, I hung on for several minutes, until a man spoke into the phone.

"*Ja, das ist* Professor Gildersleeve."

"Please tell me you speak English."

"Yes. How may I assist you?" He seemed to speak English well, but his accent was thick.

"Professor Gildersleeve, I'm a good friend of Professor Nicholas Weldon."

"*Ja, ja,* Nicholas. He will be instructing our students on a fellowship."

"That's right," I said, as relief flooded through my system. I would make up a reason for the call, end it, go back to bed, and never ever tell Nick I'd once wondered if he was a serial killer. The lie fell skillfully from my lips. "I've been trying to call his cell phone but haven't been able to reach him. I was hoping you could give me a phone number to his office at the academy."

Professor Gildersleeve didn't answer immediately. "You say you are a good friend of Professor Weldon?"

"Yes."

"Shouldn't you know his fellowship does not begin for two weeks? I do not expect to see him until then."

The relief I'd felt earlier was replaced with nausea, and I ended the call without another word.

Chapter 32

Slamming the brakes on my paranoia and suspicion, I forced myself to think rationally about what I'd learned. Nick had a fellowship in Vienna. When he left, I'd been under the impression that he would be starting that fellowship right away, but he hadn't actually said that.

Did he purposely indicate it, or was it simply my assumption? It would make sense that he'd go early, but three weeks?

I'd assumed the academy would provide housing, so it wasn't like he would need to spend that time finding a place—if my assumption was correct. And Professor Gildersleeve would have known if Nick was on the premises, even if his teaching duties had yet to start. Perhaps Nick wanted to be a tourist before getting to work, which was something I would expect of him.

But why didn't he say so? Why didn't he invite me along?

There was another possibility to consider: that he had yet to leave for Vienna and was still in San Marco. That possibility was disturbing, because at the very least, it meant he'd lied to me. He was the kind of man who would tell me if he needed space, but then again, perhaps he was concerned about what I would think if he asked for space just prior to spending a semester out of the country. My assumption was that we had a growing relationship, but maybe he thought otherwise. He'd said so and left a voicemail about taking the relationship to another level, but maybe that was just lip service. That was a lot of *maybes*. There was another *maybe* to consider, the one where he could be cheating on me and wanted to spend time with her before leaving.

There was even a worse option, the worst possible—not only was he still in San Marco, but he was also Michelangelo. If so, why would he perpetrate that kind of violence? The only thing I could think of was that he hadn't escaped his terrible childhood.

I wondered if I should share my suspicions with Baker and Ortega, then I remembered how stubborn Ortega had been about checking Baker's alibis. He'd known it—could feel it—that Baker wasn't Michelangelo. And just like them, when it came down to it, I knew it couldn't be Nick. I would call and demand to know what was going on. My thumb hovered over the call button, but I wasn't sure what to say. I determined to call him, just not now.

So much was percolating in my brain that I didn't even bother trying to get back to sleep. My one job had been completed, and as much as I would have liked to work on the Michelangelo case, that was, as Professor Gildersleeve might say, verboten. I decided to take the day off and putter about the house. So, at four in the morning, I started in on housework. Special Agent Carter, my overnight babysitter, came to the door, saying he'd seen the lights and wanted to check on me. After I told him I couldn't sleep, I made him a cup of coffee and a sandwich.

Before he took the goodies back to the car, he said, "You're spoiling me, Lise."

The act of cleaning my house was therapeutic, and eventually, I stopped agonizing so much over Nick. I told myself there was a good reason he hadn't told me everything in minute detail. As his girlfriend, I should trust him. And I would have. Going early to be a tourist was a very Nick thing to do, and I had to remember that. The next time we talked, I could tell him about calling the academy. I had no doubt that we could work the whole thing out. He would understand that everything going on had put me on edge. He would understand why I had twisted myself in knots.

I yawned long and deep. My sleepless night was catching up with me, so I took Virgil Flowers to bed, read half a page, and fell asleep.

When I woke up after noon, I decided that instead of worrying about some misguided suspicion that the man I loved was a sexual sadist and murderer, which seemed ludicrous in the full light of day, I would celebrate the successful completion of an interesting case that had earned me many thousands of dollars.

I got my phone and called Gabe. "We're celebrating tonight."

"Excellent," Gabe answered, on the phone in his office at the university. "So are we celebrating anything in particular, or just using it as an excuse to eat, drink, and be merry?"

"I recovered *The Floating Ballerina*, in which you played a part. May you forever be known as Mr. X."

"Lise, that's excellent. This party, your place or mine?"

"How about you host it, and I'll cook it? I love your kitchen." Gabe was a true foodie. His kitchen featured a bookcase with countless cookbooks, and he had the best of the best when it came to appliances, including a Cornue CornuFé range.

"Seafood fra diavolo?"

"Host's choice."

"Fra diavolo it is. And some crusty bread?"

"Crusty bread for a crusty guy."

"And proud of it," Gabe said.

Then I thought why the hell not make it a dinner party. "Mind if I bring a friend? Someone I think you'll enjoy meeting."

"The more, the merrier," Gabe said.

Ending that call, I made another.

"Delve Gallery," Adolph answered in his dulcet tone. After my invitation, he said, "I'll bring some Chianti. Should go nicely with your dish."

I went shopping, and Special Agent Teague pushed the shopping cart. After deciding on big sea scallops and fresh-off-the-boat Mayport shrimp, I flipped a coin and ended up getting fettuccini instead of angel hair. We left the produce aisle with tomatoes, scallions, onions, hot and sweet peppers, garlic, Italian parsley, and cilantro. A key ingredient was crushed red pepper flakes, but I knew Gabe always had that fiery spice on hand. En route to Gabe's, I stopped at Genelle's for a long loaf of crusty bread, which I would bake with butter and garlic.

At six on the button, I stood on Gabe's stoop with both arms filled with groceries, and I used my nose to ring his doorbell. I gave Teague a chin nod as he sat in his FBI-issued sedan at the curb. Gabe's house was a red-brick split-level built in the sixties. Gabe opened his door and greeted me. He wore off-white cotton pants and a long-sleeve white V-neck T-shirt that was tight enough to show he was in great shape for a man his age. After a peck on the cheek, he glanced past me at the dark sedan at the curb and waved at Special Agent Teague.

"Want to invite your bodyguard?" Gabe asked.

"I think he's happier watching from afar."

"Aren't you bringing a guest?"

"He's meeting us here."

Gabe took half my load and led me into his house. Framed artwork covered the walls. Not every piece held value, but many did. He'd once told Nick and me that he had a quarter of a million dollars' worth of insurance for his collection. My favorites were the ones Gabe had painted. Yes, he was an art history nerd, but he also had talent and honed skill. He had no chosen medium when it came to paint; he used oils, acrylics, watercolors, or whatever fitted his mood. His landscape and still life works were beautiful, but I preferred his abstract work. Those works were bold and insightful. Good things to have in an abstract painting. With its dark wood and leather furnishings, the place screamed "bachelor." We passed by the sunken living room, a testament to sixties architecture, and went into the kitchen.

This was the room where we spent ninety-nine percent of the time when Nick and I visited.

As I unloaded the groceries, Gabe poured us each a couple fingers of WhistlePig Whiskey. He had an ice tray that made those big pieces of ice especially for whiskey, bourbon, and rye.

"Cheers, Lise. And congratulations," Gabe said, holding out his glass.

We clinked and sipped.

After relishing the whiskey, I said, "Can I ask you something?"

Noting the reticence in my tone, Gabe put down his glass. "Of course."

"Did you know that Nick's fellowship doesn't start for another two weeks?"

"Really? But he's been gone for—what—a week?"

"You arranged it for him. That's why I was wondering if you knew he hadn't started yet."

"I knew it was this semester, but no, I didn't make note of the specific dates. Why'd he go so early?"

"That's what I want to know."

"Oh."

"Yeah."

"You haven't talked to him about it?"

"Not about that, no. And now I'm feeling like a covetous, green-eyed girlfriend, which I hate. All I can figure it he left early so he could sightsee before the fellowship starts."

"That sounds like Nick."

"But why wouldn't he say something?"

Gabe picked up his glass and took another swallow. "Let me preface this by saying I'm not taking sides here. Nick, obviously, waited too long to tell you about the fellowship. You, in turn, got angry at Nick for telling you at the last minute. Maybe, just maybe, Nick was too scared to tell you he was leaving early so he could see the sights."

I grabbed the last grocery bag and unloaded it. The fact that Nick might have been too scared to tell me was grating, but it was a plausible explanation—and I was desperate for relief.

The doorbell chimed.

"Adolph's here," I said, smiling.

"Adolph?" Gabe looked confused.

"The guest I told you I was inviting."

"But Adolph?" He shrugged and held up his glass for another toast. "To new acquaintances." Our glasses met, we drained them, and I followed Gabe to the door so as to make introductions.

Adolph stood on the stoop in a white aloha shirt, white slacks, and his bright Crocs. He held out a bottle. "Barone Ricasoli Castello de Brolio Chianti—" I thought he was finished, but he took a breath and continued. "Classico Gran Selezione."

I grinned at the Italian accent he'd thrown in. "You're talking about the wine, right?"

Smiling back, Adolph added, "A 2013. Great vintage."

"Well, if word count has anything to do with quality, that's one great Chianti." Gabe held out his hand. "Gabe Turner."

Adolph transferred the wine bottle to his left hand, and they shook. "Adolph Hurst. A pleasure to meet you."

We got to the kitchen, and Adolph put the bottle on the counter and went to the bathroom to freshen up.

Once he disappeared down the hall, Gabe leaned toward me and whispered, "Oh my God. He looks just like Sidney Greenstreet."

"Yep."

Adolph passed on the whiskey and had a glass of water instead, saying the wine would wait until dinner.

Both men were outgoing art aficionados and artists, so I knew they would either get along or end up butting heads. Either would be entertaining. I assigned them the chore of making the salad. As they worked, they talked about everything from their education to masterpieces they'd encountered and appraised. Then they moved on to artists they'd known and those they considered hacks. At times, it sounded like a couple of old gossips at the clothesline. My fra diavolo recipe took over an hour, though forty-five minutes of that was simply letting the sauce simmer. During that time, I doubted I said more than a dozen words, which was not like me at all. But I had a good time watching my old friend Gabe getting to know my new friend Adolph.

I got the bread and sliced it lengthwise before slathering on butter and minced garlic. "Ten minutes until dinner," I announced, putting the bread in the oven.

"Then let me uncork our Chianti," Adolph said.

Gabe passed him his opener, and Adolph pulled it with a pleasing pop. Adolph smelled the cork, eyes alight, and passed it to me. It smelled like any other wine cork I'd ever sniffed, but for his sake, I gave an appreciative "Mmm."

Instead of Gabe's kitchen table, we sat on bar stools at the kitchen counter.

"Ta-daaa," Gabe said, placing the bowl of salad in reach.

"Looks good." I placed steaming fettuccini into bowls. As I ladled on the fra diavolo sauce, I made sure everyone got four big shrimp and two sea scallops.

As we sat, Adolph asked if he could say grace. We held hands as he proceeded with a short prayer that included thanks that he had found two new friends. At the amen, I let go of their hands, though I noticed something on the sleeve of Gabe's shirt.

Laughing, I pointed. "Gabe, you of all people should know not to wear white if there's red sauce or red wine nearby."

He saw the stain at his wrist. "Aw, crap. You're right." He stood, checked his slacks, and added, "Hey, at least gravity didn't drop anything on my pants. Be right back."

During Gabe's absence, I took the bread from the oven and sliced it into thick pieces that were rich with the aroma of garlic. Adolph told me some more amusing anecdotes about following Ricky into the Hunker Down Tavern.

"How's this?" Gabe asked on his return. He stood with his arms held out, dressed in a long-sleeve black shirt and black slacks.

"You're dressed like a priest," I said.

"In that case, Adolph's earlier prayer still counts. Let's eat."

We tucked in. I loved fra diavolo and took to it like a shark to a seal.

I looked at the two men, thinking we were having a grand evening. Then I felt a slight pang of sadness. Only one thing was missing to make the dinner party ideal, and that was Nick. My suspicions and his not telling me he was going to Vienna early proved we still had a lot of work ahead of us. But Nick was worth the effort, and I thought he would feel the same of me. I noticed Gabe smiling at me in a fatherly fashion.

Knowing me almost as well as my boyfriend, Gabe held up his wineglass and said, "To our missing comrade, Nick."

I smiled back, eyes tearing. "Aww, thanks, Gabe."

We clinked glasses, and Adolph said, "I am eager to make his acquaintance."

After our toast, Adolph refilled the glasses. "And a toast to our very own private eye, Lise Norwood, and a successful close to the case of *The Floating Ballerina*."

I was proud that, with the help of friends, I'd found it and returned it to its rightful owner. I detailed what happened for the boys, and they laughed at the account of Eve knocking Ricky Stephens's feet out from under him with a perfectly launched bowling ball. They howled when I told them about falling into Whitt and inadvertently kneeing him in the groin.

As the laughter died down, Adolph put a hand over mine. "I understand why you couldn't show me a photo of the sketch earlier. But now, with case closed, I beg you to let me see it."

"Beg?" I repeated with a smile.

"I will get on my knees if that's what it takes." Adolph raised an eyebrow. "But it will take the both of you to get me back on my feet."

"I agree with Adolph," Gabe said. "Not about begging, but about finally seeing the sketch."

I grabbed my handbag from the back of my barstool. I brought up the photos on my cell and thumbed through. I found the photo of the sketch and handed my phone to Adolph. Gabe stepped next to him.

"My God," Adolph said breathlessly.

"Incredible." Gabe took his eye from the screen for a second as he said, "Remember you promised to ask the owner if I can write a paper on it."

"I remember," I said. "And I'll see if I can have some prints made."

They both stared intently at the screen.

Adolph's eyes welled up, and I knew that when and if he saw the actual sketch, tears would trail down his cheeks. "It's—it's—"

I stood up and joined them, taking in the magnificence of *The Floating Ballerina*. "Yeah. It's hard to put into words."

After a few more minutes of passing my phone around and admiring the sketch, we started in on a group cleanup that only took twenty minutes.

As I wiped around the stovetop, I told Gabe, "Adolph is quite the artist."

"Really? That's praise from Lise," Gabe said as he put spices back into his rack. "If she'd said, 'Adolph is an artist,' I would be polite and inquire a little about it, but when she says, 'quite the artist,' well, then I'm intrigued."

Adolph said, "Please stop by my gallery. I'll show you some recent work, plus I have a few older pieces in the back, gathering dust."

I told Gabe about Adolph's latest paintings and how I'd found one in a victim's condo.

"It's an odd feeling to have had a recent customer come to such an awful end," Adolph said. "But it did bring Lise into my life, for which I am grateful."

I kind of got choked up, so before things could get too mushy, I pointed out that Gabe was a painter as well. After dinner, we brewed three coffees à la French press and took a stroll around Gabe's house, looking at the various paintings he'd done, with him giving the history of each, including inspiration, where, and when.

"Is your studio here or at the university?" Adolph asked.

"Definitely here, within the peace and quiet of home instead of the hustle and bustle at school. I doubt I'd get anything done there."

"Working on anything at the moment? Something you can show us?" I asked.

He led us to his studio, one of the bedrooms he'd long ago converted. He had pulled up the carpet and padding, leaving a concrete floor. He'd brought in a plumber to install a stainless-steel utility sink, which was a myriad of colors from all the paintbrushes he'd cleaned over the years. His supplies were on a table and shelves next to the sink, dozens of well-used brushes, palettes, paints of all kinds and colors, and countless stained rags. Preferring to work in the harsh light of overhead fluorescent tubes and the closeness of four walls, he had put blackout blinds on the room's one window, and I'd never seen them open. Three stools of varying heights stood near the easel, which was an ancient thing that held a medium-sized canvas on it. Two or three dozen other canvases of varying sizes were scattered around, leaning against the walls or each other. A few were blank, some were covered, others were completed, but most were unfinished pieces he'd stopped working on so he could move on to other projects.

We stood before the canvas on the easel and took in an acrylic abstract that seemed in motion. Hot colors—yellows, oranges, and reds—seemed to move in currents like water. It was all backed by similar hues in darker tones. Images seemed to be hidden among the colors: an observant eye in the upper left, two shadowy figures at the bottom of the canvas, and what appeared to be the ruins of a building in the middle. When I looked elsewhere then back again, I could no longer see those things.

"Did you hide images in there?" I asked.

"Maybe, maybe not. Perhaps your mind is creating them and placing them there."

"Well, whichever it is, it's a brilliant piece." Without taking his eyes from the painting, Adolph said, "I'd be more than happy to display some of your work at my gallery, if you'd like to sell them."

"Yeah, I'd be interested."

Gabe and Adolph started to talk business, and my eyes wandered around the room. One cloth-draped canvas caught my eye. It was long, and the cloth didn't cover a portion of the left side. The only thing visible was a hand, but the way it was relaxed, with a pointing index finger, was familiar. Then it hit me—it resembled God's hand as he reached for Adam in the painting on the ceiling of the Sistine Chapel. There was a momentary chill because Michelangelo had painted that. Then I wondered if I would always connect the psycho Michelangelo with the master. God, I hoped not. I stepped closer and saw that not only was it a feminine hand, but it also had nail polish. The only visible nail was the thumbnail, and it definitely sported red polish.

I pointed to it. "What's that one, Gabe? I thought it was from the Sistine Chapel. I suppose it still could be. God as a woman."

Gabe laughed and walked over to it. "Hardly." He grabbed the cloth, and I was disappointed that instead of revealing it, he'd covered the whole painting. "I won't tell you what it's supposed to be. It was a grand idea that ended up sophomoric, and I quit working on it. I'll paint over it."

Adolph said, "I like that idea, though, God as woman in the Sistine Chapel. Could fit in my current series, don't you think?"

"And instead of Adam, God reaches for Eve," I said.

"Oooh, make it Eve Arden." Of course Gabe would come up with the idea of the Hollywood actress whose career spanned decades.

Eyes alight, Adolph said, "And I'll call it the Sistine Sisters—or something along those lines."

"I'm having an after-dinner cigar on the back deck. Anyone want to join me?" Gabe asked.

"I do," I said. "No cigar, though. I'll have another whiskey."

"And I'll bask in the company of new friends," Adolph said.

"Head on out. I'll join you in a minute," Gabe said and started for his office. I knew he had his ritual of selecting a cigar from his humidor, rolling it in his fingers, and carefully snipping the end off it.

I led Adolph back to the kitchen and poured a couple of fingers of brown liquor into my glass, then Adolph and I went out to Gabe's deck. It overlooked a small backyard, but past that was the Intracoastal Waterway, almost a mile wide at this part of the river. I turned on Gabe's deck lights, which were actually small white Christmas lights that were used year-round.

"Nice," Adolph said appreciatively.

I took a sip of my spirits. "Excuse me a minute, Adolph. I need an ice cube."

I went back in through the French doors just as Gabe entered the kitchen with a fat cigar and his special cigar lighter in one hand. He grabbed a couple of paper towels and wiped at his sleeve. When I saw the fra diavolo sauce staining the paper towel, I barked a laugh, which startled Gabe, making him jump.

"Sorry," I said, laughing. "Even in black, you still make a mess."

A half-grin broke on his face. He held up his arm. "At least I'm consistent."

"Can I get one of your big ice cubes please?" I asked, holding out my whiskey glass.

We spent an hour with our butts parked in Adirondack chairs on Gabe's deck, talking. Between conversation, we listened to nocturnal birds calling out. As the party broke up, we ended up on Gabe's front stoop. I thanked both of them for helping me bring my case to a successful conclusion.

"The FBI should get your help with that art killer case," Adolph said.

"From your lips to God's ear," I said.

Gabe said, "You always could put two and two together, Lise. It might take you time to figure it out, but you always do. Even when you were a student. It's the way your mind works. In fact, I bet you figure out who Michelangelo is before the FBI."

"I wish." I was grateful we were out in the night air so they wouldn't see me blush.

Adolph volunteered to drive me home. I'd only had one post-dinner whiskey, though, and I said I would be fine.

Passing Teague's car, I banged on the hood. "Wake up, Special Agent, time to head home." I knew he wasn't really sleeping; he was too good at his job.

"Har-dee-har," Teague said and started the car.

I got in my car. Feeling someone's attention, I turned back to Gabe's house. He stood on the front porch, rubbing his wrist, a blank expression on his face. I waved and drove away. Glancing in the rearview mirror, I saw that he still stood there, watching me.

There was a special feeling when spending an evening bonding with good friends, and I went to sleep reflecting on that and feeling content.

Chapter 33

Barry White sang to me at six o'clock in the morning. I forced my eyes open, groaned at my whiskey headache, and reached for my phone.

I intended to sound bright but came across more like Gollum coughing out, "Nick, hi."

"Morning, Lise. Sorry for the early call. I was hoping you'd be up."

"Had a late night celebrating at Gabe's."

"Oh, man, wish I could have been there."

I sat up and swung my legs off the bed. Taking a deep breath, I said, "Nick. I have a confession. I called and spoke with Professor Gildersleeve."

"I went by this morning to introduce myself in person, and he told me. That's why I'm calling, Lise. What's going on?" Instead of accusation, there was concern in his tone.

"There's a lot going on." My emotions started to get all jacked up. I tried to get control of it, but my voice was quavering. "That crazy fuck posing a woman like *The Floating Ballerina*, which, as we all know, was part of a case I was working. Not to mention that the same crazy fuck broke into my house while I was there, and—it's—it's all grating on my nerves. And... and..." My voice broke as I got to the meat of it. "And you're not here, which is fine because of the fellowship, but you haven't started the fellowship yet, because it begins in two fucking weeks." My voice turned weepy and high-pitched. "You kept the fellowship from me until the last minute, and now add to it the fact that you left three weeks before your fellowship starts.

And you didn't tell me you were going early. That gives my ego a real boost."

"Ah, Lise. I'm so sorry."

"And I'm halfway across the world, questioning your motives and questioning whether you really are in Vienna, or maybe still here in—"

"What? San Marco? No, no. Why would I—"

"And then I'm wondering if we're as rock solid as I thought, and if maybe you have someone on the side, and then worst of all I wondered—I wondered if... oh, fuck it."

Nick groaned. "Shit, this is all my fault. When I originally accepted the fellowship, I arranged to come early and take in the sights. When you got mad at me for not telling you about the fellowship, I chickened out and couldn't bring myself to tell you that little tidbit."

A little of my anger started to rise up, but I managed to put a muzzle on it. "I think we need to have a serious talk."

"Oh? Well, yeah, sure."

"Not on the phone. In person. When we see each other. If I go to Vienna or when you get home."

"Do you want me to come back now?" Without waiting for a reply, he continued, "Yeah, I'm coming back."

"What about Vienna?"

"Screw Vienna."

"Don't you dare. I'd feel a million times worse if you gave up the fellowship."

He was quiet for a few seconds. "Are we—our relationship—is it in danger?"

"I don't know," I admitted, then my stubbornness kicked in. "No. No, it's not. I love you, and I know you love me. But maybe our relationship isn't as strong as we thought."

"Baby, we can fix that. Right?"

"Yeah. We can."

"Hey, why don't you come out now?" Nick said suddenly.

"Now? I really don't have any cases right now. But it'd be awfully expensive."

"I've got money," Nick said. "And a steady paycheck and a place to stay. Hell, you'd put a lot of miles between you and that crazy-ass killer."

Wow, being with Nick and not having to worry about Michelangelo, a win-win situation. "It's not a dormitory room, is it? I don't think I could go back to dorm life."

Nick laughed. "Picky, picky, picky. But no, I have an apartment. A little on the small size, but nice. It's a couple of blocks from the university."

"Sounds good."

"Best of all, it has a really big bed and a very comfortable mattress you just sink into."

I grinned. "You sold me."

"So you'll come out?"

"Maybe."

"Come on, Lise. Get out of town, at least until they catch the guy," Nick said.

"Yeah, okay. God, I miss you, Nick."

"And I miss you."

"Give me a few days to plan things, get a flight and all."

"Sure. It's so romantic here. We'll have a great time. Hell, you can stay as long as you want, for my entire fellowship if you want."

I was instantly excited. I hated to leave my business, but to spend time in Vienna with Nick... well, it was one of those things in life that shouldn't be passed up.

"It'll be great," I said. "But I'd like to get one thing off my chest. No more secrets between us, okay?"

"I've learned my lesson."

Knowing I would be heading to Austria made both of us giddy, and I felt warm as we talked about it. When we hung up, I felt that buoyancy that love could instill in a person. Soon, I could say goodbye to San Marco and the psycho killer, and hello to Nick and Vienna. Maybe I felt a little guilty about saying that we shouldn't have any more secrets when I hadn't told him about my brief suspicion that he was Michelangelo. I would tell him, but that was one of those in-person kind of things.

I got some ibuprofen, swallowed them with a glass of OJ, and decided another hour or two of sleep would be beneficial. Sliding under my comforter, I cuddled into myself. Before I nodded off, my mind replayed the phone call with Nick, then it went back to dinner at Gabe's and his studio. I saw his new painting, the covered one where I'd seen the hand he'd painted, just as I touched on sleep, then I was instantly awake and sitting up in bed. I was panting hard, envisioning Beverly Raine mounted on her wall. Angela Lopez popped up next, dead and positioned as the Little Mermaid in the fountain in the park. Her beauty, her wounds, her blood.

I reached for my phone and brought up a number on my contacts.

After three rings, Baker answered, "Norwood. Thanks for waking me up."

"You're welcome, Baker," I said in monotone. "Angela Lopez..."

"Yeah. What about her?"

"Is there anything I don't know about the crime?" I asked.

"Whaddaya mean?"

My mouth was dry and my voice husky. "Anything you've been keeping quiet? Anything about blood?"

"What are you onto, Norwood?"

By the sound of his voice, I knew I was looking in the right place. Louder, I said, "Come on, Baker. All that blood—not all of it was hers."

"What are you getting at?"

I shouted into the phone, "Just tell me!"

After several seconds of silence, Baker sniffed. "Yeah, sure, why not. Sometimes we hold back certain details. You know, helps verify if someone confesses. If they don't know that little detail, then they're just a crazy person seeking attention or something. Sometimes that unknown detail can lead to figuring out who the guilty party is. We have one with Angela Lopez, though you seem to have figured it out."

"The blood?" I asked.

"Yeah. Some on her face, around her mouth, and on the duct tape gag. Most was her blood, of course, but a little was his. We think she gnawed through the tape and bit the killer bad enough that he bled. What's this all about, Norwood?"

My head spun enough that I felt dizzy. A remembered image came to mind—the stain on Gabe's white long-sleeve T-shirt. I'd thought it was fra diavolo sauce, but now I realized it had been redder than that.

"Norwood! Why the call? What's up?"

And the bartender at Coyote Lick had mentioned the man he'd thrown out had gauze wrapped around his arm above the wrist.

"Lise?"

Gabe had been cryptic when our dinner party ended, when he'd said I would always be able to put two and two together to find a solution.

"Lise, you there?"

My mind bounced back and forth between the covered painting in Gabe's studio and Beverly Raine mounted on her wall. Her right arm was outstretched, the fingers of her right hand relaxed, except for the index finger, which seemed to have been pointing. *Her red nail polish...*

"Lise?"

I closed my eyes. "I know who Michelangelo is."

Chapter 34

At Baker's instruction, I ran out of the house to tell my curbside FBI babysitter what I suspected. At this time of day, it was Janet Davis. She ordered me back into the house and started to push buttons on her phone.

Baker called me back, saying he'd contacted his higher-ups, then added, "Look, Norwood, neither the stain on his shirt nor the hand you saw in the painting are concrete evidence, at least not until we can check them out. But it's the first break we've had. Just don't go getting your hopes up."

I sat at the kitchen table, a cup of tepid and untouched coffee before me. *Just don't go getting your hopes up*. No problem. My hopes ran in the opposite direction. I hoped I was wrong.

I started to call Nick, to tell him my suspicions about Gabe, but my phone rang. This time, it was Ortega on his way to join his partner. "Baker and I get to go with the FBI when they visit Professor Turner. What do you think, Lise? What's your gut tell you?"

"I think—I think—I don't know. The way he looked for just a brief second when I caught him wiping at what I thought was a sauce stain—and the hand in the painting, matching Beverly Raine's. I'm worried."

"We'll let you know as soon as we learn anything," Ortega told me.

As I ended the call, there was a tap at the door, and it opened. It was Special Agent Davis. "Mind if I join you?"

"Come on in. I'll get us some coffee." I dumped my cold coffee in the sink and poured us each a fresh cup. Sitting at the table, I asked, "What's going to happen now?"

"It won't be an assault team hitting his house and office." She sipped her brew. "But we'll have enough people so that he won't be able to run. We're also using some manpower from the San Marco PD, including your friends, Baker and Ortega."

"Sorry you have to sit here and watch me," I told her.

She nodded. "Well, the good news is, if it is Professor Turner, you won't have to deal with us anymore. Life can go back to normal."

I shook my head. "That wouldn't be good news. Gabe is a friend."

Davis nodded. "You did the right thing."

"Yeah, I know. Still sucks." All that time I'd spent with Gabe, I hadn't a clue. If it was true, I wondered how long it had been going on and if there were things I'd missed. If I'd been more alert, maybe some of his victims might still be alive.

"Do you think he's killed others? Women who haven't been found?" I muttered.

She glanced at me as she took another sip. "I don't know. And we don't know for sure that it was him."

"He traveled a lot. Maybe he killed women in other—"

In a rare show of compassion, Davis put down her mug and laid her hand on mine. "Lise, don't trouble yourself with what-ifs and maybes. We'll know for sure soon."

"Yeah, you're right."

The raid was successful in that we learned the horrible truth that Gabe was Michelangelo. It was unsuccessful because Gabe had already fled by the time they hit his house. Later that afternoon, there was a group at my kitchen table that included Baker, Ortega, and Special Agent Teague, who had relieved Davis. She'd gone to join other feds as they went through Gabe's home and office.

I'd just finished the gut-wrenching chore of calling Nick to tell him that his mentor, the man he looked up to most, was Michelangelo. He refused to believe me at first, but then I'd handed the phone to Baker, who told him it was true and to let him or the FBI know if Gabe tried to contact him. Nick was dumbfounded when I got back on the phone. He was in shock, and I knew that when it wore off, it would hit him hard. Before we ended the call, I told him I would get out to Vienna as quickly as I could.

"Sorry, Lise." Baker tried to be sympathetic, but he just sounded even more gruff.

"Me too," Ortega said.

"Me too," Teague echoed. I started to sip my latest cup of joe but stood and dumped it in the sink instead. I reached down to the cabinet beside my oven and brought out a bottle of Jameson. "Anyone?"

Teague shook his head. "On duty."

"Paperwork to do," Ortega said.

Baker nodded at Ortega. "What he said."

I shrugged, got a small glass, poured a finger, and added a splash of tap water. "Suit yourselves." Sitting, I held out my glass. "To the one thing I can feel good about. To *The Floating Ballerina*."

"Ah, what the hell." Baker grabbed the bottle and put it next to my glass. "*The Floating Ballerina*."

We clinked. I sipped from my glass. He sipped from the bottle.

He gave an appreciative "Ahhh" then said, "Eve said to tell you they've recovered everything Stephens stole from his wife."

"That include the gifts he gave girlfriends?" I asked.

"Yep."

"Where was he stashing it all?" I asked.

"Right before he staged the robbery, he installed a safe in his office," Ortega said.

"A safe at work, huh?" Almost in plain sight, except his office wasn't visible from the observation post Elliot the Slim and I had set up. I shook my head and took a larger sip. "You know how hard this is to believe? I would never have believed in a million years that Gabe would be Michelangelo. Are you sure he's on the run?"

"That's the assumption we're working under. His dresser drawers were all open, and the clothes were pulled out and thrown on the bed like he packed in a hurry. Same with the closet, and a lot of empty hangers. We couldn't find his passport, and most people don't carry those around unless they're getting set to travel. A neighbor out walking his dog last night said he saw Turner drive off an hour or so after you left."

"But how did he know I'd figure it out? I mean, he knew I would. That's why he went on the run, right?"

Teague said, "You saw his painting where he was recreating what he'd done to Beverly Raine."

"I only saw a little bit of it, and it didn't hit me until later what it was."

"He knows you, knows you're smart. He knew you'd figure it out, so he bolted."

Baker sniffed. "We've found all sorts of connections to violent, deviant behavior at his house."

"Turner's a member of a couple of sadomasochistic groups, has a collection of porn in the same vein, and we've discovered snuff films on DVD, flash drives, and his home computer," Ortega said.

It made me feel sick.

"We think they're authentic," Teague said.

"Authentic?"

Teague's gaze fell to his coffee mug. "People sexually tortured to death. For real."

"Ah shit..." I drained my glass.

"His files backed up what you said about him traveling a lot," Teague said.

"He prefers Southeast Asia," Ortega said.

Teague said, "Lise, we're early into discovery, but what we've found shows he had connections in Indonesia and other locales where certain things can take place for the right amount of money."

Ortega took up the conversation. "Things that would attract a man whose tastes had grown from causing pain in the name of sex, to sexual torture, and eventually to sexual murder."

"He's in some of those films we found," Baker said. "He's torturing and killing young Asian women."

I closed my eyes. "Oh, dear God."

Baker glanced at Teague. "I'm not some big-shot fed profiler, but I'll bet any of you a hundred bucks that they'll end up saying that Turner escalated, and the occasional kill trips no longer satisfied him. He killed Kristin on a whim, and after that, he couldn't stop."

"It's the art aspect that puzzles me," Teague said. "Why go to the trouble?"

Thinking out loud, I said, "Maybe in his mind, it elevated him from being a crazed killer to the status of an artist."

"Maybe," Baker said. "He's the only one who could tell us. Anyway, it's mandatory for anyone employed at San Marco University to be fingerprinted for a background check. That's why he wiped the crime scenes, but as he has no DNA on record, he didn't worry about that. We're getting a rush on matching the DNA at his house with that at the crime scenes."

Ortega added, "Bite marks on the vics match X-rays from his dentist."

Baker put a hand over mine. "Can you think of any place Professor Turner could be hiding?"

I shook my head. "I don't have a clue."

"If he left right after that dinner party, that gives him hours to put distance between himself and San Marco," Ortega said.

"We've got his photo and bulletins out everywhere," Teague said. "If he tries to get out of the country, we'll nab him."

"Considering his sleazy connections in Southeast Asia, I wouldn't be surprised if he had some false paperwork," Baker said. "Not sure he'd be stopped on his photo alone."

"His face is already all over the internet," Teague said. "This evening and tonight, it'll be on television news, both local and national. Tomorrow morning, his face hits printed media. I think it's only a matter of time."

Chapter 35

They all stuck around for another hour or so, and I was touched, knowing they all stayed to make sure I was all right. Finally, Baker and Ortega left. Teague resumed his post in his car at the curb. Until they caught Gabe, I would still have the FBI to keep me safe. I poured another finger of Jameson and lay on my sofa to watch Humphrey Bogart and Katherine Hepburn in *The African Queen*. That helped a little, but when it ended, my heartache and confusion about Gabe returned. I wondered how Nick was doing and decided to call him after giving him some time to work it all out in his head.

Seeking solace in an unhealthy dinner, I went to Henry's, a nearby bar, and ordered hot chicken wings and a cold pint. Teague followed me over and joined me. Wings and beer didn't help. I ate a wing and a half before the thought of Gabe killing people so brutally twisted my gut. I couldn't even bring myself to finish my beer and asked for water instead.

Teague noticed. "You all right, Lise?"

"Gabe is—was a good friend. Can't wrap my mind around it."

"I understand."

"He and my boyfriend are the best of friends, so I know it's tearing Nick up."

"There are lots of victims when it comes to crimes, not just the obvious ones."

He was right. My cousin's murder was an example of that.

I smiled at Teague. "You're a good guy. I hope we can stay in touch when this nightmare is over. I'd like for you to meet Nick."

"I'd like that too."

I checked my phone for the time. There would be a little time to visit Mom before they put her to bed. "Finish up, Special Agent Teague. I'm going to introduce you to my mother."

Our two-car caravan made its way across town to San Marco Eldercare. Mom liked Teague and paid more attention to him than me, until he went to sit across the room to give us some privacy. I laid it all out for Mom, told her about Gabe and the horrors he'd perpetrated, though not in too much detail. She'd known Gabe, and had she been healthy, Mom would have been devastated. I confessed to suspecting Nick.

"God, I miss Nick," I said.

Mom looked at me, a half grin in place, then her eyes took in something above me that she found much more interesting. In my mind, however, Mom said, "Honey, if you miss your man, maybe you should go to where you're most reminded of him."

Well, duh. "Thanks, Mom." I kissed her cheek, signaled to Teague, and left.

He followed me home. I called Nick, and as I'd thought, he was having a rough time of it.

"As soon as I think I can accept the fact that Gabe was a killer, I get to thinking how he broke into your house. It makes no sense that Gabe would terrorize you of all people. I just can't understand." Nick sounded close to tears.

"I don't think we'll ever understand. And frankly, I don't know if we should waste the time trying to."

"I guess."

"Focus on the fact that I'll be there soon. A couple of days."

"Yeah, that sounds good."

"And speaking of being close to you, do you mind if I stay at your place tonight? If I can't have you, I want to at least feel your presence."

"Of course."

After we ended the call, I got my bag, put my Ruger inside it, and headed out. I walked over to Teague, and he rolled down his window.

"I'm going to stay at my boyfriend's place tonight," I told him.

"I'll follow you over."

We did the two-car shuffle to Nick's. I got out, opened the gate to Nick's driveway, and drove through. Teague followed and shut the gate. Nick's Florida Cracker house was surrounded by woods on all sides. The only illumination came from the stars and the sliver of moon above. It was creepy.

Teague stepped up next to me. "Want me to come in and look around?"

"You better believe it."

We carefully made our way through the dark to the door. I picked up a planter that hid a spare key and passed it to Teague. He opened the door, and we stepped into the foyer.

Teague handed the key back and said, "Be right back." He put his hand on the gun on his hip and went farther into the house.

He went through the rooms, switching on lights. I turned on the porch light and took a few moments to enjoy it as it shone through the stained-glass windows of random geometric shapes in a varied pastel palette on each side of the front door. Nick had made them himself after taking a course a few years ago. I switched on the hall light and smiled. It wasn't creepy anymore. It was Nick's home.

Teague returned to the foyer. "All clear down here. Let me check the second floor."

"I'll go with you."

Nick's room was the first at the top of the stairs. As Teague looked around, I put my bag on a chair and went to sit on Nick's bed: a queen-size mahogany four-poster with a carved pineapple at the top of each post.

"I'll check the other rooms," Teague said and left.

Nick's bedroom was furnished with a mishmash of antiques he'd picked up here and there, and though they were all of different styles, it fit Nick well. Though Nick was an art history professor, he only had one painting on his bedroom wall that was worth much. It was a Florida landscape by one of the founding members of the Florida Highwaymen, Alfred Hair. The Highwaymen were a group of African Americans who, from the 1950s through the 1970s, would paint colorful Florida landscapes and seascapes on Upson board. They made frames out of crown molding and sold them out of the trunks of their cars for an average price of twenty-five dollars. Years later, they valued into the thousands.

The framed picture on his bedside table was far from a masterpiece. It was the nude sketch I'd posed for the night we roleplayed as artist and model. I could feel my face flush as I realized Teague might have seen it. Hoping he hadn't, I put the picture facedown.

"Hey, Lise?" Teague appeared in the doorway, wearing a serious expression. "Can you come here a minute?"

"Sure," I said, curious as to what he wanted.

We went to the very last door in the hall. He pointed to the large padlock that hung under the doorknob. "What's up with that?"

"That's Nick's home office," I explained. "That's the only way in, and there are no windows. He sometimes brings home valuable pieces to study, so he keeps them locked up in there."

"Got a key? I'll check it out."

"No need. It's not like anyone could lock the padlock from inside."

"Then I'll head on back to the car," Teague said.

I almost invited him to stay inside then realized I wanted to be alone—well, I wanted to be with Nick. But since that wasn't possible, I wanted to be in his home, where everything I could see, smell, and touch reminded me of him. "Make sure you tell Carter I'm staying here tonight."

"I will," Teague said and left.

I went down to the kitchen. As if being a first-rate lover and art expert weren't enough, Nick loved to cook and had a wonderful kitchen filled with restored antique appliances. I opened the teal-blue 1950s Westinghouse refrigerator and found what I was looking for—a chilled bottle of Chardonnay. I filled my favorite wineglass, which was more of a goblet really, made of crackle glass with beads strung on a silver strand that ran up the stem. I took a sip.

"Yeah, that's the stuff."

I thought of calling Nick again, but a glance at his kitchen clock showed it was almost ten o'clock, so it was almost four in the morning in Vienna. If he'd somehow gotten to sleep, I didn't want to wake him. I topped off the wine and went back upstairs. I stared down the hall at the padlocked door of his office. When Teague pointed it out, I didn't think it was odd, but now I did. Nick only locked it when something valuable was inside. *What would he leave in there for the whole semester?*

I went into Nick's bedroom and got the padlock key he kept in a dresser drawer. I keyed the lock, stepped in, and reached to the side to flick up the light switch. Illumination did not bring what I'd expected. In fact, what I saw made no sense. My wineglass fell from numb fingers and shattered on the floor. A moment later, I fell back against the wall and slid all the way down as I stared at the room.

Nick's desk, computer, chair, and all the furnishings were shoved up against a wall and into corners, leaving an open area in the middle of the room. Wires and ropes in loose coils lay on the floor, which was stained with copious amounts of dried blood. Michelangelo—Gabe—had brought four stakes from Beverly Raine's place, the same as the ones he'd used to mount her on her bedroom wall, and they'd been hammered into the hardwood floor. Lengths of rope were tied to each stake.

My attention was drawn to a photo that was finger-streaked with dried blood and tacked to the wall above the desk. It was the photo I'd given Nick of *The Floating Ballerina*. Gabe had stolen it from Nick's office. This was where Gabe had made his most recent kill.

Chapter 36

Wishing I could behave like a stone-cold professional and calmly go to get Teague, I panicked and ran. I flew down the hall, down the stairs, through the foyer, and out into the night, which became darker the farther I got from the porch light.

"Teague?" His name came out soft and hoarse.

I made shambling steps to where we'd parked, finally able to detect the cars. I put my hand on my MINI Cooper and trailed my fingers as I walked past it to Teague's. Walking around the back, I came up to the open driver-side window. The lights in the house silhouetted him in the car.

"Teague," I said. "Teague, get on the horn, get more agents here. I found where Gabe killed Amanda Kellogg."

He didn't react—or move at all. I opened the door, and he fell out. Teague sprawled unmoving on the ground, his feet still in the car. He faced away from me. In the glow of the interior light, I could see the fatal wound in his neck that had bled him out. I stared numbly at the wound, at all the blood. It could've been a bullet, but I hadn't heard gunfire. A stab wound, I decided. I stood there a long time before my flight instinct kicked in. I initially started for my car until I remembered my keys were upstairs in my bag, along with my phone and Ruger. Figuring I could get to the nearest house in five minutes, I ran a dozen or so steps down the drive. A figure stepped from the darkness of the wild growth to the left, blocking my exit. I skidded to a stop and turned for the house. My phone upstairs in Nick's bedroom became my focus. As I ran, I heard rapid footsteps behind me.

Hurrying past my car, I remembered the Glock in the glove compartment, but by then, it was too late. I would have to backtrack, and he would be on me before I could get it out. I continued toward the house. Reaching the front door seemed to take forever, like I was in a slow-motion nightmare. But I did get there. I charged in and stopped long enough to lock the door. Turning, I grabbed the heavy shillelagh from Nick's cane collection in the umbrella stand.

I rushed up the stairs and into Nick's room, locking the door behind me. I grabbed my bag and dug out my phone. I brought up my contact list and pressed the phone icon next to Baker's name.

"Damn it, Norwood, it's after ten. What do you—"

"Teague, the FBI agent, is dead. Michelangelo is here; he's after me."

"At home?"

"I'm at Nick's." I gave the address and how to get onto the property.

From downstairs, Gabe—Michelangelo—called out in a singsong voice, "Lise?"

My breath caught.

"Lise, you there?" Baker asked.

"He's in the house," I whispered.

"I'm on my way. Get somewhere safe and hide. Don't make a sound. I'll call the cavalry. You'll be all right. I promise."

I ended the call as Gabe shut off the main breaker in the fuse box. I froze as the house fell into darkness. I stood still and listened, trying to detect his approach. Finally, I decided I needed to move, to take action.

"My gun," I muttered. I held up my phone for light. Tucking the shillelagh under an arm, I picked up my bag.

The doorknob rattled. Gabe hit the door hard enough that wood cracked.

Without conscious thought, I screamed, "Leave me alone!"

He hit the door again, and it swung wide, slamming into the wall. I screeched and dropped my phone and bag. My phone, screen lit, spun across the floor, barely illuminating the dark figure rushing toward me. I swung the shillelagh and connected, making him grunt. His momentum carried him on, however, and he knocked me to the floor. I hit so hard that my teeth clacked, and I lost the shillelagh. A weight straddled my belly. Strong hands closed on my throat.

I tried to say his name, but it came out choked and unrecognizable. I reached blindly, hoping to grasp the cane. When that failed, I tried to punch him. My blows were ineffective. I reached for his face with my fingernails, but he kept out of reach. So I scratched his arms. As everything went black, I took some small satisfaction that, like Angela Lopez, I had drawn blood.

Chapter 37

I woke. I breathed. *A nightmare... it was a nightmare.* Then I coughed, and my throat flared in pain like I'd swallowed barbed wire. I tried to get up, but I couldn't move.

There was a click, and light flared. The brightness was so painful, I had to close my eyes. I heard footsteps on hardwood, leisurely going in circles around my body. They stopped for a few seconds before starting up again then pausing again. I lifted my eyelids a little at a time, looking anywhere but directly into the light. I'd been tied naked and spread-eagle to the stakes hammered into the floor. We were back in Nick's office, where Gabe had killed Amanda Kellogg. A couple of feet above me dangled a construction lamp with a heavy aluminum reflector. Gabe started walking again, and I followed his progress around me. The lamp prevented me from seeing anything above his thighs.

"Gabe?"

"Call me Michelangelo."

"You tried to kill me."

"No, no, that was foreplay."

I didn't know how long I'd been out. "What time is it?"

"When I am most creative."

Where is Baker? "What are you going to do?"

"Make love to you—create art."

"A sculpture?"

"No. You of all people, Lise, deserve something unique, something I have yet to craft."

"What?" I asked.

He spoke in a voice filled with wonder. "You will be a mosaic." A butcher knife flew down and stuck in the floor, inches from my right hand.

The significance struck with a wave of nausea, and I fought to keep my dinner down.

In reverence, he said, "Before I assemble my mosaic, I will first disassemble you." *Thunk.* Another knife pierced the floor by my leg. He went on in a tone that sounded as if he were offering the greatest honor possible. "My math may be off, but considering a cut at each knuckle, wrist, elbow, shoulder, neck, thigh, knee, ankle, toes..." *Thunk.* "You shall be a masterpiece made up of fifty separate pieces."

Nick's meat cleaver fell to the floor by my head. I screamed. A handsaw dropped to the floor. A pair of pruning shears fell next to it. He stepped away and returned with Nick's circular saw in one hand and its battery in the other. Standing over me, he shoved the battery in place with a click and pulled the trigger a couple of times. The saw sang. The blade slowed and stopped. He stood there. Though his upper body was in darkness, I could feel his eyes on me.

The artist was scrutinizing his blank canvas. My mind shifted, and instead of trying to understand why, I concentrated on how I could get out of this nightmare. I tried to reach the closest knife, but it was an inch too far. I could scream my head off, but no one would hear me. Nick's nearest neighbor was too distant. All I could think to do was talk, to get him talking, hoping to delay what seemed inevitable until Baker arrived.

"Gabe? We're friends. Why?"

"Love."

"Love?"

"You've kissed my cheek countless times, Lise, said you loved me."

"I did." Though I was no longer sure it was true, I added, "I do."

"Uh-huh. A brotherly love. But, Lise, all of this *is* love. Real love. The act of love. The consummation of love." His voice was sincere and gentle as he knelt at my side and placed the saw on the floor.

I looked at the man standing over me. He was Gabe, and yet he wasn't. It was like he wore a Gabe mask that was slightly askew and twisted. A smile stretched his mouth wider than I'd ever seen. His eyes were wide and feral, reflecting madness and ecstatic joy. He didn't blink. I saw his arm was bleeding where I had scratched him. My fingernail marks merged with the scabbed bite mark made by Angela. Without warning, he brought his fist down on my left cheek. For an instant, there was no pain, then agony blazed on my face. I squeezed my eyes shut until the pain lessened. I opened my eyes to see another strike descend. I turned my head so that he smashed my temple and left ear. He lowered himself, putting his face inches from mine, and panted like some large beast, his breath sour.

"Gabe?"

He grabbed my cheeks with one hand and squeezed. He kissed my lips softly and whispered, "Michelangelo."

The two blows to the head had knocked rational thought from my mind. I felt a surge of surrealism, a feeling that there was no way this could be real. It had to be a prank. Dizzy, I grinned, wanting to be in on the joke.

"Lise, you're smiling," Gabe said. "I knew you were special. You can grasp the significance of what's to play out." He stood and raised the lamp so that it dangled inches below the ceiling. He knelt by my side again. "You of all people should understand my artistic journey. It began with my summer visits to a friend in Kuta, Indonesia. A fellow artist, he owns a private club that caters to the prurient interests of men of means. But it is out of that degradation that I've honed my art." He put his hands on my shoulders and, with his face inches from mine, asked, "Do you understand, Lise? True art?"

Come on, Baker, where are you? "I don't understand. What do you mean?"

He stared at me, eyes intense, then nibbled at his lower lip. "His connections include other locations where similar things can be attained, Bangkok, Hong Kong, Malaysia. Do you know what I've learned, Lise? Art is not a simple depiction. Art is emotion and feeling. I pursue the purest emotion—love. And love is reflected in lust. And pain is the purest feeling, an agony reflected in my art."

"I'm scared."

"Embrace it. The best inspiration and insight, for you, the model, comes from fear. Your fear heightens my love and my lust, the agony of creation, and my own fear."

"You're scared?" I asked.

"Yes, I am always frightened at the moment of transformation, when flesh becomes stone or metal or canvas."

"What?"

"Or you, Lise. You when you become fifty random pieces of colored glass put together in a way that will be creation."

Gabe stared at nothing. I wanted to say something, to come up with some strategy to snap him out of whatever spell he was under.

Gabe shifted his gaze to me. "I loved every woman who has been my muse." He stroked my cheek. "I love you, Lise. I love you most of all." His fingers traveled down my neck and to my breast, which he squeezed.

When his hand moved farther down my body, I shouted, "Don't touch me!"

"It's no coincidence that Nick is in Vienna."

"What?"

As his fingertips reached my mons pubis, he said, "I've wanted you for some time. I arranged the fellowship to get him out of the way. When the fellowship was in place, I couldn't contain my desire, and I had to act. Therefore, the first."

"Kristin Harmon," I said.

"The others were just a prelude to what I want—need—crave. You, Lise, you."

I heard a rhythmic sound—rapid footsteps on the stairs. Gabe stopped. I lifted my head.

"Lise? Where are you?"

I recognized the voice. "Ortega!"

Gabe hit me again.

My vision returned in time to see Gabe grab the knife stuck into the floor by my leg and pull it free. A second later, Ortega charged into the room, his pistol held in a two-handed grip.

Gabe launched himself at Ortega. Their bodies collided, and Ortega's gun went off. There was pain under my left arm near my armpit, and I yelped. As they wrestled, I lifted my head. I hadn't been hit, but the bullet had gone into the hardwood floor, sending a chunk of wood at least five inches long into my arm. The men continued to grapple. I heard grunts, growls, and heavy breaths. Gabe's arm pulled back, the knife in his hand, and he thrust it into Ortega. The movement repeated, over and over, piston-like, until Ortega collapsed to his knees. Gabe kept thrusting until Ortega fell on his face.

Chapter 38

My perception changed, from shock perhaps. Everything had a hazy element to it. Events progressed in a slow, deliberate fashion. Every inch of my body throbbed, feeling as if I swelled with each heartbeat. I couldn't understand why Ortega had been alone, why Baker and a whole platoon of cops weren't with him.

I lifted my head and muttered, "Ortega?"

He didn't move.

Gabe stood. Bloody fingers opened, and he dropped the knife to the floor with a clang. His other hand clutched Ortega's gun. He smiled at me as he took in my body, then his smile fell. For the first time since I'd been bound, his manic gaze narrowed.

Looking at my injured arm, he shouted, "He damaged my mosaic!" Gabe fired the gun over and over into Ortega's body.

"Stop!" I screamed.

My ears were overwhelmed with a high-pitched screech cause by the gunfire. Gabe turned to me, his expression reflecting two levels. In one, I could see the affection he'd always felt for me. And the other reflected intense lust. Terrified, I tried kicking and yanking free. Pain shot through my injured arm, so I concentrated only on the rope that bound my right wrist. I tugged and felt the rope move. Turning my head as much as possible, I looked at that iron stake. Gabe had hammered it into a seam between two pieces of hardwood flooring. I pulled, and one of the wooden boards lifted a quarter inch. If I hadn't been so traumatized, I might have laughed at how Nick's lack of home restoration skills could lead to my escape.

"What are you doing, Lise?" Gabe asked as he stood in front of the door. Then there was an explosion and a burst of red mist at his side. He spun like an Old West gunslinger and fired two shots into the hall. A grunt was followed by the sound of someone tumbling down the stairs.

> Gabe glanced back at me, wonderment in his eyes. "How about that? I hit him." Oblivious to the bullet wound in his side, he ran from the room.

I yanked on the rope again and pulled the stake from the floor. Grasping the handle of the butcher knife, I wrenched it from the wood and set to work cutting the ropes. As an amateur chef, Nick kept his knives sharp, and I freed myself in seconds. When I stood, my head swam, and I dropped the knife, though I managed to keep on my feet. My arm was on fire where the wood shard pierced me. I started to barricade myself in the room, but Gabe had shot someone, a cop, then gone after him. I bent down for a weapon and ended up with the circular saw. It was heavy and clunky, but I gripped it hard. Wearing only a cut piece of rope around each wrist and ankle, I shuffled to Ortega. He was dead.

I hurried through the door and down the hallway. Gabe stood two steps down from the top of the staircase, his back to me. He aimed Ortega's gun down the stairway. Baker lay on the floor at the bottom of the stairs, a hand over a spreading bloodstain on the front of his shirt. He held the other hand up in front of his face as if it would ward off bullets. I tried to use both hands to bring up the weighty saw, but my left arm was pretty much useless. I swung the saw backward then forward, awkwardly lifting the tool in my right hand.

Baker saw me, a pained smile grew, and I could just hear him mutter, "Atta girl."

Another step, and I pushed the saw blade against Gabe's back and pulled the trigger. The tool and Gabe both screamed as the saw cut into flesh and meat. The spinning blade caught on bone and skittered into his left shoulder blade. Gabe's hot blood splashed my face and body. Still, I squeezed the trigger. Gabe thrashed about, somehow tangling fingers in my hair. Our legs got ensnared. We fell down the stairs together, the saw bouncing with us. One roll smashed my side against a step and pushed the chunk of wood deeper into my arm. I screamed. With a loud crack, we hit the bottom. The saw skittered past us and came to rest at Baker's feet. On top of Gabe, I tried to stand then found it was a skill I no longer possessed, so I quickly crawled to Baker, who sat up a few feet away, his stomach bleeding.

"Oh God, Baker. He shot you."

"I'm okay, a little dizzy is all." He licked his lips. "Fuckin' lucky shot."

I heard a gasp behind me and turned as Gabe shifted into a sitting position, his back against the wall at the base of the stairs. He looked at his right leg. It was broken and wrenched at an unnatural angle. Next, he took in the gunshot to his side. I watched, amazed, at the amount of blood puddling the floor from the wound I'd opened in his back. His expression was tight with pain, his face pale and shadowed with gray smudges. Yet he smiled.

"Gun?" I said to Baker.

"Lost it."

"I still have mine." Gabe held up Ortega's gun. He aimed it at me then at Baker. Back and forth. One then the other, like the eyes on a Felix the Cat clock. Tick-tock, tick-tock.

"This was the perfect hideout, don't you think?" Gabe laughed and shook his head. "You told me about the sketch of *The Floating Ballerina*." Gabe spoke calmly. "As an art scholar, I had to see it. Since Nick's in Vienna, I broke into his office at the university and took it. With Nick out of the country, his home was the perfect studio to prepare a model. But the artwork had to be shared, so the actual creation of *The Floating Ballerina* was conducted back where the model was found. Created in the medium of death."

"You left that photo of the sculpture in the Medici Chapel, the one made by Michelangelo. How did you know that was what the police were calling you?"

"Remember when you were arguing on the phone with this cop?" He used the pistol to point at Baker. "You said something about the case he was working and the psycho, Michelangelo. It was pretty easy to figure out."

"But why?" I asked. "Why do any of it?"

"Why? Why? Why? Don't you understand?" Gabe paused then shouted, "Because I'm an artist!"

We heard distant sirens.

"I called for backup, asshole," Baker rasped. "You're done."

Gabe smiled at him. He brought the gun barrel up so that it lay over his lips like a finger. "Shhh. Wait a minute. Quiet please. Wait a minute." He lowered the gun, once again pointing at us. "I've just had a brilliant idea, an inspiration. My final piece, the three of us in death." Gabe gasped. "Oh, Lise, with you in the nude, and Baker and I dressed, it will be like Manet's *The Luncheon on the Grass*. A lovely tableau—no—a triptych! Yes!" The smile and wonderment left his face and were immediately replaced with a sneer. "A triptych! Who's first?"

I laughed, the kind of laugh that came out of my nose, more of a snort, like I was trying to hold it in, to hide it, but couldn't. Gabe's face reflected my confusion, and in my peripheral vision, I saw Baker look at me. They probably both thought I'd lost it. I hadn't, or maybe I had, which was why I was going to try something.

"Oh, you're funny, Gabe." I reached out and squeezed Baker's leg, trying to signal him to follow along. "You are so not a gun person."

Baker chuckled, though it sounded anything but sincere. "You got that right."

Gabe angled his head inquisitively. "What are you two going on about?"

I grinned at Baker. "Should we tell him?"

Baker shrugged then grimaced, the gesture causing him pain. "Yeah, why not?"

"Gabe?" I paused for effect. "You only have one bullet left."

Gabe looked at the pistol, as if a cursory glance would tell him if it was true or not.

"Yep," Baker said. "I was counting too. Between what you fired up in the room and the two you shot at me, you only have one bullet left."

"So that leaves the question—who will you shoot?" I said. "You hit Ortega with all your shots because you stood right over the body."

"The fact you shot me was just plain luck." Baker took his hand away from his bloody stomach as if to show Gabe.

"It's not easy to hit someone at a distance, even as short a one as between us," I said.

"Yeah, you're—what? A dozen feet or more away? You're bleeding out. I bet that gun's getting heavy, ain't it? My guess is you miss whichever one of us you choose."

I grimaced at a fresh burst of pain in my arm. "And you'll still be alive and have a lifetime of prison ahead of you."

Gabe's eyes flashed back and forth from me to Baker as he tried to assess our truthfulness. A smile broke on his face. "Well, damn." He reached up and knocked the drywall behind his head with the gun barrel. "On this canvas. A masterpiece in red to rival anything by Rothko."

A part of me wanted to try to stop him and beg him to embrace life, no matter what lay ahead. But that entreaty would be for the Gabe I'd known for so many years. Not this one.

Gabe placed the barrel of the pistol in his mouth, looked back to the wall as if checking the angle, turned back to us, and smiled around the gun. With a muted explosion, a splash of red painted the wall.

Chapter 39

Woozy and a little nauseated, I kept my eyes closed and tried to hold on to a dream I'd had about Gracie. Details were already fleeting, but I did remember that we'd been having a tea party on a grassy lawn. Even though she was a child in my dreams, her voice was older, and she told me, "You did good, Lise. Can you help me?" I woke before I could tell her I would.

I thought back to the night I'd almost died, the night Teague, Ortega, and Gabe did die. According to Baker's wife, after I'd called Baker, he'd called Ortega first because he lived near Nick's house and could get there the quickest. Then he called for backup as he ran to his car. Ortega got to Nick's first, then Baker shortly after. The rest of the police didn't arrive until after Michelangelo had already used his own blood and brain matter for his final piece.

I opened my eyes, and though the lights were off and the shades drawn, the room seemed awash in white. Licking dry lips, I craved water and tried to orient myself. I felt lingering pain where I'd been struck and knew I sported a black eye and swollen ear. My arm was tender where over a dozen stitches had repaired that damage. There were hushed sounds of hospital equipment monitoring vitals.

A nurse entered the room. "Ah, you're awake."

I nodded and felt a pain in my neck from sleeping awkwardly. "These chairs could double as torture devices," I said, sitting straighter. "Any idea when Sleeping Beauty will wake up?" I nodded to Baker in the hospital bed.

"When he's ready." She smiled, got his chart, and checked his vitals before leaving.

That night, I had been admitted at the hospital as well but only spent one night there. After stitching me up, they'd kept me mainly for observation. They'd prescribed heavy-duty Tylenol and kicked me loose, but I was still hurting. With my left arm immobilized in a sling, I was currently a one-armed private investigator.

"Really?" a gruff voice said, and I saw Baker look at me through half-lidded eyes. "I wake up and find you in my room?"

"You're just lucky, I guess," I said, a grin in place.

"How long have I been out?"

"Three days," I said. "Your wife has been here round the clock. I told her I'd sit with you so she could go home and rest and shower."

"Thanks, Norwood." Baker coughed. "Thanks for saving my life." Then he was out again.

I called the nurse and told her he'd been awake for a minute, then I called his wife.

I RETURNED TO SAN MARCO General the next day. Baker's wife and daughter were there. I told them to head down to the cafeteria, that I would keep Papa Bear company. Baker had the TV tuned to ESPN. I picked up the remote from a bedside table and switched it off.

After a few minutes of silence, I said, "I'm sorry about Ortega."

"Me too. He was a damn fine partner." Sorrow shadowed his eyes.

I nodded. "A fine person."

Baker reached with a shaky hand for a Styrofoam cup on the tray by his bed. I got it first and held it so he could sip water through a straw. He looked up at me. "Been meaning to ask. How many bullets were really in the clip?"

I knew he meant the gun that Gabe had taken from Ortega. "After shooting himself? Two."

Baker shook his head. "Why'd you work this so hard when it wasn't your job? It almost killed you."

I pictured Gracie in my mind. "I had a cousin. We were close as kids. She was murdered. Stabbed and left to die in a park in Panama City. This was a few years ago. The killer was never caught. I think it's because of her that I wanted to stop Michelangelo."

"Ah, shit, Lise. I'm really sorry."

"I've been thinking that I might go to Panama City, see if I can find her murderer."

"I'll do what I can from this end to help you."

I smiled at him. "I'll hold you to that, Baker. You know, for all your attempts at coming across gruff and mean, you're a sweet man."

Baker snorted. "Now what?"

"What do you mean?"

"Back to being a private pain in the ass?"

"Best private pain in the ass in San Marco."

From behind me, I heard, "Lise?"

I turned to find Nick. We were immediately in one another's arms. I squeaked in pain when we crushed my injured arm between our bodies, after which we held each other a bit more gingerly. We kissed, he stroked my cheek, we kissed again, then we looked into one another's eyes. In this quiet gaze, we shared our love, and when we both started to cry, we shared the shock, betrayal, grief, disbelief, and horror at learning Gabe's true nature.

We stepped apart, and I wiped my eyes, noticing Adolph standing just outside the door in the hallway. I gave him a quick hug and pulled him into the room. "Thanks for picking Nick up at the airport."

"My pleasure." Adolph approached the bed and asked, "Detective Baker, how are you feeling?"

"Like I've been shot in the gut and morphine is my new best friend."

"Thanks for keeping an eye out for Lise," Nick said to Baker.

"It's the other way around. She saved my life," Baker said. "So you two lovebirds flying to Vienna?"

Nick shook his head. "The fellowship ended before it even began. I've been recalled to San Marco University to step in for Gabe."

"Tough break."

I put my good arm around Nick's waist. "We plan to go to Vienna during Christmas break and play tourist."

"My almost-boss at the Academy of Fine Arts, Professor Gildersleeve, promised he'd show us around. Said Vienna is beautiful at Christmas."

"That sounds nice," Baker said. "And Lise deserves a good time."

Nick smiled. "I'll show her one."

Baker yawned just as a nurse walked in, and she said, "Nice of everyone to come visit, but it's looking like the detective could use a nap."

"Nah, I'm good."

The nurse's eyebrows went up, and she stated matter-of-factly, "You'll nap."

"Then we'll skedaddle," I said. To Nick and Adolph, I added, "Meet me at the little chapel down past the nurses' station. I want to say a prayer for Ortega and Teague."

They left, followed by the nurse. I went over and kissed Baker's cheek. "Get well, you ol' bear."

Baker got misty eyes and mumbled, "Your boyfriend, he's a lucky man to have you."

"Why, Detective Baker, is that a compliment?"

"Yeah, why not? You earned it." He thought a second and added, "But don't expect it to become a habit."

Acknowledgements

To Paul Meyers, who helps me get the law enforcement aspects of the story right. Anything that doesn't ring true is totally my fault. Eternal thanks to my agent, Liza Fleissig. Your belief in me is humbling. A toast to my publisher, Red Adept, and their incredible editors, particularly Alyssa Hall and Stefanie Spangler Buswell. Kudos to the guys who read my early manuscripts and make sure the stories are headed in the right direction, especially Eileen and Tim. And most importantly, a sincere thank you to my readers.

Also by Andrew Nance

A Lise Norwood Mystery
Red Canvas

Standalone
All the Lovely Children

Watch for more at https://www.andrewnance.net/.

About the Author

Andrew Nance is a writer, actor, and amateur historian. He spent over twenty years working in the radio industry up and down the east coast and still keeps his hand in as a volunteer at a local college radio station. He's had two young adult books published including *Daemon Hall* (Henry Holt Books for Young Readers), which was named an American Library Association Quick Pick for the Reluctant Reader, a New York Library Book for the Teen Age, and was nominated for an Edgar Award in YA, and for the ALA Teens Top 10 for 2008.

Andrew lives in St. Augustine, Florida with his family and can be heard playing jazz on Mondays from 5-7pm EST on WFCF, which is available on iHeartRadio online.

Read more at https://www.andrewnance.net/.

About the Publisher

Dear Reader,

We hope you enjoyed this book. Please consider leaving a review on your favorite book site.

Visit https://RedAdeptPublishing.com to see our entire catalogue.

Don't forget to subscribe to our monthly newsletter to be notified of future releases and special sales.

Made in the USA
Columbia, SC
16 July 2023